Champagne Gold

A Novel

NISSA ALEXANDROV

HEADWIND
BOOKS

DEDICATION

To *Switzerland, the place I call home.*

1

"Cheese. Heidi. Chocolate. Cows. What else?"

Pinkie flipped up the corner of his eyeshade and gave me a baleful look. "Patek Philippe watches. Specifically, a 1972 Patek Philippe watch engraved with my family's coat of arms."

I sighed. Ever since Pinkie had caught sight of his father's long-lost Patek Philippe on his cousin's wrist in a German society paper, he had been a man on a mission. I would have sympathized more, but the only thing that had ever been passed down in my family was a love of fried foods. "Enough already with the watch. When are you going to let it go?"

Pinkie pulled off his eye mask and sat up to sip his champagne. "When I'm dead, Lora. Dead and cold and buried in our family crypt wearing my father's 1972 Patek Philippe."

I looked over at him in exasperation. Usually, looking at Pinkie's tanned, rounded, immaculately attired figure made me happy. Today it just made me question whether I could strangle him with his ascot before he mentioned that godforsaken watch again.

"Can we drop this subject?" I asked. "Just for the rest of the flight. I'm trying to brush up on my typically Swiss stuff so that I can carry on an intelligent conversation with Jack Green. Dieter's counting on me to charm him into signing a contract, and since you spent a lot of time in Switzerland as a kid, I was thinking you might actually have something of value to add to the topic."

Pinkie made a great show of adjusting himself in the chair. "Well, of course I do. But I don't see what you're getting so upset about. Dieter's been leading tours of Switzerland for twenty years. Surely he can impress one little international tour operator, even without your help."

"First of all, Jack Green's not just some 'little' international tour operator," I said. "His clients are very discerning."

"By which you mean rich," Pinkie clarified.

"Right. And surely his rich and adventurous clients occasionally have need of a fun-loving and charming hostess for their luxury travels, right?"

"Surely. So all of this prep work is just so that he'll recommend you to his clients?"

"Exactly."

Pinkie narrowed his eyes at me over his champagne flute. "And yet I feel that you're holding something back."

I tried to keep my face perfectly neutral. "I have no idea what you're talking about."

"Ha! I knew it."

"What?!"

"You always give me that dead fish stare when you're hiding something. You might as well tell me. You know I'll find out eventually."

I sighed. Pinkie *would* find out eventually. He had an almost psychic ability to detect scandal. "You remember I told you that Jack Green had narrowed the choices down to Dieter and a rival tour operator?"

"Yes."

"The other guy hired Vanessa St. Germain."

"No! I love her! She's such a bitch!"

I tried not to grit my teeth. "She's a completely horrible human being, and she's been trying to drive me out of business ever since she set up shop in New York. Did I tell you that she tried to horn in on my corporate retreat gig with Mr. Yamamoto? I've been doing that gig for years! I have my own fan page in Japan!"

"Well, I don't think she stands much of a chance there. Mr. Yamamoto loves you."

"That's why he told me. Apparently she assured him that we weren't in direct competition because she focused on hostessing events for more *discerning* clients. She told him that being the daughter of a baron gave her a special insight into the needs of the elite."

Pinkie raised an eyebrow. "And the fact that you're the daughter of a librarian from the suburbs of Delaware…"

"Gives me a special insight into the creative uses of Cool Whip."

"Don't underestimate that as a selling point."

I rolled my eyes. "The point is that she is trying to steal my clients, and Jack Green is so well connected that he's like the Good Housekeeping seal of approval for the luxury hospitality industry. If I can impress him, I'm set. And if she impresses him, I might as well pack up and move back to Delaware." I pondered that idea morosely. Maybe I could get a job hostessing at Applebee's.

Pinkie slapped his hand on the armrest. "Well, we can't let that happen. I make enough of a sacrifice coming all the way out to Brooklyn to see you. Delaware is out of the question. Let's see if I can't think of something Swiss that you can use to fascinate Jack Green. It isn't the most exciting country, you know. There is their watch industry, of course…"

"Enough, Pinkie! Once we get to Hubert's place, we can talk about your father's watch again. You can write a song about it and go around singing it, for all I care."

"Yodeling," Pinkie said.

"You're going to go around yodeling it? Wouldn't that make it hard to understand the words?"

"No. You should add yodeling to your list of Swiss stuff."

"Right," I said, jotting it down. "Good call. What else?"

"Nazi gold."

I looked at him skeptically. "The dinner is supposed to showcase authentic Swiss culture. How do you suggest I work Nazi gold into the theme?"

"Maybe Dieter could have a guy dressed as a Nazi storm the dinner and glitter bomb everyone. Ooh… Then he throws some cheese and chocolate into a picnic basket, grabs a girl dressed like Heidi, and rides a cow off into the sunset, yodeling. You hit every cultural highlight in two minutes. In fact, it's a classic example of Swiss efficiency, now that I think about it. Tell Dieter not to worry about a thing—I'm here to save the day."

"Right. And that's why I am the event hostess and you are the…" I paused. "Remind me of what you are again, exactly?"

"I'm a prince."

"Well, I know that, obviously, but it's not exactly a job, you know."

Pinkie looked at me in outrage. "*Of course* it's a job, Lora. It's the hardest kind of job. I'm constantly investing in my skills. Like now," he said, taking a sip of champagne. "Veuve Clicquot Vintage 2004. I don't even need to look at the bottle. See? Do you know how much champagne I have to drink to be able to do that? That's part of my job."

"Doesn't a job generally pay something?"

"It's a charity job. Like being the Dalai Lama."

"Ah. And here I wouldn't have said you had anything in common with the Dalai Lama."

"I actually have *loads* in common with the Dalai Lama. We both have great fashion sense. We both spend a lot of time on other people's private planes."

I looked around at the private plane we were currently on. Tan leather, neutral colors, elegant but understated. "Whose plane is this, by the way? It's remarkably tasteful for your friends. No Ferrari logos, nothing gold-plated...not even a Swarovski light fixture. I feel a little cheated, to be honest."

"You're thinking of Prince Abdul's plane. This is Fish's plane."

"I thought Fish was running for Parliament," I said. "Why would he need a private plane?"

"He doesn't need a private plane. That's why he's lending it to us."

"Hmm. Something in the logic of that statement seems fuzzy to me."

"That's because you're not an out-of-the-box thinker like I am. You know what helps with that? Veuve Clicquot Vintage 2004." He rang the bell for the flight attendant. "Could we get some more champagne for my friend here?"

"Of course, sir," the young man said, collecting the bottle and refilling my glass with a flourish. I took a sip and sighed. This was ruining me for traveling economy class, which was unfortunately the only way I could afford to travel when Pinkie's friends weren't picking up the tab.

Pinkie sipped his champagne. "So. Back to my watch. Shall we go straight to Hubert's house, or shall we swing by my Patek Philippe-stealing cousin Maurice's house and demand my watch back first?"

"I thought you already tried demanding your watch back."

"I did."

"And what did Maurice say?"

"Maurice told me that his father wanted him to have the watch. So I told him that if his father wanted him to have a Patek Philippe watch, he should have bought one instead of stealing it from my father's body like some kind of ghoul. Then he threatened to have me arrested if I set foot on his property. Then there was some name calling in German." Pinkie took a thoughtful sip. "You know, German is really the best language for that kind of thing. You can just string together whatever words you like."

"I see. Dare I ask which words you strung together in this particular case?"

"I was a little upset, so I can't be precise, but I think I might have called him something like a cheese-breathed grave robber who sleeps with cows. I was going for something with local color, you know."

"Ah. I'm surprised he didn't courier the watch right over." I mentally ran through the likely chain of events if we stopped by Maurice's house to try to wrest Pinkie's watch from what I assumed would be Maurice's perfectly manicured grasp. Yelling, hair pulling, possibly some slapping—it would definitely be entertaining, but since I was too jet lagged to rescue Pinkie, I thought it would be irresponsible to encourage him. "If that was how you left it, I'm voting for going straight to Hubert's house."

Pinkie sighed. "That's probably best. I called Maurice's sister, Margrit, to see if she wanted to meet up while we're here. She's a police officer, and she's none too fond of her brother. Maybe she'll be able to help. It's part of her job to return stolen property, after all, even if her family was the one doing the stealing."

"If she works for the police, won't she have better things to do than help you prove that her father stole your father's watch twenty years ago?"

"She works for the Swiss police, so no. She's probably bored to tears from all the parking tickets she has to fill out. I bet she'll bring me chocolates to thank me for injecting a bit of excitement into her life."

Pinkie rang the bell again, and the young man appeared from the back, bottle in hand. He refilled Pinkie's glass without being asked. Obviously he was a quick study.

"Thank you, darling," Pinkie said, flashing the young man a smile that made him blush. "By the way, when are we going to be arriving in Zurich?"

"Noon, sir," the attendant said. "Right on time. Do you need me to arrange transportation, or will you be taking the train?"

Pinkie shuddered. "I never take public transportation. It's full of germs and other people. I've already arranged for a limo. Privacy, comfort, and no open container laws," he said, stroking the side of his champagne flute lovingly. "I wouldn't travel any other way."

2

I was the first out the door when the plane landed. Although Pinkie swore that he could happily live on a private jet, I was always woefully aware of the fact that every hour I spent in the desiccating atmosphere of an airplane cabin cost me at least thirty additional bucks worth of high-end moisturizer. I wondered, not for the first time, if the people at La Mer were in cahoots with airplane manufacturers.

I didn't see the car on the runway, but there was a man waiting for us on the tarmac.

"The driver's waiting for us," I called back into the cabin. "Can you snap it up a little back there?"

"I don't know why you're in such a hurry to get off of the plane," Pinkie called back, his tone peevish. "I'm finishing my champagne."

"There's probably champagne in the car. A whole fresh bottle."

"Fine." Pinkie's disembodied voice came out of the plane. There was a low rumble of conversation, which I attributed to Pinkie hitting on the flight attendant. He did love a man in uniform.

I walked across to the chauffeur, smiling. He was dressed in a dove-gray pair of pants and a neatly pressed white shirt. My eye was caught by what he was wearing around his neck. Was that…an ascot? I looked into his face and involuntarily took a step back.

"Oh my god," I said.

The man smiled, raising an eyebrow rakishly. He had dark brown hair and pale skin rather than Pinkie's uniformly golden glow, but he was otherwise a dead ringer for Pinkie. "You look…" I started.

He held out a hand. "I'm told the family resemblance is very strong. My name is Maurice. I'm Philippe's cousin. You must be a friend of his."

My eyes were immediately drawn to his wrist, looking for Pinkie's father's watch. No such luck. There went Pinkie's chance for snatching it and racing back onto the plane.

"I…uh…" I started. I glanced over my shoulder at the airplane stairs. Pinkie had still not finished chatting up the attendant. "Yes," I said, trying to be nonchalant. "Lora Godwin." I took his hand and shook it once.

"Hmm," he said, not releasing my hand. He gave me a lingering once-over that made it clear that he and Pinkie's similarities didn't extend to every aspect of their lives. I suddenly wished I were wearing something a little less fitted. Like a poncho. Or maybe a burka.

"Lora," Pinkie called out from the stairs. "Is that the…" He trailed off. "*You!*" he hissed, catching sight of Maurice. "Remove your hands from Lora at once!"

Maurice dropped my hand. "Really, Philippe. Is that any way to greet your cousin?"

"It depends on the cousin." Pinkie walked over to where we stood. I looked from one man to the other, scarcely believing my eyes. The same height, weight, face, and clothes… It was like matter and anti-matter. I wondered if the universe would end if they shook hands.

Pinkie didn't appear inclined to risk it. "What are you doing here?"

"You told me you were coming to try to steal my father's watch. It didn't take me too long to figure out your travel plans."

"*My* father's watch," Pinkie corrected coldly. "Your father stole it from him."

Maurice smiled. "Let's just call it *my* watch, for the sake of clarity. Whoever bought it originally, I'm the one who has it now, right?"

"Not for long. I'll find out a way to prove ownership. Don't worry. The truth can't hide forever."

"No, it can't," Maurice agreed. He smiled, as if this thought gave him pleasure. "Tell me, Philippe, will you be staying with your godfather on this trip? Dear, conservative Hubert?"

"Of course. Not that it's any of your concern. You're not invited to visit, if that's what you're getting at."

"Oh, I'm not angling for a visit, but if you insist on pursuing this absurd watch situation, I may have to drop by to have a little talk with Hubert."

Pinkie looked at him impatiently. "A talk about what?"

Maurice shrugged his shoulders, the picture of nonchalance. "I was doing a little research into Hubert's bank the other day and I ran across an interesting fact about a former partner of his. Jurg Hoffmann. I think you and he would have gotten along really well."

"Who is Jurg Hoffmann?" Pinkie asked. He looked genuinely confused.

"He was a partner at Hubert's bank. Briefly. Very briefly. Hubert forced him to resign, and unfortunately he later took his own life. Very tragic, really."

"I fail to see what that has to do with me or my watch."

"*My* watch," Maurice corrected him. "It actually has everything to do with you and my watch. I suggest you look into Herr Hoffmann. I'm sure you'll figure out the relevance soon enough. And when you do, I'm also sure you'll come to see that it's better to let sleeping dogs lie."

Pinkie sniffed. "I'd say that this situation is already full enough of lying dogs."

"Just offering a little friendly advice," Maurice said.

They looked at each other for a moment, silently, their expressions mirrors of haughtiness and disdain. "You may go now," Pinkie said, waving a hand in dismissal.

Maurice smiled and took my hand again before I could snatch it back. "It was a pleasure to meet you, Lora," he said, the barest hint of a leer coloring his smile. "Perhaps next time we meet, we can chat about something other than an old watch. I'm sure we'd find that we had a great deal in common."

I removed my hand, stifling the urge to wipe it on my skirt. "Perhaps."

Nodding again to Pinkie, Maurice turned and sauntered off toward a sleek Mercedes sedan that was parked near one of the buildings. He started the motor and drove off without looking back.

"What the hell?" I marveled.

Pinkie was flushed with rage. "The nerve of that man! I can't believe someone so underhanded could be related to me."

"Well, there's clearly no doubt that he's related to you."

"What do you mean?"

"I mean, you look…" I started out.

Pinkie raised an eyebrow menacingly.

"Uhh… Never mind. Who was Jurg Hoffmann, and what was he getting at with all this 'chatting with Hubert' stuff? He sounds like someone training to be a supervillain in a really bad movie."

"I have no idea. You know that Hubert belongs to one of the oldest banking families in Switzerland, right?"

"You might have mentioned it once or twice." *Or every time we passed an ATM for the last two weeks*, I thought.

"The bank has been run by partners from four families for over three hundred years. Hoffmann is one of the family names, but I never heard of a partner named Jurg. But I'm sure that if Hubert forced him to resign, he had a very good reason. Theft of other people's family heirlooms, perhaps. Maybe that's how Maurice knows him. They're part of a super-secret heirloom thief fraternity."

I shrugged. "Well then, I guess you have nothing to worry about."

"Nothing at all," Pinkie said breezily. Despite his tone, he did actually look a bit worried.

"Come on. Let's get in the limo and have a glass of champagne. That'll cheer you up."

Pinkie shook it off. "You're right, Lora. Nothing cheers me up like a nice ride in a limo."

3

"What do you mean there's no limo?!" Pinkie screeched.

The man from the limo company, a rather gnomish-looking person in a cheap black suit and chauffeur's cap, looked at us mournfully. "It's the Fat Cat."

I sneezed. "Please don't talk about cats. I'm really allergic."

The man looked confused. I couldn't blame him. I was the only person I knew who was allergic to pictures of cats. Being allergic to the word cat was something new, though. I hoped this wasn't the start of a new trend. I'd hate to be sneezing every time someone mentioned a catamaran.

"The Fat Cat is not a cat," the driver said. I sniffed experimentally. No urge to sneeze. Apparently my psychosomatic allergy was a discriminating sort.

I glanced over at Pinkie, who looked as lost as I was. "Perhaps you should explain. We've never heard of any limo-stealing Fat Cats."

"For the last two months, the Fat Cat has been terrorizing Zurich," the man said, wringing his hands in distress. "He started by painting the windows at a private bank. And then he splattered paint all over the headquarters of Chopard. Next it was Gucci. And every time, he leaves this sign, in orange paint—a fat cat in a top hat." The man dug around in his bag for a moment. "Here," he said, pulling out a newspaper. He tapped a photograph depicting the silhouette of an obese feline in a top hat sprayed on the windshield of a limousine. I looked at it closely. It was rather charming, assuming you could overlook the fact that it was keeping us from our ride.

"You see this in the picture? These are our limos. All of them completely wrecked. They will be in the shop for the next week. This kind of thing…" his lips tightened. "This is Zurich. We don't have problems like this. We love fat cats here."

"Apparently not all of you," I noted.

Pinkie held up a hand. "Okay. So there's no limo. I can deal with that. I'm flexible. What do you have instead? A Ferrari? A Porsche?"

The corners of the man's mouth turned down farther.

"A Land Rover?" Pinkie asked, his voice faltering.

Now the man looked like his puppy had just died. "The Street Parade is in two days. A million people will be here this weekend. All of the rental cars have been booked for months."

Pinkie dropped his voice to an urgent whisper. "What are you saying? Are we going to have to take a Volkswagen?"

The man winced. "Unfortunately, I was only able to find one car. But the good news is that you'll find it very convenient for parking. It's over here."

He led us around to the side of the building, where a fluorescent green Smart Car was nestled under an awning.

Pinkie looked at the car in abject horror. "You can't be serious! I can't be seen in a Smart Car. I'm a prince, for god's sake!"

"It's the only car I have. I'm sorry…the Street Parade…" The man trailed off.

"It'll be fine, Pinkie," I said, walking around the hideous plastic contraption. "It's kind of cute, don't you think?" I squinted at the writing on the side of the car. "Discount Erotik Megamart," I read. "Wait a minute. Does that mean what I think it means?"

The man winced again. "My brother-in-law owns the Discount Erotik Megamart in Dubendorf. It's his car. The good news is that he said that if you want to visit, he'll throw in a 20-percent discount."

I looked at Pinkie, who was clutching his chest. "No," he whispered.

"You heard the man," I said. "It's the Smart Car with the Discount Erotik Megamart sign or nothing. We can take public transportation if you're going to be like that."

Pinkie took a deep breath and drew himself up to his full height. "Public transportation? I don't think so." Rummaging around in his bag, he pulled out a massive pair of sunglasses and pushed them onto his face. He opened the passenger door, slid inside, and sat there, fuming. "Luggage!" he snapped at the man.

The man glanced over at my modest suitcase and Pinkie's unwieldy stack of Louis Vuitton bags. "Uh...I think we will need to put the bags in first, and then you will get in."

Pinkie let out a hiss of displeasure, but stiffly got out of the car and stood next to it in silence while the driver wedged the bags into the vehicle. Even with the cargo area stuffed to capacity, three duffel bags ended up on the passenger-side floor. "How am I supposed to sit there?" Pinkie asked. "There's no room."

"There is a trick to it," the driver said. "You put your feet on this bag, then slide in...then I close the door, and voilà!"

Pinkie followed his instructions and ended up in a ball in the passenger seat, his chin resting on his knees, arms crossed over his chest. His eyebrows were lowered in a scowl that was visible even over his Prada sunglasses. "If I find that Fat Cat, I will personally kill him," Pinkie said, his voice throbbing with menace.

I suppressed a snicker. "Is there some paperwork or something that I need to fill out while my friend here gets comfortable?"

The man gave me a serious look. "This is Switzerland. There is always paperwork. If you'll come this way?"

I trailed behind him to the office, checking out my reflection in the glass while he rustled around with a stack of papers. Ten hours on a plane—even a private plane—hadn't done me any favors. My skin looked dry, and even the lovely and hideously overpriced golden highlights Jacques had added to my hair last week weren't enough to save it from its usual limp mediocrity. At least my mascara was still good. I said a silent prayer of thanks to the scientists at Christian Dior who had decided to devote their considerable talents to developing anti-clumping mascara instead of curing cancer or figuring out nuclear fusion.

"Here we go," the man said, handing me a stack of paper that looked almost as big as the car.

I signed at least seven highlighted places, initialed three more, submitted a copy of my driver's license and passport, and was headed back to Pinkie when I suddenly caught a glimpse of someone familiar out of the corner of my eye.

"You've got to be kidding me," I said. The man looked up, startled. His face lit up as he recognized me. Tousled dark hair, a square chin, and a crooked grin coupled with dazzlingly green eyes that I'd thought about more than once in the last few weeks. I suppressed a scowl. I was going to play this cool.

"Benjamin," I said, my voice neutral.

He smiled broadly. "Actually, it's…"

"I don't care what alias you're currently going by," I snapped. Apparently I wasn't going to be playing this cool after all. "And I don't care if you're keeping tabs on me for the president himself. I don't appreciate being stalked." I felt a surge of righteous fury, and I told myself that that was fully due to the fact that Benjamin was obviously following me again and not the fact that the last time I had seen him he had kissed me, vanished, and never called again.

He held up his hands in surrender. "Lora, I'm not here following you. It's just a coincidence. I promise. What are you doing here, anyway?"

I crossed my arms over my chest. "That's none of your business. I have a life, you know."

Benjamin looked taken aback by the ice in my tone. "Wait a minute. Is this because I didn't call? You know that I would have…"

He was interrupted by a honking noise from the Erotik MegaSmart.

"I couldn't care less whether you call or not. It's not like we're dating. I just don't like you showing up every time I turn around." Another long, wailing honk came from the Smart Car.

Benjamin looked over at the car. "I must be seeing things. Is that…?"

"Pinkie," I confirmed. "Our limo got vandalized by someone called the Fat Cat. That's the only car they had."

Benjamin laughed delightedly. "I feel like I should take a photograph. You know…for his file. And maybe a commemorative plate."

"I suggest that if you want to keep your testicles, you keep your camera in your pocket. Right now is not the time to mess with Pinkie."

"Too bad." He reached out and touched my shoulder. "If you have some time while you're here, maybe we could meet up. I know this great little place…"

I shrugged his hand away. "I'm pretty sure I'll be too busy to meet," I said, giving him my coldest glare.

Benjamin's face fell. "Well, if you change your mind…" He rummaged around in his pocket for a card and held it out to me.

The horn wailed again, even more insistently. I snatched the card and tucked it into my purse without looking at it. "Fine. Have a nice trip." I headed off to the car with as much dignity as a woman walking to a fluorescent green Smart Car emblazoned with *Discount Erotik Megamart* could show.

Pinkie scowled at me as I got in.

"You know, every minute that I spend in this so-called car increases the chance that someone will see me. So I'd appreciate it if you wouldn't hang around chatting up strangers." He adjusted the side mirror to look behind us. "Even if they do have really nice butts."

I glanced in the rearview mirror, where I could see Benjamin, his back to us. I felt a pang of remorse at being so curt with him. He really did have a nice butt.

"He wasn't a stranger. That was Benjamin, that government guy who's been assigned as my semi-official stalker."

"Really? Why are you on the stalking list today? Business or pleasure?"

"Neither, or so he claims. Apparently it's just a coincidence."

"Really," Pinkie said, clearly unconvinced. "Well, they say it's a small world, but people who say that have never been on a flight to Australia. In any case, less talking, more driving. I don't want to be in this vehicle one moment longer than necessary."

I put the car in gear. "Fine. But I don't know why you're being such a drama queen about this car. What's going to happen if someone sees you in it? Is the council of princes of countries that no longer exist going to take away your secret decoder ring?"

Pinkie sniffed. "It lowers the dignity of the title. What would happen if people stopped believing in royalty?"

"They'd save about a billion dollars a year and enter the twenty-first century?"

"Despair, Lora. They'd despair. And their gray little lives would have just a little less meaning." He sighed. "Heavy is the head that wears the crown."

I debated bringing up the fact that Pinkie had never actually worn a crown, but one look at his nobly dejected expression made me hold back. "Buckle up," I said. "Let's go see Hubert."

4

Pinkie sulked silently as I drove, which gave me the chance to appreciate our surroundings. On the right side of the road was Lake Zurich, a flat blue expanse dotted with picture-perfect sailboats and ringed with colorful villages. Off in the distance, we could see the jagged peaks of the Alps, their gleaming tops still capped in white even though it was August. To our left was a scattered handful of small apartment buildings that gradually gave way to manor houses and terraced vineyards as we drove out of the city.

I shot Pinkie a glance. He was crunched up in his seat with his knees higher than his head, a scowl on his face. "Pinkie, I know you're not happy about the car, but at least look around. This might actually be the most beautiful place in the world."

Pinkie poked his head up briefly, first checking to make sure that no passing cars would be able to see his face.

"It *is* pretty," he admitted grudgingly. "I used to come here a lot to visit Hubert when I was a boy. I always thought we spent so much time here because Hubert was my godfather. Now I think we probably spent so much time here because my father needed make sure Hubert wouldn't come visit us to check on my father's investments."

"What was your father investing in?" I asked.

"Horse racing, mostly."

"Ah."

"Of course, back then I thought that Zurich was the most boring place on earth. And Hubert doesn't even live in Zurich proper. He lives in Maennedorf." Pinkie shook his head. "There is literally nothing to do in Maennedorf."

I gestured at a particularly picturesque blue-faced village clock tower. "I could put up with a little boredom if I lived in a place that looked like this."

"Well, this weekend should be pretty exciting anyway," Pinkie said. "It's Street Parade."

"The guy who gave us the car mentioned that. What kind of parade is it? Like marching bands and batons and things?"

"Hardly. Imagine a giant rave where a million people from all over the world show up, do drugs, get drunk, dress up in costumes, have sex, and dance around in the streets until they pass out."

"Sounds like your last birthday party."

"There are certain similarities," Pinkie conceded. "Turn here." He pointed to a tiny track that wound up the hill into the vineyards. The car made a protesting noise as it struggled up the slope, and I missed my vintage Jaguar, which had been recently liberated from the mechanic. Not that it would have made it up the hill with any more grace, but at least we would have looked good while our car was wheezing away.

"Look at this place," I enthused. "You didn't tell me your godfather lived in such a wonderful location. Right in the middle of a vineyard. What could be more perfect?"

Pinkie snapped his fingers. "That reminds me. There's something I need to tell you. Don't panic."

I immediately felt a wave of panic wash over me. "What did you do? You didn't send a ham to my neighbor Heather, did you? Because if I come back and find a pack of enraged vegans holding a vigil outside my apartment, I'm going to be very upset with you."

Pinkie waved his hand. "I've put that plan on hold until the next time she calls the police on me. Although the last time the police came, one of them was so adorable that I almost demanded he cuff me and take me in."

I tried not to visualize. "Okay, now that I'm not panicking about that, why don't you tell me what else I'm not supposed to panic about."

"Right. It's Hubert. He makes wine."

I looked at Pinkie in confusion. "I fail to see how that's supposed to panic me. In fact, it sounds like good news. You may recall that I have been known to drink wine. In fact, I think I had wine for breakfast this morning. I mean, that's a little out of the ordinary for me, but there's got to be some sort of advantage to changing time zones, right?"

"He makes Swiss wine," Pinkie clarified.

"Swiss wine… I don't think I've ever had that before."

"There's a reason for that," he assured me.

I rolled my eyes at Pinkie. "I'm sure I can put up with a little substandard wine. It's not like I was raised by Robert Parker, you know. When I was growing up, my dad only drank Pabst Blue Ribbon."

Pinkie looked at me, mystified. "Is that a white or a red?"

"Never mind." The chances of Pinkie running across a can of Pabst Blue Ribbon were so vanishingly small that I didn't figure it was worth the effort to explain.

We pulled up in front of a palatial peach stucco house that was flanked on both sides by formal gardens and vineyards. Large windows overlooked Lake Zurich. It was exactly the kind of house I had always wanted—elegant, historic, graceful, and out of my price range by a staggering number of zeroes.

Pinkie opened the door to the car, gingerly unfolded himself, and let out a shriek. "Aigh!"

"What now, for heaven's sake?! You forgot what the car looked like when we were driving here, and you're throwing yet another temper tantrum about it?"

"I could hardly forget a fluorescent green pod advertising sex toys, now could I?"

I looked at him. "What bothers you the most—the car itself or the fact that it advertises sex toys?"

"It's a package deal, but now that you mention it, I think it's the fact that it advertises *discount* sex toys that's the most mortifying. Discount. I mean, as if I can't afford to pay full price for my sex toys." He sniffed. "But I wasn't shrieking about that. I think this stupid car made me pull something in my knee." He took a shambling step forward, lurching like Frankenstein's monster. "I'm wounded! I would kick this pregnant roller skate of a car, but then I'd probably just break my toe, too. I'll kill that Fat Cat!"

Just then, the door to the house opened, and an elegant sixty-something man in charcoal slacks and the snowiest white shirt I had ever seen emerged. "Philippe!" he cried, spreading his arms wide in welcome.

Pinkie limped up and embraced him, submitting to the three kisses that accompany every Swiss greeting. "Hubert! It's been too long."

I joined them on the doorstep and extended a hand. "Lora, this is my godfather, Hubert," Pinkie said. "Hubert, this is my very dear friend, Lora."

I smiled at Hubert. Between his gray hair and the lines of care across his forehead, he was every bit the Swiss banker, but his eyes were kind behind his rimless glasses, and he looked genuinely happy to see both of us. "Welcome, Lora," he said, taking my hand before pulling me in to kiss my cheeks. "Philippe has told me so much about you. It's so nice to meet the special woman in his life."

I tried not to wonder what Pinkie had said about me. I'd learned the hard way that I was much happier not knowing.

Hubert gestured toward the house. "I'll send someone out to get the bags. Come in! I've got some people who can't wait to see you."

He ushered us inside a soaring foyer lined with daring modern oil paintings showing the Alps in various seasons. In the center of the hall stood a pale, serious-looking young woman I judged to be in her early twenties. She had long, dark hair pulled back into a severe bun, high cheekbones, and a complexion that was dazzlingly clear despite her lack of makeup. She didn't look like she'd be very much fun to spend time with, but that could have been my limp hair, scaly skin, and complete lack of cheekbones talking.

To her side stood a handsome thirty-something-year-old man with a square jaw, warm brown eyes, and a friendly smile that made me like him immediately.

Pinkie limped across to the girl first. "This can't be Sarina, can it? My god! The last time I saw you…"

Sarina smiled primly. "The last time you saw me I was twelve," she said, smoothing a hand over her navy linen skirt. "Surely you were expecting a few changes?"

Pinkie hugged her. "Not at all. I never age. Why should other people be different?"

"Well, you did change a little," she said. "I don't remember you limping the last time I saw you. War wound?"

Pinkie clutched his chest. "Yes, as a matter of fact. I am officially at war with this Fat Cat person, whoever he is. Thanks to his vandalizing ways, Lora and I had to drive a Smart Car here. I was folded up like origami in there. I may never recover."

Sarina shook her head at Pinkie's dramatic declaration. "Okay, I take it back. You haven't changed at all."

"And you remember Arnaud, right?" Hubert said, putting his hand on the younger man's shoulder.

"Of course," Pinkie said. He turned to me. "Arnaud's family has held a partnership at the bank for as long as there's been a bank. Arnaud, this is my friend Lora."

Arnaud smiled, revealing a deep dimple in one cheek. "It's wonderful to meet you." As we offered the traditional greeting kisses, I caught the faintest whiff of a light, crisp cologne.

Pinkie looked at Arnaud. "What brings you to Hubert's place today? Business? Or did you just come to see me?"

"Well actually..." Arnaud started.

"Actually," Hubert jumped in, "you and your friend have come on a very special night. Did you forget?"

Pinkie slapped a hand to his forehead. "August eighth. It's the partner's dinner, isn't it?" He looked chagrined. "Hubert, I'm an ass. I completely forgot. I would never have imposed…"

I poked him with my elbow. "Why are you an ass this time?"

"Every year on the same day they have a partner's dinner," Pinkie explained. He looked up. "Wait. Does that mean Gerhardt is coming as well?"

Hubert smiled. "He'll be here in a couple of hours."

Pinkie clapped his hands in glee, bouncing in his Tod's driving moccasins. "I wanted to *be* Gerhardt when I was a boy," he told me. "He was like a movie star. Always a gorgeous suit, smoking a cigarette, with a new convertible Mercedes every year and just this string of beautiful women on his arm." Pinkie sighed. "At least until Marilyn stole his heart. How is Marilyn, by the way?"

"I'm afraid she passed away a few months ago," Hubert said sadly.

"Oh god," Pinkie said, placing his hand on his heart. "I'm so sorry."

"She was ready," Hubert said simply. "She always said that thirty years in bed was long enough for even the laziest woman."

Pinkie looked at me. "Multiple sclerosis. It was such a tragedy.

But even after the diagnosis, she never lost her sense of humor."

Hubert gave him a sad smile. "She kept it to the end. But onto happier news. We're also having one more guest tonight for dinner. An old school friend of yours."

I perked up. Inbreeding and ridiculous amounts of cash meant that Pinkie's school chums were always good fun. The last time they had all gotten together, Pinkie had gone to his room in pajamas and woken up the next morning naked in a rowboat in the center of the Thames. We still hadn't figured out how they'd done it, although most of them traveled with enough pharmaceuticals to stock a small hospital, so I had my suspicions.

Pinkie clapped his hands. "Really? Which one?"

"Reiner Hoffmann."

"Reiner?" Pinkie repeated. "Really! Imagine that. It will be so *wonderful* to see him again. Why is he coming, exactly?"

Hubert beamed. "He's being made a partner. You know his uncle was one of the partners, so there's a family connection, and Reiner's really taken to the work."

Pinkie smiled even more broadly and took my hand, squeezing it mercilessly. "Isn't that lovely, Lora? Reiner Hoffmann. A partner. In Hubert's bank. Reiner."

"Lovely," I repeated, removing my hand from Pinkie's death grip and shaking it to try to restart the circulation. Whoever Reiner was, Pinkie evidently loathed him.

"I didn't know that Reiner was one of *those* Hoffmanns. What was his uncle's name again…Jurg, was it?" Pinkie's face was a mask of innocence.

Hubert's face darkened. "His uncle's name was Matthew. He was a partner with us for twenty years. Wonderful man. But you're right, Reiner did have another uncle named Jurg. I'm surprised you remember the name. This was years ago. He was a partner, briefly, but we decided that he wasn't suitable for the bank."

"Not suitable," Pinkie pressed. "Because he was a criminal of some kind?"

Hubert looked shocked. "Not at all. It was more of an issue with his…shall we say…personal life."

"His personal life?"

"Honestly, Philippe, it was a long time ago. It's just gossip at this point, and you know how I feel about gossip." Hubert shook his head, dismissing the topic. "But no need for us to stand here in the foyer. I'm sure you will want to freshen up. Let me show you to your rooms. You can relax, take a shower, catch up on your email, then come down when you're ready, and we'll have something for lunch." He turned to Sarina and Arnaud. "Shall we say one o'clock?"

Arnaud smiled at me. "Swiss precision. If you had arrived a moment after one o'clock, the whole lunch would have been ruined."

"Well thank heavens we avoided that." I smiled back at him. He was really easy to smile at, actually. The white of his shirt made his skin look tanned, and there was the faintest hint of salt and pepper at his temples… I realized I was gawking and pulled my attention back to Hubert.

"If you want to come this way…" Hubert said, gesturing down one of the halls.

I snuck a glance at my cell phone as we walked. "I'm going to have to apologize in advance. I'll probably need to leave after lunch. I'm afraid this is a working holiday for me. I'm supposed to be the hostess for an authentic Swiss dinner on Monday, and I want to see what Dieter has planned."

"Dieter Schumacher," Pinkie clarified for Hubert. "I told Lora that I used to play over at his house when I visited you as a child."

Hubert smiled. "That's lovely. Dieter's a wonderful man. Very active in the community. I'm glad to hear his business is doing well. I haven't seen him in months. I should probably swing by to say hello."

"Yes, well, I'm hoping that I'll be able to help his business do even better," I said, "but that partially depends on my ability to bone up on some authentically Swiss topics I can discuss with Jack Green, the guy he's hoping to partner with. I don't suppose you have any suggestions?"

Hubert nodded. "You've come to the right place, my dear. Let's see…there are alphorns, of course…those are the really long horns they play in the mountains. There's kirsch…that's the local firewater. Great with fondue or raclette, although I don't advise drinking too much of it unless you want a terrible headache the next day. Wrestling, of course. Most people don't know about that, but there's a very traditional Swiss style of wrestling that used to be quite popular here. Gerhardt and I were both regional champions, actually."

"That's very helpful… Maybe I can get you to fill me in on more Swissness later today. You sound like an expert."

"Well, there should be some advantage to living for four generations in Switzerland," Hubert said.

"You mean aside from peace, prosperity, beautiful views, and great chocolate?"

"Yes, aside from those."

5

Hubert dropped me off in a tastefully decorated room with a pillow-smothered bed, a tiny turquoise velvet sofa, and a large box of truffles on the coffee table. "Let me know if you need anything, my dear. The bathroom's just through that door." He smiled at me in a fatherly way. "The other door leads to Philippe's room."

I looked at the connecting door. I wondered why Hubert thought I'd need a connecting door to Pinkie's room. Maybe he thought we might want to get together and watch *Vampire Diaries*. Did they even have *Vampire Diaries* in Switzerland?

I poured a glass of water and helped myself to a champagne truffle. The thing about truffles was that you really didn't feel too guilty eating them since they were really small. I popped another one in my mouth, reminding myself that dark chocolate and alcohol were both healthy eating choices. God bless the *New York Times* health section for that little nugget of life-changing information. After devouring a third, I reluctantly put the box down and called Dieter.

"Hi, Dieter, it's Lora. We just arrived. How are things going?"

"Wonderful," Dieter said. Like many people who worked in the hospitality industry, Dieter applied the word 'wonderful' pretty liberally to any circumstance that wasn't actively terrible—and a few that were. "The entertainment is ready, the menus have been perfected, the wines have been selected…but what about you? Are you all up to date on your Swiss history and culture?"

"Absolutely," I lied. "Nothing but yodeling and chocolate for me these days."

Dieter laughed. "There's more to it than that, of course, but that's not a bad place to start. Did you find the hotel all right? Where are you staying?"

"Actually, we're not staying in a hotel. My friend Prince Philippe's godfather invited us to stay with him. Hubert Richter. He said you two knew each other?"

"Hubert?!" Dieter said warmly. "But that is wonderful. Our family has banked with Richter and Partners for generations. Hubert is what you Americans call a 'slice off the old block.'"

"Chip off the old block."

"Chip," Dieter repeated cheerfully. "And I haven't seen Prince Philippe since he was a boy. He used to come over here whenever his father visited Hubert. He very much enjoyed spending time with the stable boys, which I always thought showed that he had a great touch with the common man."

I stifled a snort of laughter. Pinkie wasn't above touching a common man, particularly one with rock-hard abs, but I didn't think it had a lot to do with his democratic sentiments.

"Yes. Even in New York, Prince Philippe is known for his love of all men. But tell me about the dinner I'm supposed to be helping you with. Did Jack Green give you any guidance on what he was looking for?"

Dieter sighed. "I asked, of course. He just said it had to be authentically Swiss."

"Authentically Swiss. That could mean anything. Did you ask him what he meant by that?"

"Of course. And he said that if he told me, it wouldn't be authentic."

Of course he did. While I'd never actually met Jack Green, he was pretty famous in the hospitality industry for being a tough customer with zero tolerance for errors. He ran a company called Authentic Tours, which led small groups of wealthy tourists all over the world. A normal tour guide could show you the Vatican. Jack could show you the pope's bathroom. Assuming, of course, that you wanted to see the pope's bathroom—but who wouldn't want to see the pope's bathroom?

A contract with Jack provided access to the world's most pampered and free-spending globetrotters. Whoever got this contract would be the undisputed leading luxury tour operator in Switzerland. Not to mention the business he could throw my way.

I had a sudden vision of myself sweeping into the opera on the arm of some gorgeous, rich business tycoon who was relying on my wit and charm to restore his soul. Good.

Then I pictured Vanessa St. Germain wiping away a tear, packing her bags, and heading back to Europe on a one-way ticket. Better.

"What do you have planned?" I asked. "I want to make sure we crush your competition." *And Vanessa St. Germain*, I added silently.

Dieter laughed. "Such passion! Not to worry. We'll be holding the dinner at my gasthaus—my inn, I suppose you Americans would call it. It's a very beautiful historic building in Staefa, overlooking the lake."

"Okay, and entertainment?"

"We will start the evening with a traditional round of steinstossen. I've hired our national champion to provide lessons to the guests. After that we'll have a bit of a competition. Break the ice, you know."

"I don't know, actually. What the heck is steinstossen?"

"Stone tossing," Dieter said. "Something like your modern shotput. Very traditional, dating back to prehistoric times. A moment to learn, but a lifetime to perfect."

"Traditional sport…check. What else do you have?"

"I've booked a musical trio. They're very big here, so it's quite a get. They sing modern songs—almost pop—but they incorporate yodeling and traditional instruments. They're really very talented."

I winced. "Pop yodeling. Sounds painful."

"You'll love it. And at the end of the evening, we'll be joined by Switzerland's finest alphorn soloist."

"That's the long horn they use in the mountains, right?" I asked, remembering Hubert's comment.

"Exactly. He's a magician. I tell you…the sound of that horn drifting out over the hills of Staefa…" He fell silent for a moment. "It will bring tears to your eyes. It's magical."

I thought about it. It didn't sound like anything dazzling, but it was Switzerland, so I wasn't sure how dazzling it could be. "You're sure that won't be too many acts?" I worried.

"They'll be short. It won't get boring. Plus, this way we're covered if someone gets sick."

I mentally ran through the schedule again. The steinstossen would take maybe half an hour, singing between courses, alphorn with dessert... That left me plenty of time to charm Jack Green without having to shout over the entertainment. "Sounds good," I finally said. "And the dinner itself?"

"Onion and gruyère tartes, a very tiny amuse-bouche version of fondue, veal in cream sauce, crème brûlée with honey crackers and walnuts...trust me. It'll be great."

I felt a rumble of hunger and rummaged around in the truffle box for another chocolate. God, these were delicious. "Do you know what your competitor is doing? What was his name?"

Dieter laughed. "Ueli. I'm sure he's doing his best, just as I am. Ueli and I have worked for many years in this industry. Sometimes together, sometimes in competition. He is good at his job. Very good. But I'm better. Don't worry."

"I'm not worried," I lied.

"Have a little faith in me. I've got perfect faith in you, and I'll tell it to anyone who asks. Like I told that other woman."

I felt a shock of alarm.

"What other woman?"

"The other hostess. What was her name? Vanessa, I think."

"You called another hostess?" I felt a wave of panic. Dieter and I had known each other for years now. If Vanessa had been his first choice, I might as well get on the plane back home now and see if I had any clients left.

"No, no," Dieter reassured me. "She called me a couple of days after Jack sent over the invite. She offered her services as a hostess. I told her I was planning on working with you."

"And she said..."

"Oh, she was very kind. Just so charming and apologetic. Did you know she's some sort of aristocrat? Apparently she spent some time in a finishing school here in Switzerland. The French-speaking part, of course."

"Of course," I grated.

"Anyway, she said you were a wonderful choice, but she thought you might still be tied up in some sort of legal business. She was very clear that none of it was your fault, of course. Just bad luck that you happened to be...how did she put it? 'Working for some dreadful criminal types.' She sounded very concerned for you. She also told me that she was available to work with you as a pair. Double-teaming Jack Green with a charm offensive. I told her I didn't think it would be necessary, but maybe I was wrong… What man could resist two such charming women?" Dieter laughed.

"Oh yes," I said, faking a lighthearted chuckle. "I'm sure it would have been a blast. Unfortunately, she's now working with Ueli, so I guess that's out of the question." I was going to crush that client-stealing witch.

Dieter's tone was smug. "I'm not worried. Poor Ueli will need all the help he can get."

"Right," I said, almost lightheaded with suppressed fury.

"So…any other questions? I've got a crew coming in a few minutes to do some gardening. I want the place to look its best when Jack comes."

I pushed my anger at Vanessa aside and tried to focus on the task at hand. "Should I come over early to run through everything? My schedule is clear. We could do a rehearsal."

"Absolutely not. If it's not fresh for you, it won't be as fun for Jack. If anything comes up, I'll call you. Otherwise, spend the next couple of days seeing the sights and getting a feel for the place. Let Hubert and Prince Philippe show you around. They can show you the real Switzerland almost as well as I can."

"If you insist," I said, picking out another truffle. Obviously, chocolate truffles were a vital part of the Swiss research I'd need to do for the dinner. "Talk to you Monday, then."

I hung up and flopped onto the bed to rest for a couple of minutes, bringing the box of truffles with me. They were without a doubt the best chocolates I had ever eaten. "Teuscher Champagne Truffes," I read off the front of the box. *Note to self*, I thought, *if you ever see a Teuscher store, avert your eyes and run away as fast as possible.*

It was very hard to focus on getting into a peaceful Swiss frame of mind when so much of my brain was engaged in wishing cold sores, head lice, and assorted other unpleasantness on Vanessa St. Germain. Honestly, I wasn't against a little healthy competition. Truth be told, it might even be nice to know someone else with the same job. We could cover for each other during vacations. We could warn each other about sleazy clients. Heck, maybe I could even hold her up as proof to my mother that an event hostess and a hooker weren't the same thing.

But Vanessa St. Germain didn't want to be my colleague or my vacation cover or my proof of virtue. She wanted to take over my client list and drive me out of business, and that was not going to happen.

I popped a couple more truffles in my mouth, feeling the jet lag hit. I really needed a vacation. Of course, I had spent a week in the Mediterranean on a private yacht not too long ago, but since part of that time had been spent being held at gunpoint by white slavers, I couldn't really say that it had been all that restful. No, I needed someplace that would relax and rejuvenate me. For the hundredth time I wondered why they didn't rent rooms at Saks Fifth Avenue. Somewhere between the handbag and shoe departments, preferably. That was the most rejuvenating place I knew.

I yanked out my cosmetic kit and dotted some moisturizer around my eyes. Pinkie had given me something new that he claimed was made with dragon's blood. I had given up trying to figure out what was in the potions he was always foisting on me. Fermented seaweed? Skin growth hormone? Gold? On a list like that, dragon's blood sounded almost plausible.

I checked the mirror critically. I had to admit that Vanessa St. Germain looked every inch the aristocrat. I, unfortunately, did not. Greenish eyes; pug nose; full lips; soft, flat, and pathetically straight hair. Also a light dusting of powdered sugar from the truffles. I grabbed one more before wiping off my chin and putting on a couple more coats of mascara, an acknowledgment, though I refused to admit it, that Arnaud was pretty adorable.

Squaring my shoulders, I headed down to lunch.

6

I could hear Pinkie talking as I came down the hall toward the dining room.

"So I'm not really clear on whether my uncle stole it from my father while he was lying there dying, but it wouldn't surprise me. That side of the family has always been willing to take whatever they could get their hands on. Did I tell you that my cousin Maurice once stole a soap dish out of my bathroom? A soap dish! The sheer mechanics of stealing a soap dish are just mind-boggling. I mean, it's both fragile and slippery... You'd need bubble wrap and a Ziploc bag to keep from getting soap scum all over your clothes when you packed it, wouldn't you? Who travels with bubble wrap and a Ziploc bag just in case they see a really nice soap dish? He's like some kind of deranged cat burglar."

"Achoo!" I sneezed.

"Lora, it's going to be very hard for you to lurk around eavesdropping if you keep up this ridiculous habit of sneezing every time you hear the word 'cat,'" Pinkie said.

I sneezed again. Arnaud looked at me, amused. "You're allergic to the word 'cat?'"

I clutched my nose, stifling another sneeze. "Can we please stop talking about it?" I held up a hand to forestall further feline conversation.

"That's impossible," Sarina said flatly, looking at me.

I gave her a tight smile. "Yesterday I would have said that Pinkie going anywhere in a Smart Car was impossible, so I guess today we've both learned something about the difference between impossible and merely improbable."

Hubert smiled at me. "Let's not just stand here. Pour Lora some wine, Sarina. The chardonnay was not bad this year, if I do say so myself. What do you think, Philippe?"

I looked over at Pinkie, who quickly stifled a cringe. "It gets better every year."

I took the glass Sarina handed me and took an experimental sip. The flavor was familiar. I took another sip, rolling it around on my tongue in the approved wine tasting way. I finally made the connection. It was Welch's white grape juice. I drank again, feeling nostalgic. From concentrate, just like my mother used to make back in Delaware. It didn't taste like wine, but I had always liked Welch's grape juice, so I wasn't complaining.

Hubert was looking at me expectantly. "It tastes like something my parents used to serve. An American vintage," I said tactfully.

"There you have it, Philippe," Hubert said, thunking Pinkie on the shoulder. "I told your father I'd get the hang of winemaking eventually. Of course, if I'd known it would have taken thirty years, I probably would have just planted roses."

Hubert snapped his fingers. "That reminds me. About your father's watch—have you checked the Patek Philippe registry? If it's registered to your father and the registration was never transferred to your uncle, you might be in a better position to claim that the watch was stolen."

Pinkie tapped his jaw thoughtfully. "Well, my father was never a big man for filling out forms, you know. Unless they were betting forms. Heaven knows how many of those he filled out. But it's a good idea. Is the store still on Bahnhofstrasse? Maybe I'll run down there tomorrow."

"Do you know the serial number?" Arnaud asked.

"No, but there aren't too many Prince von Hofstedtlers registered. It's worth a try, anyway." He looked at Hubert beseechingly. "Please tell me you have a car that doesn't advertise discount sex toys."

Hubert shook his head. "I'd offer you the Bentley, but it's in the shop, and I promised our housekeeper the Mercedes tomorrow so that she can help her sister move. Arnaud, did you bring your car?"

"I took the train," Arnaud said, shrugging apologetically.

Pinkie squared his shoulders. "Fine. Lora will drive me."

"Why do I have to drive?"

"Because it's very difficult for me to see over the steering wheel when I'm trying to protect my reputation from the damage that being seen in that so-called car would cause. And you don't have a reputation to protect, so obviously you should be the one driving."

Arnaud laughed. "Honestly, Philippe. This is Switzerland. People don't care about that kind of thing. Just tell everyone that you're really environmentally conscious."

Pinkie huffed. "Really? What are you driving these days, Arnaud? Something environmentally conscious? A Prius, perhaps?"

"My father's old Jag," Arnaud admitted. "But it hardly ever gets out of the shop, so I'm not sure 'driving' is really the right word. Given how rarely the thing works, I'd have to say it probably qualifies as the most environmentally conscious car in the world."

Pinkie looked over at me. "Lora has a car just like that. A 1968 Jaguar. Once in a while she takes it out of the shop so that I can push it off to the side of the road and get my frequent tow truck discount card punched. I think next time I get a free sandwich."

Arnaud looked over at me, his eyes soft. "I fell in love with that car the moment I looked at it despite the fact that it's left me stranded more times than I can count. I know I should get rid of it, but sometimes love really does conquer all."

Looking into Arnaud's eyes, I felt a willingness to be conquered. "But mostly it just sucks up your cash and leaves you standing by the side of the road getting harassed by strangers," Pinkie said. "Shall we have lunch?"

7

Lunch was a relaxed affair consisting of a variety of mysterious dried meats and odiferous cheeses. "We didn't know when you'd arrive, so we wanted to be prepared," Hubert explained.

"If there's one thing I can always count on from Swiss people, it's being prepared," Pinkie said, neatly folding a piece of dried boar meat into his mouth.

I swallowed a bit of sandwich. "I hope you're right. I'm relying on Dieter Schumacher's planning to make sure this dinner goes off without a hitch. We both need to make a good impression on Jack Green."

Arnaud looked at me questioningly. "Dieter's doing the planning? I must have missed something. I thought you were the event planner."

"No. I'm the event hostess."

"What's the difference?"

"An event planner knows how to fold napkins," Pinkie said.

I ignored him. "An event planner has the job of planning and organizing everything so that everyone can have a good time. An event hostess has the job of making sure everyone actually *has* one."

"How do you do that?" Arnaud asked.

"Well, think back to the last dinner party you had a really good time at."

"Let's see," Arnaud said, "The food was perfect, we had several drinks, which never hurts, but mostly I was seated next to an attractive woman who was hanging on my every word."

"Right," Pinkie said. "Only instead of an attractive woman, imagine Lora."

I shot him a murderous look.

Arnaud gave me a gallant smile. "We Swiss banker types are quite famously short on imagination, which is why it's a good thing that Lora is an extremely attractive woman. No imagination required."

"I never knew there was such a profession," Hubert said, "but as a widower, I've often wished I had someone to help me when I had to throw a client event. Helen was always so good at that kind of thing. I'm really not that clever at parties, I'm afraid." Hubert looked over at Sarina. "You see, my dear, there are all kinds of jobs out there to consider."

Sarina rolled her eyes. "I need a job where I'm making a difference. Not just flitting around trying to charm a bunch of overprivileged rich people into drinking. No offense, Lora."

I narrowed my eyes at her. Sarina didn't appear to have any charm to speak of, but I was pretty sure that when it came to getting people to drink, she was second to none. She was driving me to drink even as we spoke. I took a healthy swig of my Welch's grape juice and tried to remember what it had been like to be a spoiled little princess with a streak of moral superiority that ran straight to the bone. Oh wait—I had never been one of those. No wonder I was so unsympathetic.

Hubert looked at me apologetically. "My daughter wants to go work at a girls' school in Pakistan when she graduates. I'm trying to convince her that there are other jobs out there that don't involve putting herself at risk."

"Your father is right," I told Sarina, "but even if you do decide to go into a field like international aid, I think you'll find that learning how to keep people entertained and happy is a pretty valuable life skill. It's a lot easier to get people to listen to you when you've got a lot of booze and a little charm."

Sarina's mouth tightened. "It's an Islamic country. Alcoholic drinks are out of the question."

"So trust me—you'll need a lot more charm," I said.

Arnaud flashed me an amused look and put his napkin on the table. "Lora, did you and Philippe have plans for the afternoon? It's such a beautiful day that I was thinking about going for a short bike ride. Perhaps you'd like to join me?" He glanced over at Sarina. "Of course you're welcome to come as well, Sarina."

Sarina looked at him with a touch of condescension. "I have work to do. I have grant applications to write, you know. Every moment I spend indulging myself in some frivolous activity is a lost opportunity to make a difference in the world."

"Of course," Arnaud said, his face absolutely serious except for the faintest twinkle in his eye. "I wouldn't want to distract you from making a difference in the world."

Pinkie pushed back slightly from the table. "Well, I for one love riding bikes in the country."

I stared at him in disbelief. Pinkie loathed any form of transportation that wasn't being piloted by someone else. I didn't think he owned a single pair of shoes that could hold together for longer than the distance between a limo and the foyer of Prince Abdul's apartment building, which is where he lived when he wasn't crashing with friends in ridiculously expensive flats in the world's most fashionable locations.

"Unfortunately," Pinkie continued, "that wretched car has simply destroyed my knee." He rubbed it and gave Hubert a pathetic look. "I think I'll go and lie down for an hour or so and see whether that helps."

I looked at him suspiciously. Perhaps my memory was playing tricks on me, but I seemed to recall that he was rubbing the other knee when he got out of the car.

Hubert looked concerned. "I'm so sorry, Philippe. We might have some aspirin or something..."

"No aspirin," Pinkie said, putting on a heroic look, "but perhaps some ice. I'd hate to have it swell up. Oh, and as long as I'm going to be stuck inside, maybe I'll take a look at some of the old photo albums. Coming back here has made me nostalgic."

"You? Nostalgic?" Hubert chuckled, but I could tell from the way his face softened that he was touched by Pinkie's sudden interest in the good old days. "Actually, most of the photo albums are on the bookshelf in your room, so help yourself. And I'll have the housekeeper make you an ice wrap."

Pinkie waved a hand. "No, need. If she can just bring up an ice bucket and a towel, I'll make it myself. I hate to cause a fuss."

Now I knew something was up. Pinkie loved to cause a fuss.

"I'll send her right up," Hubert promised.

Arnaud looked at me. "That leaves just you and me." I felt a little tingle in my stomach. I was usually pretty good at telling when men were interested, and I was definitely getting an interested vibe.

"It sounds lovely, but I should warn you that I haven't ridden a bike since I got my driver's license, about ten years ago."

"Ten years ago?" Pinkie chimed in. "Really, Lora? I bet it seems like longer. Like half a decade longer."

It occurred to me that maybe Hubert had ensured I had a connecting door to Pinkie's room so that I could creep in and smother him in his sleep.

"Pinkie, don't you have to go ice yourself?" I asked sweetly.

"I do," he said, limping off regally toward the stairs. He had definitely switched legs since he had hobbled out of the car. I shook my head.

"Let me just go up to change," I told Arnaud. "I'll meet you back down here in five minutes.

8

I went up to my room and changed into pants, helping myself to a few more truffles while I was there. Given their addictive nature, it occurred to me that the white powder on the outside might be cocaine rather than sugar. Really, given the relative calorie count, cocaine might actually make them healthier.

I gave the box a hard look. I must have eaten at least ten since we had arrived, but the level in the box didn't appear to have gone down at all. Apparently Hubert had a really competent household staff. Or maybe the box was one of those magic tablecloth things that never emptied, no matter how many truffles you ate. Maybe black magic made them irresistible. I popped another into my mouth. Who was I to resist the forces of darkness?

Arnaud wasn't in the living room when I returned, and while I waited for him to join me, I examined the photographs on the mantelpiece. By far the majority of the pictures were of a lovely brunette with a mischievous look and a keen sense of fashion.

"Helen, Hubert's wife," Arnaud said as he came into the room. "She really was a lovely woman, wasn't she?"

"Beautiful," I agreed. "Sarina looks a lot like her." Sarina had inherited her mother's strong cheekbones and almond eyes, but her skin was much paler, and there was a pinched look around Sarina's mouth that I associated with librarians and people who gave you dirty looks when you ordered mimosas at brunch.

Arnaud nodded, coming over to join me at the mantelpiece.

"She does, although Helen was much more carefree than Sarina has ever been." He picked up a photograph of Helen standing in front of a vintage Porsche. "She really was a hellion in her youth. Much younger than Hubert, of course. It was a bit of an odd match in some ways—Hubert so serious and conservative, Helen so young and wild. But it worked. Hubert adored her."

I picked up a photograph of her in a room lined with books. "That was taken in the firm's library. A couple years after they got married, Helen decided that she was going to give Hubert a birthday present—a history of Richter and Partners. The bank is the oldest private bank in Switzerland, you know, so there was a lot to look at. What was supposed to be a three-month project ended up taking her years to finish. She had just completed the final draft when she died in a boating accident off of the Cayman Islands."

"Hubert must have been devastated."

"He was, of course. Hubert grew up in this house, but I think she was really the one who made it a home for him. She was one of those people who really seemed able to do anything she put her mind to. When she was here, even the wine was good. She made Hubert upgrade to modern equipment. God knows what he was using before. Probably barrels from the eighteenth century."

We stood for a moment in silence. "So," Arnaud said, breaking the gloomy atmosphere, "are you ready for our trip? I was thinking that we could bike over to the next town. It's called Staefa."

"Staefa..." I said. The name rang a bell. Suddenly it came to me. "That's where Dieter's place is. I didn't know it would be so close."

Arnaud nodded. "I've been there many times. Dieter was always inviting us over when we were kids. He claimed it was so that he could exercise the horses, but I really think he just liked having people around. When he figured out how to make a living throwing parties for other people, his father breathed a big sigh of relief, I can tell you. His place is about fifteen minutes away by bike, if you want to see it."

"Great! But I should warn you that I wasn't kidding about not having been on a bike in a long time."

"Well, you know what they say about riding a bike, right?"

"That it will get you stoned in some countries?"

Arnaud laughed. "Not this country. Swiss people love bikes. No, you really do never forget."

Arnaud and I went around to the front of the house, where two bicycles had been pulled onto the circular drive. They had baskets and headlights and overall looked just like something that you'd expect to be riding in Provence in the springtime to pick up a bundle of flowers and a baguette.

I looked down at my fitted blue pants. I kind of wished I was wearing a full, floral dress that would flutter appealingly as I pedaled. Of course, knowing me, it would probably get caught in the chain and send me plunging down into the grape terraces, where I would lie, bloodied and scratched and not remotely appealing.

"So," Arnaud said, walking me over to the bike. "Brakes are here. You only have six gears, here," he said, operating a thumb switch. "And voilà…it's just that easy."

I nodded, feeling nervous. "Let me just take it for a spin around the driveway."

I pushed off, managing to get the pedal most of the way around before it suddenly encountered an unexpected obstruction. "Aigh!" I yelled, slamming on the brakes and jumping onto my feet. "I think there's a problem with the bike. The pedals are stuck."

Arnaud was obviously struggling not to laugh. "It works better when you put up the kickstand."

"Right," I said, flushing. "Kickstand. Check."

I put up the kickstand and set off again around the circle, gaining in confidence as I rode. I had forgotten how much fun riding a bike could be. Maybe I could get one when I got back to New York. Of course, riding a bike in Brooklyn and riding a bike in the vineyards of Switzerland probably had about as much in common as Velveeta and Camembert. I pulled to a stop in front of him. "I'm ready. Let's go."

Arnaud set off down the road, which was lined with vineyards and rose gardens. The grape terraces were laid out on steep slopes facing the lake to catch the sun. The road sloped gently downhill, requiring little effort on my part to keep up with Arnaud.

"There's no traffic here," he called back over his shoulder. "Why don't you pull up beside me?"

I pulled my bike even with his, and he gave me an easy smile. I felt a warm glow of pleasure that had nothing to do with the bike or the view. "See, you haven't forgotten how to ride after all. Did you bike a lot when you were a kid?"

"Until I got my driver's license. But just around the neighborhood. Most Delaware drivers think of bikes as target practice."

"Delaware? That sounds familiar. Is that a city?"

"Technically it's a state. For reasons nobody has ever understood, Thomas Jefferson actually called it the Diamond State, making that probably the United States' earliest example of false advertising. Of course, when I was a kid they took that off the signs and replaced it with 'Home of tax-free shopping.' Delawareans were totally fine with blowing off one of the founding fathers if it led to more sales at the Christiana Mall Sunglass Hut."

Arnaud laughed. "Sounds like a very pragmatic place. Was it settled by Swiss people? We're quite the pragmatists, you know."

"I have no idea, but it wouldn't surprise me. It's actually the least transparent banking jurisdiction in the world. It's a point of state pride."

"Ah. Maybe that's why it sounds familiar. Maybe we should open a branch there."

I took in his perfectly tailored button-down shirt, English shoes, and chinos. "Well, if you do decide to open a branch there, make sure they send someone else to staff it."

"You don't think I could make it on the rough and ready American frontier?" Arnaud asked, feigning outrage.

"Cowboys and pickup trucks maybe, but I don't think you could make it through lunch at TGI Friday's without booking your return flight. But enough about deep-fried cheese."

"Okay," Arnaud said, "let's talk melted cheese instead. Tell me about this dinner that Dieter's got planned."

I sighed. "Imagine for a moment that you're a deranged egomaniac who owns a tour company called Authentic Tours. You're looking for a Swiss partner to help host your clients en route to Asia. Rich clients, high expectations, big profits. But…it has to be 'authentic.'"

Arnaud looked thoughtful. "What does 'authentic' mean when it comes to Switzerland?"

"That's the thousand-dollar question. Actually, it's more like the hundred thousand-dollar question, which is why this is such a big deal for Dieter. He's got some stuff lined up that sounds okay, but I'm wondering if we shouldn't try something bigger, Swissier. Something really impressive. I mean, if you had to give me an example of something Dieter could do with some guests that really typifies 'authentic Switzerland,' what would it be?"

Arnaud thought about it for a moment. "Aha! Maybe he can let them take out the garbage. You start with your cans, of course, then three colors of bottles, then corks...those are separate. Batteries, milk bottles, PET bottles are all separate, too. Paper and cardboard need to be tied with recycled string into neat little packages. Light bulbs and electronics have their own rules. Umm...let's see...DVDs are different, and old bread is collected so that they can use it for animals. And god help you if you put your carrot peels in the trash at all. Those go in the composting bins. Then you put whatever's left into a bag, and put a sticker on it showing that you've paid your garbage taxes."

I looked at him, slack jawed.

"That is how Swiss garbage works? You need to put all of those tiny containers outside your house every week?"

"Oh no," Arnaud said, laughing. "You need to haul all of those tiny containers to the grocery store, the electronics store, the farm, or the recycling center. They only pick up paper and cardboard."

"I give you points for authenticity, but I think that's too authentic for this particular purpose. The problem is that when people say they want to experience 'authentic' culture, it usually means they want to experience an American movie about what that culture was like fifty years ago. I can tell you that every American I've ever known who's talked about 'authentic' Japanese culture is talking geishas, not liver-damaged workaholics playing pachinko and reading comic books."

"Did Dieter try just asking the deranged egomaniac what he was looking for?"

"Of course. And do you know what he said?"

"If you just did what I told you to do, it wouldn't be authentic."

"That's amazing. Maybe you have a future as a deranged egomaniac."

"Who says I'm not already one?" Arnaud pulled his bike to a halt and pointed up ahead of us. "We're here. Dieter Schumacher's house is right over there."

I examined it critically. The house was a half-timbered rustic building with colorful window boxes and an old barn attached. The shutters were painted in brightly colored wavy sunbursts that would have been garish in America but seemed natural here.

"Looks pretty authentic to me," Arnaud said. We parked the bikes and wandered over into the field.

"Me too," I started, before I was interrupted by a low clanking noise that sounded like someone beating a soupspoon against a Honda.

"What the heck was that?!" I asked, spinning around. I turned in the direction of the clanking and found myself face to face with a cow that had somehow managed to creep up behind me.

"Aigh!" I yelled, stumbling backward. I threw my hands up in self-defense. Arnaud grabbed me around the waist to keep me from falling.

"I'm guessing you're not too familiar with cows," he said, trying not to laugh.

"I'm perfectly familiar with cows. But mostly when they're in steak form."

The cow nudged me gently with its nose and mooed. I patted it lightly on the head. "Good cow," I said, hoping that it was, in fact, a good cow and not one of those bad cows that stampeded and trampled innocent event hostesses to death.

Arnaud gave the cow a speculative look. "Cows are very authentic. Is Dieter planning on doing anything with cows?"

I looked at the cow thoughtfully. "Not that I know of. But that could actually be pretty interesting. Dinner in a big tent under the stars, cows all around…"

"Two problems with that. First, the weather in Zurich is miserable. Sunny, cloudy, apocalyptic hail…you never know what to expect."

"And second?"

The cow let out a loud 'whooshing' noise, and suddenly we were engulfed in a choking miasma of methane. I stumbled back, coughing.

"That. Cows are gassy."

I shook my head. "I'm officially crossing cows off of my authentic Swiss list. Let's hope Dieter's up to speed on the whole farting cows thing."

"This is Switzerland," Arnaud said drily. "Everybody's up to speed on that."

9

Arnaud and I poked around a bit longer in Dieter's fields, taking a couple of photos of the cows, the house, and the mountains off in the distance before taking a seat outside a tiny, windowless building on the edge of Dieter's property. "Are you thirsty?" Arnaud asked, rummaging around in the basket of his bike.

"You brought water? You're amazing."

He pulled a split of Veuve Clicquot and two crystal flutes from his bike basket. Filling them both, he handed one to me. Ice cold. "I brought champagne. Does that make me more amazing or less amazing?"

"That makes you Captain Amazing. Too amazing, as a matter of fact. Obviously you're hiding a dark and revolting secret."

Arnaud raised an eyebrow. "Dark and revolting? Really? Like what?"

I peered at him as if I were reading his soul. "You put mayonnaise on french fries."

"Ooh. Good guess, but I actually hate mayonnaise."

"Really? Me too. Did you also spend a weekend begging to be put out of your misery after eating potato salad in the summer in Tennessee?"

"Greece."

"Okay, so not that." I looked at him again. Gosh, what else could be wrong with an attractive thirtysomething partner in a private bank with great taste in cars and a loathing for mayonnaise?

"You're not a cat person, are you?" I asked, valiantly suppressing the urge to sneeze.

"More of a dog person. I had a schnauzer growing up. Most stubborn dog in the world. He barked every time anyone came near the house and drove my mother to distraction by hiding sticks under the rugs where they would trip you when you weren't looking. He lived to be seventeen years old. My mother always said he was too stubborn to die."

"Hmm. Then it's probably something I can't see, like a love of leopard print thong underwear."

"What's wrong with leopard print thong underwear? I love thong underwear."

"Oh my god...you're not wearing thong underwear now, are you?" I asked, blushing. "I mean, it's none of my business, of course. I was just kidding. Some men find them very comfortable," I said desperately.

"They make thong underwear for men?!?" He started laughing. "You thought I was wearing..." We both started laughing then, and before I knew it I was wiping tears away.

"I don't suppose you have a pack of tissues in that magic basket of yours?" I asked.

"Will this suffice?" He pulled out a neatly folded handkerchief and held it out to me.

"Old school."

"It's Switzerland. It's what we do."

"Speaking of old schools," I said, gesturing to the small building behind us, "is that what this building is? It looks too small to be a real house."

Arnaud looked at it. "This? No, it's not a school. It's not a house, either. It's a fallout shelter."

"A fallout shelter?" I repeated, looking at it in surprise. "Like for nuclear bombs?"

"Yep. All private houses were required to have one until just a few years ago. This one, if I recall, is pretty decent sized inside." He made a half circle with his hands. "The building is just to cover the entrance. Under the house it's like an igloo."

"Can anyone just go in?"

He shook his head. "Dieter put this one in when he renovated the farm. I think he was expecting a few more grandchildren than he ended up with. If you want, maybe you can get him to show you around after your dinner. It's probably very interesting—Dieter is pretty high up in the Swiss military, you know. He takes the whole preparedness thing pretty seriously."

"Well good, because he'll need to be prepared if he's going to make any progress with Jack Green." I took a sip of champagne, feeling a little better about the dinner. Clearly, a man who built a fallout shelter large enough for his yet-to-be born grandchildren could be expected to plan ahead for even the unlikeliest contingencies. I'd still have liked something more earth shattering than throwing rocks and yodeling pop stars, but it would probably be fine, which meant that I just had to hold my own against Vanessa. Which reminded me that I should probably be interviewing Hubert about wrestling and fondue and other Swiss stuff rather than pedaling around the countryside with Arnaud.

I looked at my watch. "I hate to say it, but we should probably head back." I stood up and brushed my pants off, handing the empty champagne flute back to Arnaud. "This was so lovely. Thank you for inviting me."

Arnaud smiled. "It was my pleasure. Now, before we set off again, is there anything you wanted to tell me?"

I looked at him in surprise. "I don't think so." Actually, I wanted to tell him that I was fully available for some romance later in the evening, but under pressure, I couldn't figure out how to say that without sounding slutty. "Why?"

"Because the way back is all uphill," he said, winking. "You'll need to save your breath."

10

I was going to kill my personal trainer. An hour a day, five days a week of abs, push-ups, plyometrics, lunges, squats, running, medicine balls, and whatever else the gorgeous and scrawny of Hollywood were swearing by that week, and I was still panting like a woman in labor by the time we got back to the house.

My mother used to tell me that ladies didn't sweat, they glowed. As we pulled up to the house, I was uncomfortably aware of the fact that I was glowing like crazy.

Arnaud nodded approvingly. "You did really well. Most people need to take a break on the way back."

There had been the option to take a break on the way back?! Now I felt needlessly sweaty, which is the worst kind of sweatiness. I sighed. Given the amount of truffles I had eaten earlier, I should probably be thankful for the exercise. I had probably burned off at least one, maybe one and a half of those sinful little nuggets. Which left somewhere around twenty to go.

I looked at my watch. "If it's all the same to you, I think I'll sneak in and try to take a shower before anyone sees me. What time is…"

"Lora Godwin! Thank heavens I caught you. How wonderful to see you again!" A musical voice interrupted me, and I turned to see a strikingly patrician woman with thick blonde hair leaving Hubert's house. She wore a jade-green dress cinched with a wide belt that called attention to her ridiculously tiny waist.

"Vanessa St. Germain," I said, trying to unobtrusively unstick my shirt from my stomach. "What an unexpected surprise. Are you here to see me?"

"I was, but Hubert told me that you were out. What a charming gentleman. He told me you were out with one of his partners." She turned a dazzling smile on Arnaud, who smiled back in return. "You must be Arnaud. What a pleasure. I hope I'm not interrupting?" She widened her emerald eyes at Arnaud innocently, and I squelched the urge to shove her.

"Not at all." Arnaud looked to me for an introduction. "Arnaud, this is Vanessa St. Germain. She's a hostess as well. She's going to be helping Ueli with the dinner for the Jack Green contract."

Arnaud raised an eyebrow at her. "So you're Lora's competition?"

Vanessa gave a tinkling laugh and tapped him on the arm playfully. "Not at all. Dieter and Ueli are competing for the same contract, that's true, but Lora and I are really more colleagues than competitors, wouldn't you say? I mean, we do the same job, but we don't exactly run in the same circles."

"Really," Arnaud said, shooting me an unreadable look.

"Definitely. For example, if you want to see something in Brooklyn, Lora's definitely your girl. I don't know too much about the outer boroughs. Or if you had hired a bus and you needed someone to take you on a tour…"

"Were you here for some reason?" I asked, cutting her off.

"Oh, sorry," she said, fluttering her eyelashes. "I didn't mean to prattle on. I can see I'm keeping you from the shower."

Arnaud let out a tiny cough that I suspected was a stifled laugh.

"I just came over to leave you a little gift. You know, just to wish you good luck, even if we are on different sides of this particular competition. I thought you might find it useful, and I knew you'd understand the sentiment behind it. I left it in the entry."

"How kind of you," I said, making my voice as chilly as possible. "I didn't get you anything."

"Nonsense," she said, placing a hand on my shoulder and tilting her head endearingly at Arnaud. "You introduced me to Arnaud. I think that's the best gift I'll get all week." She smiled again, oozing charm.

"The pleasure is all mine," Arnaud said.

"Well," I cut in, "it certainly was lovely of you to stop by. All the best for your dinner. I'm sure you'll do brilliantly."

"Well, I must admit, I do have something dazzling planned. But I really can't talk about it. You understand."

I smiled and said nothing, letting the silence stretch between us. I pointedly looked at my watch.

"Well, I guess I'd better head out," she said, her voice chipper. "Best of luck, Lora."

"Same to you." I stood next to Arnaud, and we both smiled at her as she got into a Porsche and revved the engine once, extending a hand out the window in a wave as she pulled out of Hubert's driveway.

"So," Arnaud said.

"So."

"Colleagues."

"Apparently."

He stifled a smile. "Should we see what she left for you?"

"Let's."

The gift turned out to be a green box of champagne truffles from Teuscher and a glossy hardcover book about Switzerland. It was tasteful, lovely, and packed with information.

"Kind of her," Arnaud said, his voice neutral.

"You bet."

"You don't sound convinced."

I wondered whether to tell him that the truffles were intended to make me fat and spotty prior to the dinner and the book was a subtle jab at my lack of knowledge about "authentic" Switzerland. Even though I knew I was right, I was pretty sure that Arnaud would think I was a paranoid lunatic if I spelled it out for him. Men were such simple creatures.

I smiled at him instead, evading the comment. "I just wanted to thank you again for the bike ride. But after that workout, I think I'm off to the shower. Do you know what time we're supposed to meet for dinner?"

"Drinks start at six in the parlor. Gerhardt and Reiner should be here then."

"Great. I'll see you then." I smiled at him, tucked the book under my arm, and headed for the stairs, pleasantly aware of a tingle at the back of my neck where Arnaud was watching me. At least I hoped that was the cause. It could also have been sweat rolling down into a big spot on the back of my shirt. I picked up my pace, just in case.

Once I got to my room, I set the truffles aside and flipped the book open to the inside cover. *Best of luck on your dinner. If you need any advice on what to see while you're here, I'm happy to help—my years here in school have made me practically a native! Warmest wishes, Vanessa*, the inside flap read.

I felt my cheeks burning, and I grabbed a couple of truffles from Hubert's box and tried to stand still. The Swiss, blessed with a climate that rarely got hot, were not big fans of air conditioning, which meant that standing naked on the central air conditioning vent, which I had long ago determined to be the fastest way to cool off after riding the subway, was out of the question here. I walked over to the connecting door with Pinkie. Maybe I could steal his ice pack to cool down a bit.

I knocked softly on the door.

"Mmm!" I heard back.

Loosely interpreting that as "Come in," I opened the door. "You wouldn't believe who was lying in wait for me when I came back…" I started.

Pinkie looked at me guiltily, a split of Veuve Clicquot still clutched in his hand. "Pinkie!" I said, taking in the scene. "What are you doing?"

Another two splits were chilling in the ice bucket that he had commandeered for medical purposes. Photo albums were opened all over the bed. Clearly, Pinkie wasn't taking this trip down memory lane without provisions.

"Did you fake a knee injury so that you could get ice for your Veuve?!"

"Not only. Also so that I wouldn't have to go hiking or biking or cow tipping or whatever other Swiss thing Arnaud was going to propose." He gave me a dark look. "The Swiss are never happy unless they're sweating, sunburned, and being eaten alive by bugs."

"Where did you even get Veuve? I thought Hubert only served wines that he produced."

"He does, which is why I had to pack my own survival kit." He gestured to a Louis Vuitton duffle that was unzipped to reveal a stack of Veuve splits.

"Let me get this straight. You brought a full bag of Veuve Clicquot to Switzerland so that you wouldn't have to drink Swiss wine, and then you faked a knee injury so that you could get an ice bucket? That's low, Pinkie, even for you."

"I prefer to think that I brought a full bag of Veuve Clicquot to Switzerland and faked a knee injury so that *we* could avoid drinking Swiss wine." He popped the cork and handed me a split.

I took the bottle. "Well obviously that's completely different."

I took a long sip. God. If there was anything better than a cold bottle of Veuve Clicquot after biking uphill for twenty minutes through the world's most beautiful vineyards, I had no idea what it was. It sure as heck wasn't a cold bottle of water. I sipped for a few moments in silence so that I could be a little less glowy.

Pinkie looked at me closely. "My god. Did you go for bike ride or a swim? I think you're actually dripping."

I frowned at him. "Uphill is not my forte. And we can't all fake knee injuries, you know."

"What were you prattling on about when you came in? Someone lying in wait, I think you said…?" Pinkie asked, clearly trying to change the subject.

"That witch Vanessa St. Germain."

"She was here?"

"She left me a book. On Switzerland."

"Telling you that you better do your homework, I assume."

"Exactly! She's trying to rattle me, Pinkie."

Pinkie shook his head, a smile of appreciation on his face. "I tell you, Lora, you almost have to admire the girl."

"I have to do no such thing." I gestured to the photo albums spread across the bed. "But on a less revolting topic of conversation, do you mind telling me what you're looking for here? Since when did you develop an interest in history?"

Pinkie lifted his chin. "I was a classics major at Oxford, Lora. I've always had an interest in history."

I cocked an eyebrow at him.

"Okay, actually I had an interest in the teaching assistant in the classics department. It's practically the same thing. But in this case I wanted to figure out what Maurice was talking about with this Jurg person."

"Just let it drop, Pinkie. Hubert clearly adores you. Don't let Maurice upset you. I doubt you'd be able to figure it out from old photos, anyway."

"You underestimate me, as always, Lora. Maurice said that Jurg was dismissed because of something that we had in common, right?"

"Right," I said, taking another sip.

"And Hubert said that it wasn't criminal. So we're looking for something personal that led to his dismissal."

"Right."

"So look at these pictures." Pinkie walked over to the bed and tapped a photo of Hubert and his wife standing next to two younger men. All four wore boating outfits, and the location had a certain sun-drenched intensity that made me think of Santorini. Hubert's face was filled with happiness as he looked at his wife. Pinkie touched the younger man on the left. "This is Jurg."

I picked up the photo and looked at it closely. Jurg's white pants and linen shirt were tailored close to his elegantly slender frame. His jutting cheekbones and hooded eyes gave him a severe look that was belied by a full, almost sensual mouth. One hand held a cigarette loosely, the other a drink. His mouth was twisted slightly in a wry smile. The young man standing next to him looked altogether like a simpler soul, with friendly bright blue eyes and a corn-fed wholesomeness that came across even in the photo.

"Who's the friend?"

Pinkie flipped the picture over. "*Jack*, it says. Honestly, why do people even bother labeling photographs if they're going to do such a poor job? Jack indeed."

"So?"

"Now this one." This time Jurg was sitting in full ski gear at an outdoor bar, the inevitable cigarette in hand. The man sitting next to him, a dark, intense-looking type, held himself rigidly, clearly uncomfortable in front of the camera. Jurg looked cold. A full ashtray on the table was flanked by a pair of beer steins.

"Still not getting it."

"Now look at this one," Pinkie said, pulling out a photo with Jurg and a different man, both in evening dress, emerging from what looked like the opera.

"You think Hubert asked him to leave because he had a social life? Wasn't this back in the days when you were *supposed* to have a life outside of work?"

"Isn't it obvious?"

I looked at the photos again. "Not to me."

"He's gay, Lora."

I blinked. "Well, maybe, but so what? You think Hubert fired him because he was gay?"

"What if he did?"

I shrugged. "Well, yes, I can see how that would be disappointing, but you have to remember that times were different, and you're always telling me that Swiss bankers are the most conservative people on earth. I mean, even if that were the reason Hubert fired him, you're gay, and he obviously doesn't hold it against you, right?"

Pinkie looked away guiltily.

I sat back on the bed. "Wait a minute. He does know you're gay, right?"

Pinkie remained silent.

Something in my mind suddenly clicked. "Wait a minute. Is that why we have connecting rooms? Does Hubert think we're sleeping together?"

"Maybe," Pinkie said, sniffing. "You could do worse, you know. In fact, you have done worse fairly recently," he pointed out. "At least I'm not a murderous white slaver."

"That was a one-time thing, and I didn't know he was a white slaver when I slept with him. It's not that. It's just...come on..." I gestured at Pinkie, resplendent in a pink ascot, his tiny bottle of Veuve clutched in his hand like a security blanket. "Even if you didn't come right out and say it, don't you think he's noticed? And why would he even care? Nobody cares anymore. It's not a thing."

"It's not a thing for people now, but Hubert isn't really living in the now. He hasn't kept up with popular culture since the '70s."

"I'm pretty sure there were gay people in the 1970s," I told him, taking another sip of bubbly.

"Yes, well, when it comes to Hubert, we're looking more at the 1870s. And I'm not trying to keep it a secret. It's not like you go around announcing that you prefer to sleep with men. Although given the way you were gawking at Arnaud, you might want to consider a neon sign or a tattoo across your forehead. More discreet, you know."

"Well, I'd agree that you're not hiding anything, but even if Hubert didn't know, he seems like a really sweet guy who loves you very much. I'm sure he'd be fine with you being gay."

"I would have thought so, too, until I saw these pictures. But what if Hubert really *did* fire Jurg because he was gay? You can see from the pictures that they were social friends as well as business partners. What if Hubert really thinks that being gay is some kind of perversion?" Pinkie touched the picture of Jurg, biting his lip.

I put my hand on his arm. "Okay, worst-case scenario: Say that charming old Hubert, your godfather, who has loved you since you were a child, is a rabid homophobe. You really think your cousin Maurice would out you to your godfather over a watch?"

"God, yes," Pinkie said with feeling.

I shook my head. "So...you're going to let Maurice have the watch?"

"Of course not. I would never allow myself to be blackmailed like that."

"So you're going to tell Hubert."

"Uh...probably. But not just yet." Pinkie slouched down and nibbled nervously on a cuticle.

"Pinkie, if he doesn't stand by you when you tell him, he's not worth having in your life."

Pinkie sighed. "It's different when it's family, Lora. I never told my father, either, because I knew he'd be so disappointed." He shook his head. "They were just raised in a different time. I don't blame them. It's like how I feel about snowboards. People tell me there's objectively nothing wrong with them, but I can't help thinking that anyone who prefers a snowboard to pair of skis is a deviant. It's just a generational thing, I guess."

I snickered. "I'm not sure it's exactly the same, Pinkie. And anyway, I don't buy that whole generation gap thing. Hubert's an old man, sure, but he doesn't seem out of touch. Even if he did fire Jurg for being gay, I'm sure his opinions have changed over time."

Pinkie gave me a doleful look. "Swiss bankers never change. That's why people trust them." He took a sip of champagne, his face clouded with worry.

"Speaking of changing," I said, glancing at my watch, "I better get into my room and get ready. Is there anything I need to know about this partner's dinner that we've accidentally crashed?"

Pinkie stood up, closing the photo album with a snap. "Don't worry about it. It's not really a business thing. It's just a chance for all four of the partners to get together and talk about ancient history."

"Unless Arnaud is much older than he looks, I doubt he'd have much to add to that conversation."

"Oh, trust me," Pinkie said, rolling his eyes. "Every partner can go on and on and on about ancient history. Arnaud heard all the stories from his father, who heard the stories from his father, and all the way back to the founding of the bank. It's like four crusty old guys have been forcibly downloaded into Arnaud's brain."

"Eww. Why do you say things like that?"

"Just so you're not shocked when he asks you to wear a corset. Although given the amount of those truffles you've eaten since you got here, I can't imagine that would be too shocking. Frankly, *I'm* on the verge of asking you to wear a corset."

"What about Reiner? I gathered from your earlier attempts to pulverize my hand that you weren't too fond of him. Am I to take it that he's some sort of half-wit?"

Pinkie snorted, shaking his head in irritation. "They should be so lucky. Stupid people are never an issue. They're usually afraid of messing things up, so they rarely do any damage. I'd go so far as to say that stupid people are the very bedrock of society. Reiner isn't stupid at all, more's the pity. He's hard working and diabolically clever."

"Really? *Diabolically* clever? Do you hate him because he's hard working and smart, or did he actually do something evil?"

Pinkie narrowed his eyes. "I suspect him of many things, but I've never been able to prove any of them."

"You know, Pinkie, people can be hard working and smart without being evil."

"I suppose it's theoretically possible, but trust me—Reiner isn't one of those people."

11

Five minutes after my shower, I was in front of the mirror smearing on some concoction that Pinkie told me was a "base layer," which meant that it did basically nothing, as far as I could tell. I had never quite figured out how something called "base layer" could possible cost three hundred dollars an ounce. Honestly, if you're charging that much money for a skin cream, it should cover any and all layers that need to be covered, and it should protect you from sun, time, parking tickets, and possibly bullets.

With my makeup mostly under control, I turned my attention to my dress, a sea foam-green silk sheath that Pinkie assured me coordinated beautifully with my eyes. Unfortunately, it wasn't coordinating well with my waist. I had promised my personal trainer that I'd try to stick to a paleo diet while I was here, but given how quickly I'd surrendered to the siren call of non-caveman-produced chocolate truffles, I figured that wasn't going to work.

I pulled out my phone and scrolled quickly through my list of diets, looking for one that was optimally suited to the environment. Atkins, cabbage soup…chocolate diet! Obviously that was the right one to follow. I felt immediately better now that I was following a sensible eating plan. Of course, I wasn't really sure exactly how the chocolate diet worked, but it seemed pretty obvious that eating chocolate was a big part of it, and clearly I had that covered.

I pulled the dress off again and yanked on a miserably constricting set of Spanx. As a fan of breathing, I usually tried to avoid shapewear, but desperate times called for desperate measures. I shot a speculative look at the box of truffles sitting innocently on the nightstand. Maybe the problem was that I wasn't eating enough of them to boost my metabolism, I thought, grabbing another truffle.

To compensate for my wider hips, I put on a couple of extra layers of mascara. Maybe people would be so distracted by my bewitchingly long lashes that they wouldn't even notice the fact that I was risking compression fractures just to get the zipper of my dress up.

All of the primping and breath holding was worth it when I saw Arnaud's face light up as I came down the stairs. "Lora!" he said. "You look lovely. I think the fresh air did you good."

I smiled at him. "Yes, the fresh air," I agreed, secretly thanking the new bronzer Pinkie had magicked up from somewhere. Fresh air, given its eye-reddening pollen and wrinkle-causing sun, was public enemy number one on my list.

"Let me introduce you to Richter and Partners' newest partner," he said, steering me over to a whippet-thin young man with thinning hair and a penetrating gaze. "Lora, this is Reiner. Reiner, this is Lora Godwin."

"Reiner. How lovely to meet you." He took my hand in his, and I tried not to wince at its slight dampness. Given my own bout with exercise earlier on in the day, I was hardly one to make a fuss over a little stickiness in the palms, particularly on a night when Reiner was being brought in as a partner, surely the culmination of years of effort that had started with the careful selection of his parents (or at least his uncle).

"Arnaud didn't tell me he'd be bringing a guest," Reiner said smoothly, looking at me with disconcerting intensity.

"That's because she's not my guest, unfortunately," Arnaud said. "Philippe is here."

"Prince Philippe?" Reiner asked, his eyes narrowing.

"No need for titles among friends, old chap," Pinkie said, striding into the room. I wondered how long he'd been hovering outside, waiting for the right moment to make his entrance. My bet was on quite some time.

"How surprising to find you here," Reiner said, holding out his hand to inflict his damp mitt on Pinkie. "I don't suppose you're being brought in as a partner too? Finance was never your thing, was it? All those...numbers."

Pinkie gave Reiner his most charming smile. "Definitely not. I'm more of a creative type."

"Really? And what have you created..." Reiner suddenly stopped cold, his mouth snapping shut as Sarina walked into the room.

If Pinkie had timed his moment well, Sarina had no need to worry about timing. In a simple, conservative ivory dress, her hair down, blue eyes sparkling, she was gorgeous. She shook her head a little bit, causing waves of dark, glossy hair to swing in what I could have sworn was slow motion. I let out an inward sigh. Maintenance—even the best maintenance Pinkie could beg, buy, or steal on my behalf—was never going to make me a beautiful twenty-two-year-old. Arnaud handed me a glass of wine and leaned over to whisper in my ear. "She cleans up well for such a humorless child, doesn't she?"

Two points for Arnaud: one for noticing my distress and another for his use of the word "child" to refer to a college-aged student. Oh, and two additional points for the wine, now that I thought about it. A man who was quick to distribute alcohol always got bonus points in my book. Sarina gave her father a kiss on the cheek and came over to where we were standing.

I squelched down my jealousy and gave her a smile. "You look lovely, Sarina. How is your paper going?"

"Fine," she said shortly, taking a glass of wine from Pinkie, who was manfully choking down Hubert's latest vintage with an enthusiasm that I attributed to Reiner.

"What paper is that?" Reiner asked.

"In preparation for the volunteer work I plan on doing in Pakistan, I'm studying the role of patriarchal tribalism on women's education initiatives."

I raised an eyebrow. "I would have thought the role of patriarchal tribalism was pretty much to stop women's education initiatives."

"I'm sure it looks like that to the uninformed, but as an academic I need to look past the simple answers and dig into the cultural underpinnings. It's possible that what looks like misogyny to a Western eye is really only a misunderstanding of a deeply entrenched protective instinct. Of course, I'm sure this kind of discussion isn't interesting to someone in your line of "—she paused for half a heartbeat—"work."

Pinkie took my elbow to hold me back, probably anticipating bloodshed.

I was saved from having to respond by Reiner, who was hanging on her every word. "That sounds fascinating," he said, taking a step closer to her.

Sarina took an involuntary step back, either defending her red pumps from Reiner's handmade wingtips or defending her person from the naked hunger on his face. He looked like he wanted to suck on her ear, and it was pretty obvious from her expression that she wouldn't allow her ears to be sucked without a fight.

My mental pictures of the slimy and self-righteous children that a Sarina-Reiner coupling would produce were interrupted by the sound of the doorbell.

"It's Gerhardt!" Pinkie said, putting his drink down in what I assumed was preparation for jumping, spaniel-like, all over the new arrival.

When Gerhardt was shown in, I suddenly got a much better understanding of where Pinkie's sense of style came from. Gerhardt had to be at least sixty-five, but, as my aunt Hester used to say, "I wouldn't kick him out of bed for eating crackers." With his gorgeous silver hair, perfectly tailored suit, and commanding presence, he was what every woman pictured in her mind when she imagined a handsome duke sweeping her off her feet. The silver-topped cane he leaned on added an almost rakish flair, and I wondered whether Pinkie's bad knee might stick around long enough for him to indulge himself in a similar prop.

"Gerhardt!" Pinkie said, stepping forward to greet him, arms outstretched, "I couldn't believe my luck when I heard you were coming!"

"Philippe?" Gerhardt asked. Clearly Hubert hadn't filled him on the fact that Pinkie would be there. "My god! Hubert, you didn't tell me. You really can keep a secret, can't you?"

"Four generations of Swiss banking does tend to teach that particular skill," Hubert agreed.

"What have you been up to, Philippe?" Gerhardt asked, returning his embrace before accepting a glass of wine from Arnaud. "It's been years."

Pinkie shrugged gracefully. "You know. Travelling, spending time with my friends... Oh, and speaking of friends, you must meet my dearest friend, Lora." Pinkie grabbed Gerhardt's hand and dragged him over to stand in front of me. "Lora, this is Gerhardt." He said it with such a flourish that I wasn't sure whether I was supposed to kiss him on the cheek or swoon at his feet.

The correct answer was neither, apparently. Gerhardt took my hand and kissed it. "Enchanté," he murmured. I had always found the whole hand-kissing thing annoying and pretentious, but apparently that had been more a response to the person than to the actual kiss, because I suddenly felt just like a princess.

I smiled at him and took a step back to compose myself. "It's lovely to meet you."

I heard a little stifled laugh from the side and looked over to see Arnaud struggling to keep a straight face. Clearly, he was used to Gerhardt's effect on the fairer sex.

Pinkie stepped in between us, quick to reclaim Gerhardt's attention. He drank in the sight of him, touching his own pink ascot lightly as he took in Gerhardt's more restrained burgundy one. A slight frown creased his forehead as he looked at the cane. "Have you hurt yourself?"

Gerhardt shook his head. "Just getting old, I'm afraid. My knees. Not a problem most of the time, but stairs are out of the question these days."

"No more skiing?" Pinkie asked.

"No more skiing, no more wrestling, no more second floor," Gerhardt admitted ruefully.

Hubert clapped a hand over Gerhardt's shoulder. "After a lifetime of being beaten by Gerhardt in every possible sport, I finally have a fighting chance."

"I wouldn't go that far," Gerhardt laughed.

Hubert gave him a fond smile before turning his attention back to the gathering as a whole. "Now that we're all here, allow me to make a toast." He raised his glass, and we all followed suit. "To old friends," he said, toasting Pinkie, "to new friends," he said, raising his glass to me, "and to new partners," he said, finally raising his glass to Reiner. We all drank.

"And now to dinner," he said, placing his glass on the table and ushering us into the dining room.

12

An hour into the meal, I remembered how much fun dinner parties could be when I wasn't the hostess. Freed from the responsibility of making everyone get along, I laughed at Arnaud's jokes, put up with Pinkie's over-the-top remarks, and listened to Gerhardt and Hubert reminisce about their early years in the bank.

"I couldn't help notice the Discount Erotik Megamart car outside, Philippe," Gerhardt said, a mischievous twinkle in his eyes. "Is that yours?"

"'Mine' is a word I'd use loosely here," Pinkie said, making a sour face. "I arranged for a limo for our trip here, but it was apparently defaced by this Fat Cat person. Since when did Switzerland start having problems with class warfare?"

Hubert rolled his eyes. "The Fat Cat again. Did you know that our bank was the first victim? Orange paint all over the windows. Ten thousand francs worth of cleaning. But I don't think it's fair to call it class warfare, Philippe. Switzerland doesn't have that kind of thing. Even our poorer residents are doing fine by any reasonable standard."

Sarina snorted. "Poor people in Switzerland might not be worried about where their next meal is coming from, but that hardly means they're happy about being at the bottom of the social pecking order, watching bank bosses and corporate CEOs get richer every year. Obviously the Fat Cat is just someone who is tired of seeing some people take everything while so many are just scraping by."

Gerhardt shook his head indulgently. "Sarina, mark my words. This Fat Cat person isn't some poor, oppressed member of the lower classes. People from the lower classes are too busy working to take part in such foolish behavior. Revolutionaries have always come from the upper classes. They're the only ones who have the time."

Hubert jumped in. "I think that dignifying that Fat Cat vandalism with the term 'revolutionary' is a bit much, don't you?" he asked, looking at me. "I mean, spray painting the windows at Gucci? It's not exactly changing society for the better."

I tilted my head, considering. "I don't know. Their fall collection looks pretty appalling. If it's spared us all an epidemic of leather hot pants, I'm willing to say that society has been changed for the better."

A chuckle rippled around the table, and the tension eased.

"Speaking of leather hot pants," Arnaud said, "perhaps Gerhardt has some advice for your Swiss dinner on Sunday."

"Swiss dinner?"

I nodded. "One of my clients is trying to make a deal with a high-end US tour agency. They bill themselves as selling 'authentic cultural experiences.' My client is supposed to host a dinner that showcases authentic Swiss culture."

"The client is Dieter Schumacher," Hubert helpfully supplied.

"Well," Gerhardt said, "there aren't too many people more authentically Swiss than Dieter. I think you should be able to relax."

Pinkie snorted. "This *is* Lora relaxed. She's a little Type A."

"I'm not Type A. I just like to be prepared. Dieter's got some kind of sport activity planned, along with a couple of musicians. I'm not worried... I was just wondering if there were some lesser-known aspect of Swiss culture that would be more dramatic."

Pinkie held up a hand. "For the record, I voted for Nazi gold, so if you were going to say that, I got there first."

Hubert adjusted his glasses. "Well, I have to admit that Nazi gold is both authentic and dramatic."

"Really?" I asked. "What does Nazi gold have to do with

Switzerland?"

Hubert shook his head. "The Swiss were neutral during the world wars, but neutral doesn't always mean innocent. In World War II, most of the Swiss banks accepted gold from Nazis—gold that was often looted from Jews and other people terrorized by the Nazi regime."

Reiner interrupted. "To be fair, Switzerland was surrounded by Nazi territory, so you can't blame them too much for cooperating."

Hubert held up a finger admonishingly. "While Reiner's technically correct, that's not all there was to it. Especially in the German-speaking part of Switzerland, there was a lot of support for the Nazis. Nobody wanted to live under them, of course, but the Swiss weren't exactly lining up to keep people from dying under them, either. And money, in those days at least, was considered to be a completely amoral thing. As your banker, it was my job to take your money, keep it safe, and provide you with a way to access it when you needed it. It wasn't my job to figure out whether you had come by that money honestly."

"That was back in the days when secret Swiss bank accounts really were secret," Gerhardt noted nostalgically. "Today you need to prove not only whom the money is for, but where it came from and how it was earned. I must say that when the laws started changing, I was against it, but I have found that we've had far fewer supervillains visiting the bank since they were passed."

Hubert chuckled. "Back in the old days, you'd just open an anonymous account, set up a password, and you were ready to deposit your ill-gotten gains. My father never knew the names of some of his clients."

Despite my firm belief that Nazi gold was not going to help my dinner party situation, I couldn't help but be interested. "So how would that work, exactly?"

"Well," Hubert said, "imagine that you want to make a deposit of gold bars. You bring the gold to us. We inspect it to make sure that the bars are pure, and then we set up a segregated vault for you."

"A segregated vault?"

Hubert nodded. "It's like a safe deposit box in that it holds physical items, but it's like an account in that we know what's in it and we track the value for you. We give you an account number. You set up instructions for how we authenticate access. It could be a number of things. Passcodes, signatures, identity documents—sometimes all three. When someone shows up who can authenticate themselves according to your instructions, we provide access to the gold. Minus the bank charges, of course." Hubert took a sip of wine. "Back then, that was all there was to it."

Gerhardt shook his head. "God, I miss those days. These days you can't spit without hitting a compliance officer or, heaven forbid, an American IRS agent."

I shook my head. "Okay, but as a client, that seems pretty risky. What if I get run over by a bus when I am leaving the bank? What would happen then?"

Hubert looked at Reiner. "Reiner, as the newest bank partner, perhaps you'd like to answer Lora."

Reiner nodded seriously. "The gold would stay with us. We would keep track of the balance for you, deducting the fees for storage."

"Forever?"

"Or until the fees for storage were higher than the value of the account."

I looked at him suspiciously. "That sounds like a pretty sweet deal for the bank."

"It depends on how the contract is written, but in general yes," Hubert agreed.

"Why would I open a box like that?" I asked. "Why wouldn't I just sell the gold and open a regular account? That way I would earn interest, and I wouldn't have to pay you any storage fees."

"Usually because the global situation is very unstable," Arnaud said. "Like at the end of World War II. People in Germany were running their whole economy on cigarettes for a while there. And when you're talking a lot of money, cigarettes aren't usually the best method of storage." He smiled.

"But what happens if my gold gets stolen?"

Arnaud shook his head. "The chances of gold getting stolen out of a modern bank vault are virtually zero. And if you've given us the gold to store, it's protected. We guarantee the contents, and the vaults are insured, of course."

"So, no offense," I said, "but two hundred years after I die, my great-great-great-great grandson comes into your bank, gives you the account number and password and what?"

"We give him your gold," Hubert said simply.

"No questions asked?"

"No questions asked."

I thought about that. "I've gotta say that if I had hundreds of millions of dollars of other people's stuff stored in my bank, I'd be pretty tempted. Especially for the older, anonymous accounts. I mean…if they've been sitting there for decades already, chances are nobody's ever going to claim them, right? If you made a little personal withdrawal, who would know?"

Arnaud laughed. "That's why Swiss bankers are such boring people. It's because if we stopped to think about how much fun we'd have if we broke the rules, we'd be out of business."

"It's also why a family bank like ours has to be so careful with whom we bring into the partnership," Gerhardt said, nodding at Reiner. "We need to be absolutely certain that they are above reproach. Once the trust of our clients is broken, the bank is over."

"Literally, in our case," Hubert agreed. "The partners are jointly liable for bank assets, so if the bank goes down, we'll all get a chance to see what being poor in Switzerland is really like."

Gerhardt looked across the table at me, his eyes twinkling. "Does that help you understand Switzerland any better?"

"Yes, but probably not in a way that easily translates into dinner entertainment."

"Nazi glitter bombs," Pinkie reminded me. "You'll regret not doing it."

"Not as much as I'd regret doing it, I'm pretty sure."

13

"Arrarkarr!"

I scrabbled on the nightstand for my phone. If my brother had remotely installed alarm clock functionality on my phone, I was cutting off his Lone Star Steakhouse delivery account and he was going to have to go back to living on Red Bull and ramen noodles like all the rest of his hacker buddies.

I got my hand on the phone and held it up. Apparently whatever was making that goat-in-a-blender noise wasn't my phone. I noted with horror that it was seven in the morning. Surely if it were really seven, I would feel less like collapsing in exhaustion than this, right?

"Arrarkarr!" I heard again.

As someone who spends more of my time in Barneys than barnyards, it took me a few seconds for my brain to finally identify the noise as a rooster. I would have thought that a country known for precision timepieces could do a little better than a rooster for a wake-up call, but perhaps the Swiss liked to preserve the charm of beginning their day with an animal shrieking at the top of its lungs. Not that I was finding it very charming in my current jet-lagged state. But it least it was a late-rising rooster—with the way I was feeling, a rooster that got up at the crack of dawn would have been chicken and dumplings by dinner.

I stumbled through my morning ablutions, taking special care with my eye makeup. I frowned at my reflection and added another few layers of mascara, hoping that the shade from my luxurious, feathery lashes would help hide the puffiness from my efforts to convince Hubert that I enjoyed his wine. I hadn't been the only one living out that little fiction—while dinner had finished at around ten, only Reiner had had elected to take the train back to his apartment in Zurich. Arnaud and Gerhardt had both stayed over.

Flipping through the wardrobe, I looked for something eye-catching that was appropriate for a trip downtown with Pinkie. We were supposed to go try to hunt up his watch today, and the snooty staff at Patek Philippe was probably more likely to be open to talk to us if I didn't show up in jeans and flip-flops. I came up with a red dress that Pinkie had gotten for me from the Prada outlet in Milan. It was knee length, sleeveless, and buckled at the waist with black leather. Every time I wore it, I felt like a million bucks, probably because the original price tag had been something pretty close to that.

As I walked into the dining room, I became aware that something was very wrong. The breakfast dishes had been shoved to one side to make space for the paper. Arnaud, Gerhardt, Pinkie, and Hubert were huddled around it, reading. Sarina was sitting at the edge of the table, one hand plucking distractedly at the tablecloth as she listened to the conversation.

"What's going on?" I asked.

Pinkie shook his head. "It's the Fat Cat."

"What? Did he hit the Versace store?"

Arnaud looked up at me. "Wow."

"What?"

"You look spectacular."

Three pairs of eyes swiveled my direction. Gerhardt, I could see, had not lost his appreciation for the female form.

"You're very kind," I said, blushing.

"Can we get back to the murder, please?" Sarina interrupted. "I'm sure Lora would agree that a brutal murder in the center of town is more important than what she's wearing."

I stifled my irritation. Objectively, murder probably was more important than what I was wearing, but honestly, it wasn't like we couldn't talk about both.

"The Fat Cat got murdered?"

"The Fat Cat murdered someone," Pinkie corrected.

"Really? How do they know it was the Fat Cat?"

Hubert scanned the article quickly and translated the essentials. "A body was discovered last night outside of the Hotel Opera. Swiss papers don't release the names of murder victims, so no word yet on who it was, but it looks like whoever did it landed a blow to his head and then pushed him over the balcony. They found the victim on the street two floors below, with the sign of the Fat Cat stenciled on his chest. Preliminary tests show that the paint and the stencil are a match to those used in the vandalism."

"Hmm," I said, trying to maintain a concerned expression while sneaking a croissant from the sideboard. While I was sure that murder was a big deal in Switzerland, people from Brooklyn were a little more blasé about it. If I skipped breakfast every time someone in New York got murdered, I'd be a heck of a lot thinner.

Pinkie tapped the paper. "Imagine someone cold blooded enough to murder a man in public right in the center of town. I tell you, Hubert, it does leave at least one large question in my mind."

"You mean, who would want to do such a thing?"

Pinkie waved that question away. "Plenty of people, I'm sure. Murderers are a dime a dozen in America. I'm surprised Switzerland has so few, honestly. Maybe it's the weather. No...my question was whether the Street Parade was going to go on as usual. There are literally a million people in this city who have come here for dancing, drugs, and casual sex. It would be a shame to let the murderers and terrorists win, don't you think?"

Hubert skimmed down farther in the article. "The Street Parade will go ahead as scheduled, but police presence on the streets will be strengthened. All police are being called to active duty today."

Pinkie scowled. "I was planning on meeting my cousin Margrit downtown today when we go to Patek Philippe. Now she'll probably be too busy catching a murderer to help me recover my father's watch from that thieving brother of hers." He sighed dramatically, presumably at the lack of consideration of murderers.

Hubert looked up. "Ah yes. Your watch. I had almost forgotten." He took off his glasses and polished them thoughtfully. "Did you know that Richter and Partners was the bank of the CEO of Patek Philippe for a time? Arnaud's father was quite involved in the account. He used to go to all the watch exhibitions. Some really amazing pieces."

Pinkie looked up. "Really? Was he managing that account in

1972?"

Hubert looked at the ceiling, calculating. "1972? Yes…yes, I believe he was. Why?"

Pinkie's face was suddenly animated. "That was the year my father bought the watch! It was a few months before I was born. It was a custom order. Do you think he would have talked to your father about it?" he asked, looking at Arnaud.

Arnaud shrugged. "If your father mentioned it when he was visiting, it's possible. My father would have been more than happy to make an introduction. But how would that help you?"

"The personal ledgers for the bank," Pinkie said. "You still keep them, right?"

Hubert nodded. "We do, of course, but I think the chances of finding something in Arnaud's father's ledger is pretty slim. We mainly use them for scheduling, as you know."

"But you once told me that you also made personal notes about clients, right?"

"Of course. Birthdays, kids' names, that kind of thing."

"Well, what if that ledger has a note about the watch?"

Hubert looked dubious. "It seems like a long shot, Philippe."

"Still… It's worth a try. Where do you keep the ledgers? Are they here in the house somewhere?" Pinkie looked around as though the ledgers might be hiding somewhere in the china cabinet.

"The house?" Hubert said, looking mildly horrified. "No, of course not. They're in the records vault at the bank."

"They contain personal information about our clients, Philippe," Gerhardt said reprovingly. "They are not for public consumption."

"But…" Pinkie said.

Hubert held up a hand. "Gerhardt's right. But let's do this: I'll call over to the bank and tell them to let you take the ledgers for just that one year. You can bring them straight here—without opening them—and I'll look through them to see if I can find something to help you."

A cherubic smile broke across Pinkie's face. "Hubert, have I ever told you that you're the best godfather in the world?"

Hubert gave him a kindly smile. "Many times when you were a child, but not recently."

"You are. And as the best godfather in the world, please tell me that you have managed to locate some alternative transportation for me to get downtown."

"What?" Arnaud asked, laughing. "You're still trying to get out of the Erotik MegaSmart car, Philippe? Today of all days, you should be thankful for something that's easy to park. It's Street Parade, don't forget. It's going to be complete madness."

Hubert shook his head. "Arnaud's right, but even if he weren't, I'm afraid that I wouldn't be able to help. The housekeeper is taking the Mercedes into the shop. It's apparently developed something of a rattle." He shrugged apologetically. "The train picks up right down the hill, you know. It's really the easiest way to get into town, especially today."

Pinkie sighed and rolled his eyes like a teenager. "I'm afraid that's not going to work for me. But I guess if there's any day that a Discount Erotik MegaSmart car will go unnoticed, it's Street Parade."

"Great," I said, dusting the telltale croissant crumbs off of my fingers. "Does that mean that you're driving?"

"When hell freezes over."

14

"Come on," I said to Pinkie. "It's not that bad. Nobody's even looking at us."

"Thank god for small favors. I told you that Fat Cat was no good. First, he's bothering the Gucci store. Then he's defacing my limo. Then…murder. It's a natural progression."

"I hardly think that spray painting the Gucci store is a natural progression to murder. Otherwise Banksy would be a serial killer by now."

"You don't know who Banksy is," Pinkie pointed out. "He probably *is* a serial killer. These social revolutionary types are always one tiny step away from violence."

We passed by a bus stop. I spotted a giant, hirsute man in a green latex Speedo and dog collar. A tiny Asian girl wearing a tie and pink hot pants held his leash in one hand and a riding crop in the other.

"Did you…?" I started.

"Street Parade," Pinkie said in a breezy tone. "If that's the weirdest thing you see today, it'll be because you weren't paying attention. Listen. You can already hear the music."

Sure enough, even with the windows up, we could hear a rhythmic thumping. It was as though we were standing outside of a nightclub, except today the nightclub was the city itself, and a million people had shown up for the party.

I glanced along the side of the road at the next bus stop.

"Pinkie, look… Some of them have Fat Cat signs."

Pinkie glanced over at the crowd of girls, most of whom were wearing bikinis and combat boots. All of them had the unmistakable orange Fat Cat insignia spray painted onto their bodies.

Pinkie shook his head in sorrow. "This parade used to be all about drugs and sex. And suddenly it's about social justice and income inequality. It's a tragedy, really. I tell you, Lora, kids these days are on the wrong path." He sighed. "We'll have to park in the bank's lot. At least the car will be safe there from any marauding Fat Cat wannabes."

I turned onto the street, inching forward slowly as our car was surrounded by a pulsating mass of aging drag queens. "You know, Pinkie, public transportation might have been easier today."

"And that is why you'll never be royal, Lora. It's not about what's easy. It's about what's correct. Turn here."

We pulled into the bank parking lot, and a guard with a clipboard sauntered over to the car to take our names. "Prince Philippe von Hofstedtler," Pinkie announced. "I'm on the list. We'll be leaving the car here while we run some errands before returning to the bank."

The guard looked at the car skeptically before checking the list. He checked the car again, then checked the list again. I could see Pinkie's face turning red under his golden tan. "Is there a problem?" he snapped.

"Uh…no, sir," the man said, making a small tick on his list.

Pinkie stroked his ascot, as if deriving comfort from the touch of silk. "Good."

He strode across the garage, his back ramrod straight. I smiled tightly at the guard and followed him into the elevator. The moment the doors closed, Pinkie's chin went up. "I am tired of living like a peasant!"

I rolled my eyes. "Honestly, Pinkie. Less than twenty-four hours ago we were on a private jet drinking vintage Veuve. Twenty minutes ago we were having breakfast with the partners of one of the oldest private banks in Switzerland. I hardly think that driving a Smart Car downtown is going to turn you into a turnip farmer."

Pinkie shook his head. "Of course not. I'm a prince. Nothing can turn me into a turnip farmer. It's just that I'm not accustomed to having to deal with this type of thing." He patted my arm. "It's easier for you because you grew up lower class."

"I didn't grow up lower class, you ass! I grew up middle class. Middle class. You know, that class that makes things actually function."

Pinkie waved a hand. "Middle class, lower class… It's all relative."

"It's not all relative! There are official definitions used in actual government reports. Honestly, sometimes I just want to slap you."

Pinkie perked up. "Really? Where?"

"On the face, you idiot."

Pinkie looked disappointed. "Oh. I was hoping for somewhere more fun."

I held up my hand to forestall further comment. "We're here." The elevator let us off in a small foyer with an ornate door leading to the bank and a pair of glass doors that led to the street. I consulted my phone. "I guess we're behind the actual bank building. Patek Philippe should be a few doors down to the right."

We left the foyer and walked over to the store. I glanced at the store's window. Unlike New York stores, which went by the *If you have to ask, you can't afford it* method of display, the Zurich stores preferred to put the price tags right next to the merchandise in the window, which is how I knew that the simplest model on display was an eye-popping fifty thousand dollars. *Typical Swiss efficiency*, I thought. *You know you can't afford it without even thinking about having to ask.*

As we approached the door, a security guard hit the button to open it, while another guard stood behind him with a neutral yet watchful expression on his face. A polished woman in a conservative blue dress smoothed her perfect blonde pageboy haircut before walking toward us, a polite smile of welcome on her face. "Can I help you?" she asked in lightly accented English.

"Yes, my dear," Pinkie said. "I need to check the registration on a watch. It's a family heirloom that has come into some dispute."

The woman's face clouded. "Dispute?"

"More like robbery. My father purchased the watch in 1972. I thought it was lost with the rest of his estate when he died, but it's recently turned up on the wrist of my cousin. I just need to check the registration so that I can prove to him that it belongs to me."

The woman shook her head. "I'm afraid, sir, that our files are private. If you had the watch with you and were willing to provide an identification document, we would be able to verify your registration, but we obviously must protect the privacy of our clients. I'm sure you understand."

"I understand. Unfortunately, my father, Prince Wilfred von Hofstedtler, passed away some years ago and…"

"Prince Wilfred was your father?" the woman asked.

Pinkie blinked. "You knew him?"

"I'm from Kuh Eierstein!" she said, excited. "The Wunscht family!"

"Oh my heavens! The Wunscht family! Of course, I knew your father as well. Bernd Wunscht, right? And that makes you…" he looked at her appraisingly. "Gertrud?"

"Isabella," she said, laughing. "Gertrud is ten years younger than I am."

"Well, I never would have guessed! You look like you just graduated from university! You must give me your secret!"

I sighed internally. This could take a while. Pinkie was spectacularly charming when he wanted to be, and nothing made him want to be charming more than someone who had something that he wanted. Still, I had to admit that being able to pull a family name out of the hat like that after what…twenty years?…was pretty impressive. I was pretty sure you could line up every single person I went to high school with in Delaware, and I wouldn't be able to recognize a single one.

"But of course, I'd be happy to take a look at the records for you," she said. "It's not as if you're some impoverished family member scrabbling over an inheritance. I mean, you're Prince Philippe!"

Actually, I thought silently, *it's exactly like he's some impoverished family member scrabbling over an inheritance.* But I could see that all the flattery was having its desired effect. Pinkie looked happier and more relaxed than he had since he saw the Discount Erotik MegaSmart, and Isabella was positively star struck.

I wandered over to the window and looked out at Bahnhofstrasse, which I had heard was the most expensive shopping district in the world. The window across the street was filled with flowers and chocolate. *Teuscher*, the sign said. Teuscher! The source of those magical truffles that I had been living on since we got here. I felt my world contract around the store. Did I dare go inside? What other wonders might be in there? I was partial to white chocolate as well. What if there was a white chocolate champagne truffle? The very thought caused my pulse to quicken.

As I watched the store, the front door opened, and a shapely woman in a blue sheath dress came out, flipping her long blonde hair over her shoulder as she tucked three tiny green boxes into her Prada handbag. Something about her looked familiar, and I squinted through the crowds. "Vanessa," I said out loud, realizing who it was.

"What?" Pinkie asked, breaking off in mid-sentence.

I waved a hand, and he went back to chatting about the tractor assembly plant that Kuh Eierstein was apparently famous for.

In a city crammed with a million drunken revelers, I couldn't believe that I had managed to run into Vanessa. But then again, maybe it wasn't so strange. Teuscher had undeniably great chocolate. Maybe she was placing an order for the dinner on Monday. Maybe the "something spectacular" that she had referred to was something made out of chocolate.

I nibbled on a fingernail, wondering if I should go in and pretend I was a colleague in the hopes of getting some competitive intel. Catching a glance of myself in the mirror, I quickly discarded that plan. Whatever competitive intel I could gain wouldn't be worth the extra pounds I would pack on the second I walked into the store.

I tore my attention away from the chocolate store and tuned back into Pinkie's conversation with Isabella.

"Let's take a look at those files," she said. "Do you have the serial number?"

Pinkie shook his head. "Just the name and the year—1972. Can't you just type it in?"

Isabella shook her head, frowning. "The older records are on paper. The good news is that the company did get around to scanning them in, so we can access them from here. The bad news is that we sell almost fifty thousand watches every year."

Pinkie bit his lip. "But not back in the '70s, right? I didn't think Patek Philippe really hit the mainstream until they came up with that ad campaign."

Isabella smiled. "You never actually own a Patek Philippe. You merely look after it for the next generation."

"I love that ad," Pinkie said. "It makes me want to go out and have some kids."

I felt my jaw go slack with shock. This was the first time I had ever heard Pinkie talk about kids without referring to stickiness, whininess, or contagiousness. Maybe being around his godfather was giving him a new appreciation for family. I tried to picture a son of Pinkie's. Did they even make ascots for babies?

Isabella's voice brought me back to the present. "We probably sold fewer watches back in those days, but certainly still tens of thousands. If you can get me the serial number, I can check it for you quickly, but otherwise someone would have to look through thousands of entries."

Pinkie sighed. "Well, it was a long shot. I'll have to see if I can find some other way." He took Isabella's hand in both of his and looked deeply into her eyes. "It was lovely to see you again, Isabella. Please tell your father that I remember him fondly, and give my best wishes to your sister."

Isabella flushed. "They'll be thrilled. I'm only sorry I couldn't help you find what you were looking for."

Pinkie gave her a tragic look. "Well, maybe something will come up. We'll be in town for the next couple of days. If you think of anything, I'd be very grateful if you'd give me a call." Reaching into his pocket, he pulled out a card and handed it to her. I hadn't known that Pinkie even had cards and I found myself wondering what was on them. Was "prince" like part of the name or was it a job description? Did they have coats of arms on them? Maybe a little cow or a tractor factory? I craned my neck over the counter trying to catch a glimpse, but Isabella tucked it into her bag before I got a look.

"Of course, Prince Philippe."

"No need for the prince," Pinkie said, waving the title away. "We're practically family. Philippe, I insist."

"Philippe," Isabella repeated breathlessly.

We walked out into the day, where hordes of semi-naked people of all ages were roaming the streets with open bottles or standing around swaying to high-volume techno. The thumping of the club music was already giving me a headache. "Well, that was a dead end," I said.

"Not at all. Isabella is in there combing that list even as we speak. I'll have my answer by the time we leave town."

"What do you mean? You didn't ask her to do anything."

"Of course I didn't ask her to look through ten thousand

registration entries. She'll do it without being asked."

"Because she's just that nice a person?"

"Because she's one of my subjects. Of course she wants to help out her prince."

"You don't have subjects. It's a courtesy title, remember?"

"Hearts and minds. I wouldn't expect you to understand."

I sighed. "So what do we do now?" I asked, neatly sidestepping a Brit in a fireman's uniform who was sloshing his beer around. I suddenly wished I'd worn something waterproof, or at least Scotchgarded.

"My god," the fireman said. "You are a vision…a vision. Lady in red, that's you, I tell you…burning hot, baby. I can put out that fire…"

I shook my head and took Pinkie's arm. "You know, I'd really like to get out of here before some drunken naked person ruins my Prada dress. I'll never find another one like this."

"Right," Pinkie said, his eyes tracking the fireman's rear end speculatively. I snapped my fingers in front of him to bring him back to reality. He shook himself. "In that case, let's go meet Margrit.

15

Despite the fact that she was working, Margrit, Pinkie's police officer cousin, had agreed to meet us for coffee. "Fifteen minutes," she had told him. "Someplace away from the station. It's impossible to do anything there today. The whole place is filled with drunk, high, naked whackos. Even more than usual."

The coffee shop was a few blocks away from the Patek Philippe store, and I braced myself for Pinkie's complaints about the walk. His attention was fully occupied by the troupe of hot-pant-clad sailor boys ahead of us, however, so we got there without him really noticing the distance.

In comparison to the madness on the streets outside, the coffee shop was fairly deserted, with only a few elderly people eating croissants and drinking espresso placidly, seemingly unconcerned by the wave of S&M-inspired insanity outside.

Margrit turned out to be a six-foot-tall Viking blonde in a beautifully cut gray suit and Hermès scarf. She looked like a private banker or a politician—except for the holster and gun she flashed as she bent over to kiss Pinkie.

I lingered behind Pinkie as he and Margit said their hellos. Finally, Pinkie turned to introduce me. "Margrit, this is my friend Lora."

Margrit looked at me appraisingly with icy eyes. I withstood her scrutiny for a few seconds, valiantly suppressing the urge to confess to all of my recent wrongdoings.

Margrit finally gave me a small smile. "Lora. Lovely to meet you. How do you know Philippe?"

"We met at a bar in New York."

Margrit chuckled. "Since when did you start bringing home girls from bars, Philippe?"

"Margrit, really, you know I can spot talent a mile away."

Margrit quirked an eyebrow at me. "And what talent did Philippe spot in you, exactly?"

"Probably the ability to put up with him."

Margrit laughed warmly. "You're right. That's definitely a talent."

Pinkie took a sip of his espresso. "So how is life in the Zurich police force, Margrit? Parking tickets and graffiti keeping you entertained?"

Margrit shook her head. "Not these days. I'm working on the Fat Cat case, like every other detective in town." Her blue eyes sparkled.

Pinkie frowned. "My god. You look positively thrilled. Maybe someone else can get brutally murdered, and we can throw a party."

"Sorry. It's just that homicide investigations in Zurich aren't all that common and are usually pretty obvious. You go in, you arrest the boyfriend, you book him, and he confesses. We're not exactly loaded with master criminals here."

Pinkie snorted. "Given the concentration of banks in this town, I'm pretty sure you are loaded with master criminals. Just not the kind of criminals who get prosecuted."

Margrit shrugged. "Not my department." She sat back in her chair and fixed her eyes on Pinkie. "So enough with the pleasantries, Philippe. Why don't you tell me why you're really here."

Pinkie looked hurt. "Can't I just stop by Zurich to visit Hubert and see my lovely cousin? Do you really need to be so suspicious all the time?"

Margrit tilted her head to the side and smiled, waiting.

Silence.

"Fine!" Pinkie said, throwing up his hands in surrender. "It's your thieving brother, Maurice."

Margrit sighed. "What now?"

"He's got my father's Patek Philippe watch. I came to get it back."

Margrit shook her head. "I'm afraid you're out of luck. Our father gave that watch to him before he died. The watch is his."

"But your father stole it from my father. Probably took it right off his still-warm body."

Margrit shrugged. "He didn't even get there until the day after your father died, so even if he stole it off the body, I doubt the body would still have been warm."

I spluttered, almost spitting out my coffee. Most people I knew wouldn't be so blasé about having their parents accused of what boiled down to grave robbing. Margrit caught my look. "The men in my family aren't exactly poster children for the German nobility. One of the reasons I went into homicide was because I figured it was only a matter of time until one of them got busted for fraud, and that was an arrest I didn't want to make. So far, so good, though." She knocked on the table.

"So can you help me get my watch back?"

She looked up, considering. "Probably not," she finally admitted. "You'll need to have something to prove it was your father's. Better yet, something that proves your father bought it and gave it to you. A will or something. Otherwise it's your word against his, and he is the one with the watch."

Pinkie squared his shoulders. "Well, I've got a couple of options that might work for that. We're going to check the registration. And Richter and Partners had Patek Philippe's CEO as a client when my father bought the watch. I'm hoping there might be a mention in their partner ledgers from that year about that purchase. We're going over there right after this to pick them up, as a matter of fact. If I find proof, will you talk to him? I'd rather handle this quietly."

"Of course. Having a family member get busted for grand larceny isn't likely to help my career." She looked at me. "Do you have any siblings?"

"One brother. He still lives back in Delaware where we grew up."

"Well, I hope you thank your lucky stars every day that he's not always one step ahead of the law."

I grimaced. "I'm hoping he's two or three steps ahead of the law, but it's hard to tell sometimes. He has some issues with information security."

"Issues?"

"He doesn't believe there's any information that should be secure from him."

"Ah…a hacker. We've got a few of them here as well, although the best ones operate mostly out of Eastern Europe, I hear."

"The best ones you know about. But I doubt he'd make it onto your radar. He prefers to spend most of his time annoying the US government."

Margrit laughed. "Then we're actually more or less on the same team. Since the US government decided that banking secrecy was an international crime, Switzerland's main industry has been hit quite hard. I don't think we'd really be too sad to see the American government embarrassed by a rogue hacker."

I smiled. "Well, thanks for the support, but hopefully it won't come up."

"Hopefully. In any case, I think we've got our hands full for the time being with this Fat Cat murder. It's turning out to be quite an interesting case."

"Ooh," Pinkie said, rubbing his hands together. "Tell us all about it."

"Pinkie hates the Fat Cat. Thanks to him, we've been driving around town in a Discount Erotik Megamart Smart Car."

Margrit laughed. "Please take a picture for me. Something for my scrapbook."

"Hmmph," Pinkie grumbled. "Just tell me—first, are you close to catching this person, and second, can I kick him when you do? I promise not to leave marks. Not many, anyway."

Margrit shook her head. "I don't know how close we are. There are some very strange aspects to this case."

"For example?"

"For example, the victim's body was found underneath the balcony of his hotel, right? So he fell from the second floor onto cobblestone streets, which almost certainly would have been fatal. Except that his skull had been almost crushed by a blow before he fell."

"So someone killed him upstairs and then threw him over the balcony?" I asked.

"Or he fell over the balcony in the struggle, but after the blow had been landed."

Pinkie leaned forward. "But the papers said there was Fat Cat vandalism on the body. Was that done in the room as well?"

"That's the weird thing," Margrit said, rubbing her head. "There's spray from the orange paint on the street. Clearly, the painting was done there after the murder."

I shook my head. "Now I'm completely lost. Someone killed him upstairs, then took the elevator back downstairs so that they could tag the body with an orange cat in a top hat?"

"That's what it looks like," Margrit said. "Only there's no elevator, so the guy had to go down two flights of stairs that went straight by the front desk in order to get out of the hotel."

"What did the front desk guy say?" Pinkie asked.

"He said nobody came in or went out between 11 p.m. and 5:30 a.m., when people started leaving for the early flights. The body was found at 5 a.m. by a street sweeper. And the guy was killed at 12:26 a.m."

"How do you know it was 12:26?" I asked. "I watch *CSI* literally all the time, so I'm kind of an expert in this, and I thought that it was hard to pin down time of death with any real accuracy."

"It is, unless they land on their watch. We double checked the time with the medical examiner, and he agreed that it looked right to him."

"Ah," I said. "I guess that's why you're the detective."

Pinkie frowned. "So someone killed him inside the hotel and then went out and spray painted a fat cat sign on the body, but nobody entered or left the hotel."

"I know," Margrit said, the sparkle back in her eyes. "It's a real mystery. I've got people examining the hotel now, looking for ways someone could have climbed out one of the windows. It's crazy. I tell you, this is going to be the case that gets me into Interpol. Assuming I can solve it, of course."

Pinkie snorted. "Well, you've got the von Hofstedtler brains, coupled with your own family's understanding of criminal deviance. If anyone can solve it, it should be you. But let us know if we can help. Since we live in America, we probably see way more murders than you do."

Margrit chuckled. "Thanks, Philippe." She suddenly snapped her fingers. "Maybe there is something."

"Really?" I asked.

She looked intently at Pinkie. "You were a classics major, right?"

"Yes. Don't tell me that you've found a use for an undergraduate degree in classics? That really would make you the world's best detective."

"What does the saying 'When defeat is inevitable, it is wisest to yield,' mean to you?"

Pinkie looked at the ceiling, trying to recall. "I think it's from Quintilian. He taught rhetoric in Rome. Sometime around Emperor Nero, if I'm right. You know, the guy who fiddled while Rome burned. What on earth does that have to do with anything? Is this a fiddle-related crime?"

Margrit looked at us closely. "Do you promise to hold what I'm about to tell you in the strictest confidence?"

"Yes," Pinkie breathed. He loved the idea of holding things in the strictest confidence. He wasn't actually capable of doing it, but he loved it just the same.

"The murdered man had a slip of paper in his wallet that had that quote and a phone number. We're still trying to figure out what it means."

"Whose phone number was it?" I asked.

Margrit took a sip of coffee. "It's for a bakery in Albania."

"Albania," Pinkie said, stroking his chin thoughtfully. "A very high-crime area. Loads of Mafia types there. Do you think it's a front for a criminal organization? White slavers, maybe? If so, you should talk to Lora. She's practically an expert in white slavers. She actually slept with...ow!" Pinkie said, rubbing his shin where I had kicked him.

Margrit looked at me.

"It's a long story. Did you have anything to add about the quote?" I asked Pinkie pointedly. "Something relevant, perhaps? Something to justify the many years you spent at Oxford?"

"Well, Quintilian was a humanist who lived during a particularly rough period of history and managed to survive it, which was something of an accomplishment back in those days. But it's hard to see what that has to do with an Albanian bakery. I mean, surviving Albanian baked goods might be occasionally challenging, I suppose.

"But I must admit that it's kind of a nice quote, particularly for when you're feeling lazy," he continued. "Like, I could ask Lora if she wanted any truffles, and then she could say 'No,' which is what she always says right before she starts shoveling them into her mouth with both hands, and then if we were in a hurry I could say, 'When defeat is inevitable, it is wisest to yield' so that we could skip the angst and go right to the shoveling."

Margrit and I looked at him in silence. "How do you keep from throttling him?" she finally asked me.

"It's challenging sometimes," I admitted.

Margrit looked at her watch. "God. I've got a briefing in ten minutes. Where are you guys headed?"

Pinkie took a last sip of his espresso. "Back to Hubert's bank. We need to pick up those ledgers. I hope they'll help us prove that your father was a lying thief."

Margrit sighed. "Good luck with that, I guess. If you're heading straight there, you can come with me. There's a shortcut by the police building. I'll show you."

We left some money on the table and walked out into the sunshine. A wall of sound hit us. Techno music, shrieking, loud conversation and...yes...someone retching somewhere close by.

Margrit scowled. "I hate Street Parade."

"I think it's kind of fun," Pinkie said, checking out two young men who appeared to be naked except for G-strings made of tinfoil.

"That's because you don't have to walk through piles of vomit to get to your office."

"Hey, girls," one of the tinfoil-clad young men said, "loosen up a little, will you? It's Street Parade. It's all about the love, baby." He smiled beatifically and moved in, arms open as if to give me a hug.

Margit stepped in front of me, unbuttoning her jacket so that he could see the gun. "You're going to want to keep moving."

"Fine, babe," the guy said, holding up his hands. "Love a woman with a gun, though. Sexy as all shit." He made a gun out of his thumb and forefinger and pointed it at her, winking. "Maybe later, right?"

"Don't count on it," Margrit said.

We waded through the crowd back toward the police station, passing a gang of bikers, a gaggle of at least twenty Japanese school girls, and a woman who was completely naked except for a large paisley pattern rendered in fluorescent body paint. I couldn't help but notice that the current fashion for full-body hair removal had apparently skipped some segments of the Swiss population.

Finally, the police headquarters came into view. In all the insanity, I noticed a man dressed completely normally walking out of the building. It was weird how normal dress was what made you stand out the most during Street Parade. The man looked up to speak with his companion, and I inhaled sharply. It was Benjamin. Of course it was Benjamin. He showed up in Russia. He showed up in Bulgaria. He showed up in Malta. With a million people descending on the city of Zurich, he showed up on the same block I was walking on.

I ducked behind Pinkie so that I was out of Benjamin's line of sight, feeling a little ashamed now of my conversation with him at the airport. Benjamin worked for the government, after all. I had accused him of stalking me when he was just doing his job. And now that I saw him walking out of the police station, it seemed likely that he really was just here on business. I hadn't been fair. I fingered my purse where I had tucked his card. Maybe after the yodel fest tomorrow night I would see if he was available for dinner. Maybe a late dinner…

"The bank is right through there," Margrit said, breaking a chain of thought that was turning increasingly raunchy. "Just follow the street. It's a couple of blocks. You could walk it, but it's probably easier to take the tram for two stops."

"Right," I said, forcing my thoughts away from Benjamin's sparkling green eyes and broad shoulders. "It was great to meet you, Margrit."

"You, too," she said, taking my hand. "Take care of my cousin for me, will you?"

"I don't need taking care of," Pinkie said, sounding like a petulant five-year-old.

Margrit flashed me a conspiratorial smile. "Of course you don't."

16

We were not lucky enough to stumble across another batch of naughty sailors, and Pinkie was soon complaining about the walk.

"The Swiss," he hissed, stopping to examine his foot for blisters. "When will they learn the difference between walking distance and driving distance?"

"She didn't tell us to walk it. She told us to take the tram for two stops."

"That's because there's a strong strain of evil in that family. She knows I don't take public transportation. Ever." He limped on, muttering under his breath.

The front of Hubert's bank was more impressive than the elevator we had come out of, but it was still more understated than I was expecting. The granite building was old and solid, with carved eagles perched above a door that looked like it was strong enough to withstand an entire Mongol invasion. Only a discreet brass plaque with a bell beneath it informed passersby that this was, in fact, a bank. Clearly, they weren't catering to the walk-in trade.

When security buzzed us in, we were met by a well-groomed gentleman in a beautifully cut gray suit. His erect carriage and unlined face made his age impossible to guess. "Prince Philippe," he said, taking Pinkie's hand and pumping it energetically. "It's been so many years. The last time I saw you, you were just a boy."

"Ludwig!" Pinkie said. "When Hubert told me that he'd call the bank manager, I had no idea that it was still you."

"Who else would it be?"

"I can't imagine. I bet if I come back here in twenty years, it'll still be you."

"Probably. I have no plans to retire."

"Thank heavens for that! The place would fall apart without you."

It was days like these when I started to believe Pinkie's claim that being a prince took a lot more effort than one would think. Pinkie never forgot names or faces or hobbies or gossip. And unlike a lot of the nouveau riche types that I hostessed for, Pinkie seemed to know just as much about the chauffeur as he did about the lady of the house. Sometimes more, depending on how good-looking the chauffeur was.

"Lora, this is Ludwig," Pinkie said, introducing me. "He's been manager of this bank forever, as far as I know. I think they cloned him years ago."

"It's a pleasure to meet you," I said formally.

Ludwig smiled. "It's so wonderful to meet one of Prince Philippe's friends. Is this your first time in Switzerland?"

"It is."

"Is it what you expected?"

I glanced back out into the street, where a man in a rainbow afro wig and a loincloth was making out with a woman dressed in a costume that evoked a fairy princess with a serious bondage fetish. "Well, Hubert's house yes...but Zurich..." I struggled for something politic to say about a city that had been overrun by naked people on drugs. "Let's just say that it exceeds my expectations in some ways."

Ludwig chuckled. "It's not always like this, you know. It's only during the Street Parade that the streets are filled with lunatics. Normally they're just filled with 'the gnomes of Zurich,' which is what they call people like me." His smile faded. "But this year, of course, it's not just the Street Parade. We have this Fat Cat killer on the loose... It's just not very Swiss." He shook his head as if to dispel his gloomy thoughts. "Can I offer you a chocolate? Teuscher champagne truffles from right around the corner. I think they're the best in Switzerland. Have you tried them?"

"I really shouldn't," I said, hesitating.

"When defeat is inevitable," Pinkie whispered.

"Maybe just one," I said, helping myself to three.

"Hubert called to tell me that you would want to pick up the ledgers from 1972. Shall I fetch them for you, or would you like to come down into the vault?"

Pinkie clasped his hands together. "Ooh, the vault. I used to love going down there as a kid."

"You certainly did." We followed Ludwig down a flight of stairs and waited for him to unlock a large, heavy door. "We were forever concerned that you were going to get accidentally locked in and suffocated. You could be quite a trial as youngster, you know."

"As opposed to now," I said, elbowing Pinkie.

Ludwig slid smoothly into tour guide mode. "This vault is one of the oldest in Switzerland. The vault chambers are carved directly into the stone underneath Zurich, making them exceptionally secure."

We came to yet another door, this one guarded by a small, wizened-looking woman who might have been a hundred years old. "Herr Achermann," she said, acknowledging Ludwig. She turned to Pinkie. "And Prince Philippe. How nice to see you again."

Pinkie smiled at her. "Frau Backer! My heavens, you don't look a day older than you did when I used to come here as a boy."

Frau Backer rearranged her wrinkles in what I took to be a smile. "I see that you're still as charming as ever. I hope I won't have to chase you around in the vaults again. I don't think I'm up to it at my age."

"I don't think I'm up to it at my age, either," Pinkie admitted.

Ludwig cleared his throat. "Frau Backer, Prince Philippe and his friend here will be taking a few ledgers out of the bank. This has been approved by Herr Richter."

Frau Backer tapped a few keys on the computer screen and nodded. "I see. Ledgers from 1972. I'll need you to leave your bag here, I'm afraid," she told me.

Ludwig looked at me apologetically. "No bags allowed inside the records room. Mr. Richter's policy."

Philippe rolled his eyes. "No exceptions for friends and family? Come on, Frau Backer…" He fluttered his eyelashes at her.

Frau Backer gave him a stern look. "Mr. Richter didn't make an exception for Mrs. Richter, so I doubt he'll make one for a mischievous boy like you, Prince Philippe."

Pinkie shrugged at me. "What can I say? Frau Backer is completely incorruptible, even in the face of my considerable charms."

"It's not a problem," I said, sliding my Louis Vuitton tote across the desk.

Ludwig entered a string of numbers on the keypad at the side of the door then put his hand on a blank panel above the keys. A line of light ran over his palm, and the screen flashed green. The door opened, revealing a set of stairs going even farther down into the vault.

"Is that new?" Pinkie asked. "I don't remember seeing any of this *Mission Impossible* stuff the last time I was here."

Ludwig nodded. "New in this case is a relative term. About ten years ago, we upgraded the security system for the vaults. Handprint sensors, video surveillance, password locks..."

Pinkie raised an eyebrow. "I can't believe Hubert agreed to that. He's always such a stickler for keeping things exactly the same."

"Well, even Mr. Richter had to realize that anyone looking to store something in the vault wasn't going to be impressed with the previous security system."

"What was the previous security system?"

Ludwig gestured us through the door and down the stairs. "The bank manager had to open the vault area, where the handprint scanner is today. The main vault required the keys of two bank partners to open the main door, and then of course, you had to have the key to whatever box you wished to access."

"Sounds pretty secure to me."

Ludwig sniffed. "It worked quite well for more than two hundred years, so I'd tend to agree with you. But clients like to see flashing lights and key codes and video cameras. I blame American movies."

We came to the bottom of the stairs, where we were face to face with two heavy metal safe doors. "The one on the left is the one with the company records," Ludwig said. He pulled out a key and unlocked the door

"Just a key?" Pinkie asked. "No retina scan or killer drones? Are you sure that's enough to protect the fifty-year-old records that are in here? I mean, what if someone wanted to find out what kind of wine Hubert's grandfather brought to a dinner party seventy years ago? You could have a scandal on your hands. Actually, given Hubert's family wines, you would definitely have a scandal on your hands."

Ludwig shook his head. "You joke, but this is Switzerland. Even records from seventy years ago have the potential to embarrass people. Especially records from seventy years ago. A dark time in our history, you know."

I looked at Pinkie. "Nazi gold again? I'm starting to think you might have something there. But I'm still not convinced about the glitter bomb."

Ludwig walked ahead of us and rooted around on the bookshelves, finally coming up with four large, leather-bound folios that looked like they should be set up against a rock with a bunch of witches dancing around them, throwing mysterious items into a cauldron.

"These are the books for 1972," he said. "Each partner kept one. While these are not considered highly sensitive documents, I'd appreciate it if you'd make sure they didn't leave your care. A private banker is in some ways very much like a priest, you know."

"Because they work in a fancy building and take all of your money?" Pinkie asked.

"Because they hear a lot of secrets," Ludwig said, giving Pinkie a stern look.

"Do we need to get them back quickly?" I asked. "I mean, do the bank employees still need access to them for some reason?"

Ludwig shook his head. "No. We keep them because they're part of our history, but nobody uses them anymore." He stroked the cover of one of the books. "The last person who looked at these books was Mrs. Richter."

"Hubert's wife? Helen?"

Ludwig nodded. "She spent many hours down here doing research when she was writing the history of the bank. Herr Richter published the book after her death." He gestured to a glossy printed tome that must have been five hundred pages. Several copies were shelved next to the ledgers. I wondered who would willingly read a five hundred-page book about Swiss bankers. Probably other Swiss bankers.

Ludwig gathered up the four ledgers. "Shall I ask someone to take these to your car?"

"No need," Pinkie said, taking them from him. He turned around and handed them to me.

"Why are you handing them to me?" I complained. "We're looking at these to try to see if we can get your watch back.

Shouldn't you be the one carrying the books?"

"I would love to carry the books if it weren't for my knee injury." He gave a halfhearted limp and looked up to see if I was buying it.

"Prince Philippe, you haven't changed at all," Ludwig said reprovingly. "Lora, let me take those for you."

"I'm fine," I said, ignoring Pinkie's hobbling gait. "They're not that heavy." We left the vault and returned to Frau Backer's desk.

"If I could just see the spines of the books…" Frau Backer murmured. I turned the books spine out, and she tapped a few keys. "You're all checked out." She slid my purse across the desk, and I dumped the books into it. Pinkie always mocked me for carrying such a gigantic purse, but that was because he didn't have a travel companion who expected Kleenex, hand disinfectant, sunglasses, and breath mints to materialize upon command. If Pinkie traveled with someone like himself, one of them would need to drag a rolling suitcase wherever they went.

We said our goodbyes and made our way back down to the parking lot, where the Discount Erotik MegaSmart was awaiting us. I put the books on the tiny back ledge and climbed into the driver's side. Pinkie sighed dramatically. "Have I told you how much I hate this car?"

"Yes," I said, putting it into gear. "Several times." We pulled out into the street, weaving at a slug's pace through crowds of drunken revelers.

Pinkie looked at the crowd. "Let's call Hubert to see when dinner is. Maybe we can hang around downtown until then. It's been a while since I've been to a cultural event."

"I'm not sure this qualifies as a cultural event," I said, carefully steering around a heavily tattooed man wearing nothing but a Fat Cat mask and a conservative gray tie dangling down to cover his penis. "You really want to see a bunch of crazed club fiends drunk and out of control and dancing in the streets?" I looked at him. "Never mind; of course you do. I don't know why I even ask these questions."

Pinkie pulled out his phone and called Hubert, putting him on speaker. "Hubert…it's Philippe. We got the books from Ludwig. And by the way, you should have told me that Ludwig was still working there… What has it been now…twenty years later?"

"Well, of course he's still working for us after twenty years.

Where else would he be working? He's practically family."

"I know. But in addition to having been there for twenty years, I couldn't help but notice that Ludwig isn't aging normally. Do you really think the vaults are safe under the care of a vampire?"

Hubert chuckled. "Pretty sure. Are you going to come back for dinner or stay downtown at the parade?"

Pinkie shot me a glance. "Well, I'm voting for the parade, but Lora seems to think that there's something wrong with a million half-naked people dancing in the streets. She's from the American suburbs, you know. Terribly puritanical."

I punched him in the arm.

"Well, perhaps if she wants to come back alone, you can stay there for a while on your own. Actually, it might be a good thing. I was hoping to ask her for a favor." I could hear the stress in his voice over the phone.

"You're on speaker, Hubert," I said. "And of course I'm happy to help out however I can. What's up?"

"It's Sarina…"

"What's wrong?" *Aside from the fact that your daughter is a self-righteous brat*, I silently added.

Hubert sighed heavily. "She's gotten some positive feedback on that grant proposal she's submitting. To teach at a girl's school in rural Pakistan. I thought for sure she would change her mind or the application would fall through. But it's looking like she really might go there, maybe as soon as this fall. I know that most fathers would be proud to have a daughter who cares so much about other people, but…"

"But you're worried, of course. It's understandable. But what would you like to me to do?"

"I thought maybe you could talk to her. I mean, I know you don't know each other very well, but Philippe tells me you've met all kinds of people…"

I shot Pinkie a suspicious look.

"And I just thought maybe an outside perspective would help. Truth be told, it's times like these when I wish Helen were still here. She could talk people into anything. I see some of that skill in you as well."

Despite my belief that Sarina wouldn't listen to a thing I said, I couldn't help but be flattered.

"That's very sweet, Hubert. If you think it would help, I'd be happy to talk to her, but if she's really got her mind set on it, it might be best just to try to prepare her for it rather than fighting her."

"As Quintilian said," Pinkie said pompously, "'When defeat is inevitable, it is wisest to yield.'"

Hubert was silent for a moment, and when he spoke again a strange tone had crept into his voice. "Philippe…would you mind telling me where you heard that quote?"

"Oh, Margrit told me they found it on that Fat Cat victim. Why?"

I hit the mute button. "That was told to you in confidence, Pinkie! It's a murder investigation, for heaven's sake!"

Pinkie looked at me, puzzled. "Margit knows I can't be trusted with secrets. And it's Hubert. He won't tell anyone. He's a Swiss banker, for heaven's sake. He thinks it's like some kind of sacred trust."

I unmuted the phone. "For the record, Hubert, that was told to Philippe in the strictest confidence."

"Of course. This is important, Philippe. Was there anything else found with the victim?"

"A phone number for a bakery in Albania. It's probably a cover for a heroin smuggling operation or something."

"I don't think so," Hubert said, his voice heavy. "Philippe, would you please call your cousin Margrit and tell her that I need to speak with her in person? I'll meet you at the police station as soon as I can get there. This can't wait."

"What can't wait?" Pinkie asked, breathless. "You can tell me. I won't tell a soul."

Hubert let out a hollow chuckle. "Philippe, you forget that I've known you since you were a child. You've never been able to keep a secret. Just meet me at the station. I think I may be able to shed some light on our Fat Cat's victim."

17

I put the car in gear to pull it back into the bank parking lot. "Where are you going?" Pinkie asked.

"I'm parking the car so that we can walk back to the police station."

"Over my dead body. We're *driving* to the police station."

"There are about a billion people out in the streets. How do you expect me to drive there?"

"Slowly," Pinkie said, settling back into the seat and crossing his arms over his chest.

I ground my teeth and pulled the car out into traffic, narrowly avoiding running over a group of teenage girls in occupational uniforms ranging from sexy cop to naughty maid. I slowly crept the car forward, waiting for the people around me to move.

"Pinkie, I know you hate walking, but today is not the day for driving around," I said, trying not to squash a Jack Russell terrier wearing a pirate hat. "We are literally the only ones stupid enough to be out here in a car."

Pinkie glanced in the mirror. "Not true. There's an ambulance right over there. That counts as a car, doesn't it?"

"I doubt they're out in an ambulance because they're too lazy to walk two stops and too stuck up to take the tram."

A jester with bloodshot eyes banged on our window. "Hey…are you guys giving out free samples?"

Pinkie turned to look at him and gave him such a withering

glance that guy jumped back as if he'd been stung. "Honestly. Switzerland is a rich country. Don't you think people should be able to afford their own sex toys instead of looking for free handouts?"

"Probably all the free condom giveaways have ruined the market," I said, weaving around a man in a Borat-style swimsuit and beer hat.

"Turn here," Pinkie said, gesturing at the entrance to the police parking garage. There was a big sign in German and English that read, *Parking for Police Vehicles Only.*

"We can't park there. Look at the sign."

Pinkie rolled his eyes. "Lora, we're bringing evidence that's important to the Fat Cat killer case. Do you really think they're not going to let us park here? We're like deputies. In fact, I bet this qualifies as a police vehicle."

I pulled up in front of the barrier, and a man in a police uniform walked over and said something in German.

"Sorry," I said. "I'm afraid I don't speak German. My friend and I are here to see Detective Margrit von Hofstedtler. We have some evidence on a case she's working on."

The man looked at the car. "You can't park here. Official vehicles only."

Pinkie cleared his throat. "Excuse me. We are here to provide evidence about the Fat Cat case. I'm sure she would be fine with us parking here."

"It is not up to her," the police officer said. "She is a homicide detective. I am responsible for this parking garage. There's a public parking garage at the end of the street. You can park there and walk back."

"Are you seriously telling me that someone is trying to bring evidence that might break open a murder case, and you are not going to let them park in the police parking garage?" Pinkie asked, his voice filled with disbelief.

"Yes," the officer said, straightening his uniform.

"What if the killer ends up killing someone else while we're standing here fighting about parking?"

The policeman regarded Pinkie impassively. "Then your evidence will be twice as important. Rules are rules, sir. Now, I'm going to have to insist that you move this"—he paused, taking in the erotic advertisements plastering our car—"vehicle."

Pinkie took a deep breath to argue, and I cut in before he could say something to get us arrested. "Thank you, Officer. We'll park down the street."

"Can you believe that!?" Pinkie hissed as we drove away. "This country is going to hell in a handbasket!"

"This country officially has the highest standard of living in the world. I hardly think that counts as hell in a handbasket."

"Just because it's a rich country doesn't mean it's a good place to live. Money doesn't buy happiness, you know."

"Actually, having never had enough money to even rent happiness, I wouldn't know." We turned into the parking garage, and I took a ticket from the machine. I surveyed the cramped space in disbelief. "My god…are all the parking garages in this country so tiny?" I eased our microscopic car around a hairpin turn in the parking ramp. "This car is the size of a roller skate, and I'm still afraid I'm going to scrape it." I winced as I inched around another parked car.

Looking around the garage, I was struck at how tiny all of the spaces seemed. Was it my imagination, or were there twice as many posts as there needed to be? How on earth did normal-sized cars park here? I eyeballed the closest space. "I don't think I can fit this car in any of these spaces unless we crawl out of the trunk."

"Don't be ridiculous. There's a BMW 7 Series behind us. Obviously the parking places are larger than they look. Or maybe the Swiss are just better at parking than Americans are."

"Look, If the Swiss are so much better at parking, why don't you park the car? You're German, right? It's practically the same thing. And I'll take your job of doing what, exactly? Oh yes…making obnoxious comments from the passenger seat."

"First of all, Swiss and Germans aren't even remotely similar."

"You mean aside from the common language, cuisine, and architecture?"

"Yes, aside from those. And secondly, those weren't obnoxious comments. They were helpful comments. I was trying to help you park by appealing to your sense of patriotic pride."

"Appealing to my sense of patriotic pride just makes me want to go out and get a Big Gulp and a box of Twinkies. We Americans aren't competitive about our parking abilities. We make the parking spaces big enough to hold Hummers. That way, everyone wins."

I glanced at the matchbox-sized parking space in front of me and then in the mirror at the BMW, which had pulled to a stop behind us. As I watched, wondering how on earth the driver was going to shoehorn that behemoth into a space, the rear window slowly lowered and a small pipe came out and turned toward us. I frowned. Not a pipe…

"Oh my god," I yelled, slamming the car into reverse. "They've got a gun!"

Pinkie scoffed. "Don't be silly—it's Switzerland." Just then the unmistakable sound of a bullet rang out in the garage.

"Oh my god!" Pinkie yelled. "They have a gun!"

"That's what I just told you," I shrieked, stomping the gas pedal. The little car paused for a moment, as if paralyzed. "Come on, you tiny piece of junk! Go! Go! Go!" The car finally engaged, jerking to a start and squealing as we rounded the corner.

My heart was pounding in my chest. "Oh shit, oh shit, oh shit. This is Switzerland. Why are we being chased by people with guns?!" I squealed around another corner as fast as I could take it without running the car into the wall.

I risked a glance over at Pinkie. "Why are people trying to kill us?! What did you do?!"

"Me?! What makes you think it was me?!"

"Who else would it be?!"

"You're the one who slept with a white slaver!"

"You've probably slept with worse! Did you screw over someone on a drug deal?"

"How many times do I have to tell you…I don't deal drugs!"

"Did you screw over someone on an introduction to a drug dealer?!"

"Just drive, Lora!"

I goosed the engine again and pointed the car onto the ramp going down a level. In the rearview mirror, I could see the BMW struggling to make the tight turns. I whipped the car down to the next level and flipped around a corner as fast as I thought I could take it. It felt like we could walk faster than we were driving, but at least the tiny car could get around the corners better than our pursuers' massive sedan.

Another gunshot came out of the BMW, echoing in the parking garage. I tried to squinch myself down below the window. Surely the Tupperware that the car's body was made of would at least slow a bullet down, right?

I heard an engine roar and saw the BMW come around the corner, sparks flying as its mirror scraped the wall. The powerful sedan didn't even slow down. I didn't know how hard you had to hit a BMW to make it stop working, but I was pretty sure that it if we so much as tapped a post, our car would shatter like a Lego toy dropped from the top of the Eiffel Tower.

"Ausfahrt!" Pinkie yelled, pointing.

"What fart?!" I yelled back, feeling the outer two tires come off of the ground as the car tilted alarmingly.

"Follow the signs for the exit. Ausfahrt! If we can get out of the garage, maybe we can lose ourselves in the crowd!"

I rocked to the side and maneuvered the car around another tight curve. Thanks to our small size, we were gaining on every turn. Another shot sounded on my right as the BMW leaped forward to close the gap in the open parts of the garage. Gaining wasn't going to be good enough.

Pinkie looked ahead. The parking barrier was down. "Ram it. As soon as we're through, get out of the car and run into the crowd. Don't worry about me. Just run. Stay in the crowd. Find a policeman and call Margrit."

I spared a quick glance for Pinkie, my best friend in the world. He reached over and squeezed my knee. "I love you," he said simply. I felt tears prick my eyes and swallowed a lump in my throat.

Accelerating toward the barrier, I braced myself for crunching, airbags, and impact. "Ahhhh!" I yelled.

The nose of the Smart Car tapped the barrier, which clattered to the ground. The tires rolled sedately over the fallen barrier, and then we were out in the street.

Pinkie blinked. "That was anticlimactic."

"Run, you idiot!"

Wrenching the door open, I fled toward the largest group of people I could find, hoping Pinkie was doing the same.

I slammed into several colorfully dressed young men, causing some grabbing and comments as they tried to figure out whether I was moshing, throwing myself at them, or just too wasted to stand up. "Get out of the way!"

I spared a quick glance behind me. The BMW had pulled to a stop behind our car, and a man in a suit was standing outside of it, looking for us. I scanned the crowd frantically, searching for cover, but as I did so I realized that my flame-red Prada dress was hard to miss in a crowd that was scantily clad in what seemed to be little more than black latex underwear.

I had to ditch my dress. My priceless, beautiful, irreplaceable dress. Why couldn't people try to kill me when I was wearing yoga pants?

I ducked into a large crowd of dominatrices, yanking at the side tie on the dress desperately. The little leather buckles on the side were hard to open, designed to save the wearer the embarrassment of being publicly naked. Of course, now that my life depended on my being publicly naked, the bloody thing was acting like it was stapled shut.

"Dammit," I panted, fumbling the last buckle open with shaking fingers. I shed the dress like a skin, handing it to one of the girls in the crowd. "It's Prada. Give it a good home, okay?" I choked back a sob and ran on.

Now clad only in black underwear, I ducked into a throng of people outside a Veuve Clicquot bar, then joined another crowd heading back the way I had just come. I spared a glance over toward where I had last seen my pursuer. There he was. A tall man wearing sunglasses and a suit, he didn't blend in any more than I had. He was scanning the crowds, looking for the red dress.

"Hey there, luv," a good-natured voice chimed in my ear. "You wanna come get a drink with me? I'm meeting some friends up there."

I spared a glance at the guy propositioning me. He was a massive, thick-necked man in jeans, a biker vest, and a spiked collar, covered in tattoos. His nose was crooked, as if it had been broken and set incorrectly. He looked like someone who enjoyed drinking and brawling, particularly when done together. Any woman in her right mind would have kept her distance.

"You know what? That sounds great." I allowed him to drape one arm over me and pull me close to his side, completely not caring about the fact that his hand was wandering pretty freely over my butt. If he could get me to a place where I could call the police, I was willing to put up with a little groping.

I ducked into the doorway with him and followed him upstairs where a large crowd had already gathered. I snuck a peep at street level. My pursuer was still looking at the crowds but was also talking into a cell phone. I reached over and pulled my unwitting rescuer over in front of me, relying on his bulk to shield me from any chance glimpses from the street.

The man smiled at me, revealing unexpectedly pearly teeth. "My god. You are a friendly thing. My name's Jimbo. Tell me what turns you on, luv, and I'll make your dreams come true."

I peeked around him. My pursuer was heading back toward the parking garage, presumably having lost me. I felt my knees buckle with relief. "What would really turn me on right now would be a cell phone, Jimbo," I said weakly. "I need to call the police. Someone just tried to kill me."

18

Twenty minutes later, I was standing in the police station, still in my underwear, when Margrit walked in. I fell on her like she was my long-lost sister. "Thank god, Margrit."

"Ahem," I heard behind her.

I felt my stomach drop. Of course he would have to be here. I looked over her shoulder. "Benjamin," I said flatly.

"Benjamin?" Margrit said, looking at him with her eyebrows raised.

"It's a middle name," Benjamin said smoothly. "Jonathan is my first name."

I felt a familiar surge of irritation at Benjamin's stupid spy games, but it was followed closely by a wave of gratitude that he was here. People could complain all they wanted about the government intruding into their privacy, but when bad guys were trying to kill you, the US government, particularly its dodgier elements, was a good friend to have in your corner.

"You two know each other?" Margrit asked, looking from Benjamin to me with a sharp expression.

I raised my eyebrows at Benjamin, loath to stand between him and whatever government-approved fairy tale he was going to spin.

"We ran into each other in Russia a few weeks ago. I had a chance to show Lora the sights."

Margrit looked at him skeptically, and then her mouth quirked upward in a surprisingly naughty grin. "And now she's repaying the favor," she said, gesturing to my conspicuous lack of clothing.

Margrit took in Benjamin's sudden flush and then glanced outside the glass wall of the office, where several officers had gathered, apparently to comment on what I now remembered was thong-backed underwear.

"Before we figure out what's going on here, do you want me to see if I can find you something to wear?" she asked.

"Please," I said, feeling as if every part of my body was blushing. She stormed out of the office, magically dissolving the knot of patrolmen.

Benjamin determinedly fixed his eyes on my face. "I swear, I'm not following you," he said, holding up his hands to forestall any outrage on my part.

"You keep saying that, but you keep showing up. How do you explain that?"

"Maybe you're following me."

"Why would I be following you?"

"Because you find me devastatingly attractive?" he tried, smiling in a way that actually was pretty devastatingly attractive.

"I'm here on a job. A job for an upstanding Swiss citizen. What are you doing here?"

"I'm here on an investigation; I told you."

"What kind of Swiss crime requires the US government to send the spook brigade to Switzerland? Let me guess—chocolate smuggling. Wait, no. Cow tipping. Oh, I got it. Tax evasion."

Benjamin gave me a pained look. "I can't really talk about it."

"Of course not. Why don't we just sit here in silence, instead?"

I fixed my eyes on the ceiling and ignored Benjamin. I was worried about Pinkie. Surely Pinkie got out okay. Hiding Pinkie in international crowd of drunken partygoers was like hiding a Dalmatian in a vat of chocolate chip ice cream. He'd just disappear.

"Are you okay?" Benjamin asked.

"Let's see… My best friend and I were attacked by killers in a parking garage. We both had to make a run for it. He could be dead for all I know." I sniffled and swiped at my eyes.

"I'm sure Prince Philippe will be fine. I've seen his file. He's very resourceful."

I nodded miserably, taking some comfort from his words and hoping he was right.

"Why do you think someone would be trying to kill you? Are

you hanging out with white slavers again?"

I gave him a watery smile. "I've given up on that. And to answer your question, I have no idea. Maybe Pinkie's managed to piss someone off. He has a bit of a gift for that."

Benjamin looked at me, and I could see real concern in his eyes. He took a step closer and reached for my hand.

Margrit chose that moment to come back into the room, bearing a Burberry trench coat. She looked at Benjamin pointedly, and he took a step back. "Sorry it took so long. I don't usually keep a change of clothes in the office, but any experienced Zurich native makes sure there's always a raincoat on hand."

I shrugged into it, rolling up the sleeves to compensate for the five-inch difference in our height. "Thank you. Did you hear from Pinkie? Is he okay?"

"Philippe is fine. He called in just a minute ago, and I sent a car to pick him up."

"Thank god," I said, blinking back tears of relief.

"Hubert is also coming in. Arnaud's bringing him. But let's start with you. I left you less than an hour ago, fully dressed, heading into the bank. What happened?"

I pulled the coat more tightly around myself. "We left the coffee shop and went to pick up those ledgers from the bank."

"What kind of ledgers?" Benjamin cut in.

Margrit shot him an annoyed look. "May I remind you that this is a Zurich police matter, completely unrelated to the reason you're here. I'm willing to allow you to stay, in light of your acquaintance with Lora, but you're not running this show."

Benjamin held his hands up in surrender, looking chastened.

"Just personal ledgers. From fifty years ago. Records of client birthdays, social events...that kind of thing. Nothing financial. Hubert was going to take a look through them to see if they had anything about that watch Pinkie's trying to wrest away from your brother."

Margrit made a *Get on with it* motion with her finger.

"And then we called Hubert, and he was complaining about his daughter, Sarina, who is apparently trying to go test her theory about patriarchal tribalism by pissing off a bunch a patriarchal tribal types. Anyway, I told him that he might just have to give in, and then Pinkie butted in with that comment. 'When defeat is inevitable...'"

"It is wisest to yield," Benjamin finished, shooting Margrit a look.

Margrit rubbed her head. "I should have known Pinkie couldn't keep a secret."

"Yes, you should have. Honestly. Anyone who's ever met him knows that. Anyway, Hubert got all worked up and asked him where he had heard that, and when Pinkie told him, he told us that he needed to talk to you."

"So why didn't you come to the police station?"

"We tried to, but the parking Gestapo wouldn't let us park there, so we had to go down to the parking garage down the street. So we pulled in, and I was trying to figure out how anyone in Zurich ever managed to get their car into those tiny spaces, and then I noticed a car behind us. And I saw the window roll down, and that's when I heard a gunshot."

"What kind of car?" Margrit asked.

"A BMW, black, 7 Series, I think."

Margrit made a note. "And the plates?"

"I didn't see."

Margrit leaned forward. "Are you sure that it was a gun?"

I looked at her disbelievingly. "What else would it have been?"

"I don't know. A pipe. A cane. An umbrella."

"I heard gunshots."

"How many?"

I thought back. "I don't know. Five? Six?"

Benjamin leaned forward. "Did they hit your car?"

"No. Why? You think I'm imagining this?"

Benjamin shook his head. "No, but something's not right. You were in the Smart Car, right? It's small, but it's not that small. And it's not fast, particularly in a parking garage."

"So?"

"Did you hear other cars being hit? Windows shattering, that kind of thing?"

I played back the scene in my head. "No," I said, finally. "I don't think they hit anything."

Margrit looked at Benjamin with raised eyebrows. "You don't think they were being shot at?"

"I don't think someone was trying to kill them," Benjamin corrected. "Your guys are running the scene, right?"

Margit nodded.

"Then we should have our answer. "Tell them to look for crimped cases. If they were firing blanks, I think we can assume whoever it was, was trying to scare you—not kill you."

Margrit looked at me appraisingly. "Scare or kill, it begs the question—why would someone want to do either of those things to you? Do you have any enemies?"

I sighed, looking up at the acoustic-tiled ceiling. "Well, there's Lady Featherstone. She tried to kill me a while ago."

Benjamin smiled. "I think you're safe on that front. I've asked our guys to keep an eye on her, and she's turned into something of a shut-in since you last spoke with her. Apparently she's developed quite an irrational fear of Russian mobsters."

"Ah, Russian mobsters. I wonder where she got that from." Of course, I knew where she had gotten that from. She had gotten that from a trip I had hostessed for a Russian oligarch who had threatened to pulp her if she ever bothered me again.

"And then there are the members of that white slavery ring I helped bust…"

"But they're all in custody, so you should be safe there," Benjamin said.

Margrit rubbed her temples. "I'm sorry. I must be confused. I thought you were an event hostess."

"I am. I've just had a couple of more dramatic events recently. Oh…wait." I suddenly thought of an actual enemy. "Vanessa St. Germain."

Margrit raised her eyebrows. "Another white slaver?"

"No. Another event hostess. She's been trying to steal my clients, and she's hostessing a competing dinner in Zurich this weekend."

Margrit's forehead creased as she gave me a skeptical look. "Another event hostess? Has she threatened you in any way?"

"Yes. She left a book and some chocolates for me."

"A violent book?"

"A coffee table book about Switzerland."

"I see. And was there a threatening inscription in this coffee table book?"

"Yes. Let me see if I can remember. She wished me good luck on my dinner, and she offered to share tips on what to see here since she went to school in Switzerland and was 'practically a native.'"

"That was the threat? Offering vacation tips?"

I sighed. "She wasn't trying to help me. It was more like a really subtle way of telling me that she was more qualified to put together an authentic Swiss dinner than I was. Like I was so clueless about Switzerland that I needed a coffee table book to help me. You have to read between the lines with someone like that. She's like the Moriarty of event hostesses."

"Huh," Margrit said, obviously unconvinced. "Well, I'll add her to the list. What about Philippe? Any enemies you know of?"

I thought about it. "Well, he has been in a really terrible mood recently, especially since he saw your brother wearing that watch. Frankly, I've been tempted to shoot him several times, and I'm his best friend."

"I heard that," Pinkie said, walking into the door on the arm of a handsome young police officer. While he still wore the slacks from earlier, from the waist up he was naked and sparkly. He had accessorized with star-shaped sunglasses and a large, fuzzy Uncle Sam-style top hat.

Benjamin stifled a snort of laughter.

"What the hell, Pinkie?"

"Well, I had to blend in, didn't I?"

"And the body glitter? When did you have time to stop and get sprayed with body glitter?"

"I didn't stop," he said, outraged. "I just kind of ran by a big glitter gun. Twice." He twisted around under the lights, turning his arms so that they reflected the light from the fluorescent bulbs. "But it looks good, right? Maybe I should wear it more often."

Margit snorted. "Can we please get back to the topic? Aside from Lora here, and possibly me, can you think of anyone else who'd like to kill you?"

Pinkie struck a thoughtful pose. "Well, there are plenty of people who resent my fabulousness."

"But I would think they fall mainly into the category of 'people who would like to see you split your pants on national television' than 'people who would like to murder you in cold blood in a parking garage in Zurich,'" I pointed out.

"Probably. But honestly, if I split my pants on national television, I would probably murder myself out of embarrassment."

"Of course you would," I said, rolling my eyes.

Pinkie tapped his finger against his chin thoughtfully. "I'm sure it's related to this Fat Cat thing. I mean, I'm a prince, right? I'm probably like the number one target."

I shook my head. "I hate to break it to you, but if the Fat Cat is targeting people with money, you're not qualified."

Margit's phone rang, and she looked at it. "That's the team that was processing the scene. Give me a minute." She listened intently on the phone.

"You said you had collected some ledgers from the bank," she said to me.

"Four of them. They were in a Louis Vuitton shopper in the back."

"Well, they're not there now. I think we're going to have to talk with Hubert about what was in those books."

Benjamin shook his head. "I think we might be overlooking the obvious here. Isn't it more likely that someone saw a thousand-dollar bag in an open car and just helped themselves? I mean, I know Zurich is pretty low crime, but a Louis Vuitton in an open car has to be pushing it, even for here, right?"

Margrit sighed. "You're probably right, but we should ask Hubert about it anyway."

"Where is Hubert?" Pinkie asked. "I thought Arnaud was bringing him to the station."

"I told the desk to put them in the other room when they came in," Margrit said. "They're probably there now. Why don't we all go talk to them? Maybe Hubert knows something that can shed some light on what's happening here."

19

When we walked into the interview room, Hubert was pacing back and forth in what for a Swiss banker probably passed for a frenzy of nerves. Arnaud sat calmly at the table scanning his telephone, a slightly worried look the only indication that he was aware of the events of the day.

"Margrit," Hubert said, taking her by the arms. "Thank heavens you're here. I have some important information about the Fat Cat victim."

"First, there's something you should know," Margrit said. "Someone may have just tried to kill Philippe and Lora."

"Kill them?" Hubert asked, blinking owlishly.

"Someone shot at us in the parking garage near the police station," I said. "We had to leave the car behind and make a run for it through the Street Parade."

Arnaud looked up, shocked. In three steps he was by my side, holding my arms as he looked down at me in concern. "My god, Lora…are you okay?" I gave him what I hoped was a reassuring smile. "We're fine." Arnaud reached down and took my hand in a supportive gesture that somehow felt natural despite our short acquaintance.

Hubert clutched his chest. "Shooting in Zurich? I never thought I would see it. Thank god you're unharmed, Philippe. I would never have been able to forgive myself if something had happened to you." He grabbed Pinkie around the shoulders and pulled him into a tight hug, heedless of the body glitter he was getting all over his suit jacket.

"I'm sorry, but would somebody make some introductions?" Benjamin asked, his tone suddenly icy.

"Ooh…I will," Pinkie said, freeing himself from Hubert's embrace. "This is my godfather, Hubert. He is a partner at Richter and Partners. Given the fact that you work for the government, that probably doesn't mean that much to you, but if you were fabulously rich, you'd recognize that as one of Switzerland's oldest private banks."

A muscle in Benjamin's jaw twitched.

Oblivious, Pinkie continued. "And this is Arnaud, who is also a partner in the same bank. I guess you've already met Margrit, since you seem to know each other."

Benjamin nodded tersely, his narrowed eyes fixed on Arnaud, who was still holding my hand.

Pinkie gestured to Benjamin with a flourish. "And, Arnaud and Hubert, this is Lora's government-assigned stalker. And what name are we going by today, Mr. Stalker?"

"Benjamin is fine," Benjamin grated.

"Benjamin," Pinkie repeated, smiling brightly.

"What does a government-assigned stalker do, exactly?" Arnaud asked, looking from me to Benjamin.

"I'm not a stalker," Benjamin said curtly. "Lora came up on a watch list a few weeks ago. I checked her out. She's clean. That's it."

I opened my mouth to object. He had kissed me. He had implied that he'd be watching out for me. He had even asked me out to dinner. I snapped my mouth shut. Clearly that was not a topic for this situation.

"Will someone please tell me why someone would be trying to kill Philippe and Lora?" Hubert asked, bewildered.

Benjamin shook his head. "It might not have been a murder attempt. Lora and Philippe heard shots, but there was no damage to the car. I'd think that any half-decent shot could hit a Smart Car at ten yards. They're not *that* small."

"Try sitting in one before you make that call," Pinkie muttered.

"Well, that's good news, but I still don't understand why someone would someone be trying to terrorize Philippe and Lora," Arnaud said.

"That's what we were trying to figure out. We were wondering if it might be because of what was in the bank ledgers they picked up," Margrit said. "The books were taken out of Philippe's car when he and Lora ran into the crowd to get away."

Pinkie raised a finger. "Ahem. I'd just like to point out that it's not *my* car. It's the car that we got stuck with when our limo got vandalized." He looked around the room. "Is someone writing this down for the record? Not. My. Car."

"The bank ledgers?" Hubert's faced creased with confusion. "Absolutely not. They were just records of appointments and such that took place more than forty years ago. They would have names, meeting times, maybe a note or two as to kids' birthdays or favorite drinks. No notes as to money or account holdings. Why would anybody take them? Most of the people in those books are long dead."

"Probably because they were in a really nice handbag," Margrit said wryly.

"Wait a minute," Pinkie said, his eyes suddenly narrowing. "I know someone who would have wanted those books. Someone who is absolutely amoral and evil to the core."

Hubert looked concerned. "Who?"

"Maurice," Pinkie said, looking at Margrit.

"Don't be ridiculous. Maurice can be a jerk, yes, but he's not a killer."

I wondered whether we should tell her that he was also a blackmailer. That might not make him a killer, but I figured it put him a couple steps up from jerk. "But wait—how would he have known? Did you tell him?" I asked Pinkie.

"Of course not."

"Goddammit," Margrit said.

Pinkie looked at her. "You told him?"

"He called right after I dropped you two off to tell me that you were trying to steal his watch and he wanted me to have an official chat with you to warn you off. I told him you were going to check out the bank's ledgers from that time and that I was on whoever's side ended up with the most evidence." Margrit looked doubtful. "I really don't think he could have found contract killers in that short a time period. It couldn't have been more than forty-five minutes."

Pinkie looked at her. "A lot can happen in forty-five minutes."

Margrit shook her head. "This is ridiculous. I'm calling him."

She pulled out her phone and hit a button. We could hear the ringing, but nobody answered. "I'll find out whether he was involved."

I winced at the tone in her voice. It was almost enough to make me feel sorry for Maurice. Almost.

Margrit looked back at me. "Tabling the question of whether my brother was involved for now, are you sure it wasn't just kids having some fun with you? It is Street Parade, after all. People aren't exactly on their best behavior."

"They definitely weren't kids," I said, "but today I saw an eighty-year-old woman wearing nothing but a G-string and pasties, so I'm not sure that Street Parade insanity is age-dependent."

Margrit chuckled. "You're right. Look. We need to see what the crime scene guys come back with before we can figure out what happened in the garage. And let me assure you that if Maurice had anything to do with it, I will make sure he is arrested. In the meantime," she said, turning her focus to Hubert, "you were coming in to see me about something else. Something about the Fat Cat victim. Something related to that quote that Philippe was supposed to not mention to anyone else. Ever. Under any circumstances."

She gave Pinkie a steely glare, and he had the good grace to look abashed.

"Yes," Hubert said, pulling an envelope out of his pocket. "But before I tell you, I need everyone in this room to sign this paper."

Margrit looked at him skeptically. "What is it?"

"It's a paper stating that you will hold what I'm about to tell you in the strictest confidence and that none of you will be able to benefit personally, directly or indirectly, from what I'm going to tell you. I should warn you that there are strict civil penalties for breaking this agreement." He looked hard at Pinkie.

"Why are you looking at me? I'm like Fort Knox."

"More like Johnny Knoxville," Benjamin said, rolling his eyes. He scanned the paper quickly. "I'm okay with this," he said, signing.

The paper was duly handed around and signed by everyone in the room.

"Now what?" Margrit asked, clearly impatient with the legal precautions.

Hubert carefully folded the paper and tucked it into his pocket.

"That paper found in the dead man's wallet—Philippe said there was a number below it."

"There was," Margrit said. "A telephone number for a bakery in Albania, we think."

"An eleven-digit number starting with 355?"

"Yes."

Hubert took off his glasses and polished them. Even Arnaud looked grim. "It's not a phone number. It's an account number. For an account that's been in our bank since 1945."

"Since 1945?" Margrit asked.

"The end of World War II," Hubert clarified.

"I know when the end of World War II was," Margrit said with a touch of asperity. "Whose account is it?"

Hubert shook his head. "There's no name on the account. It's just an account number. Whoever provides the current senior partner of the bank with the account number and pass phrase is to be given access to the account."

"Do you know what's in the account?"

"Gold. We took possession of the bars in 1945, and we've been keeping them in a segregated vault ever since."

"How many bars are we talking about?" Benjamin asked.

Hubert pursed his lips. "Two thousand bars, one kilogram each."

There was a stunned moment of silence. "How much is that worth?" Margrit asked.

"In today's prices, roughly seventy-five million francs," Hubert said. He looked over at Benjamin. "Or eighty-three million American dollars."

Benjamin let out a low whistle. "And it's been unclaimed all these years?"

Hubert nodded. "It has. But if your victim had that note in his pocket, my guess is that he was coming to claim it."

"Let me ask you something," Benjamin said. "You say that account was anonymous, right? You don't have any notes or anything on who owned the account?"

"No," Hubert said. "Anonymous means just that."

"Who would have opened an anonymous account containing physical gold at that particular point in time?" Benjamin asked.

Hubert shifted, looking uncomfortable. "It was a very dark time," he hedged. "Lots of confusion. People across Europe trying to find safety for themselves and their assets. It's impossible to say with any certainty, especially so many years later."

Benjamin took a step toward Hubert. "But I think we can make a reasonable guess, right? In 1945, the Allies were rolling into Germany and Austria. Anyone who had eyes could see that the Nazi Party was on its way out. So if you had managed to loot seventy-five million francs from people you had done your best to exterminate, where would you send it? Where would it be safe? Where would you be able to trust that your blood money would raise no questions?"

"Switzerland," Arnaud said shortly. "But that was a long time ago."

"The legal climate was completely different back then," Hubert said. "A banker who judged his clients based on how they made their money would have been considered completely unprofessional. But times are different now. Such a thing could never happen again today. There are laws in place…"

"I know," Benjamin said. "But what would have happened if that man had shown up on your doorstep tomorrow and given you that quote and account number?"

"We would have given him the gold," Hubert said.

"And you wouldn't have cared about where it was going?"

"It's not that we wouldn't have cared," Hubert objected. "It's that we wouldn't have been able to ask."

"Well, in this case, you probably should have asked," Benjamin snapped. "Because Horst Mueller, the man who was killed last night, was not the kind of person who should have had access to eighty million bucks' worth of liquid assets."

"We don't know anything about any Horst Mueller," Arnaud interjected. "And it's not our place to research people taking money out of the bank. If he was putting money into the bank, it would be a different story. Then of course we'd have to do our due diligence on him. What was he? A terrorist? An arms dealer?"

"A German businessman. Who happened to be deeply involved in the right-wing political scene. You know, those *Foreigner, go home* parties that preach racial purity."

"As terrible as you and I may find that, it's not a crime," Hubert said.

"It's not," Benjamin agreed, "but funneling money to neo-Nazis is, as is planning terrorist attacks in Israel."

Hubert looked at him searchingly. "Those are very serious accusations. I assume you have some proof of this?"

"If we had hard proof of this, Horst Mueller would never have left Germany. What I have at this point is just chatter. Chatter on websites that we monitor about what some very unpleasant people can accomplish with seventy-five million francs."

Hubert shook his head. "It's easy to be glib about what should be done, but in Switzerland and Germany, just as in America, people must actually commit a crime before being punished for one. Even if we had been aware of this so-called chatter, it wouldn't have changed our actions. We would have been legally obligated to turn the money over the Herr Mueller."

Benjamin looked as though he wanted to argue further, but Margrit put a hand on his arm to stop him.

"We're not here to argue over Swiss history or bank policies. We've been trying to figure out why a vandal who supposedly acts against the 1 percent would murder a moderately successful German businessman, and now we have at least one possible scenario. Our moderately successful businessman was about to become very, very rich."

"But how would someone who spray paints cartoons onto Gucci stores have any idea that Mueller was about to become very rich?" Benjamin asked. "You're thinking that the Fat Cat killer is lurking in right-wing terrorist chat rooms?"

"I'm not thinking anything at this point. I'm just trying to link up what we know so that we can figure out how this impacts the investigation."

Hubert shook his head in confusion. "None of this makes any sense." He looked visibly distressed by the idea that his bank could be even tangentially involved in a murder case. "What are we going to do now?"

Margrit looked at him. "I think the next step is to take a look in that vault." She looked at Pinkie's glitter-bedecked form. "And as much as it pains me to say it, I guess you two will be joining us. I can't spare a team to watch you, and until I know if someone actually tried to kill you, I can't let you run around loose, either."

She looked at me. "Are you okay to come like that, or should I try to rustle up some additional clothes?"

"I'm fine. Given what we've heard today, I would imagine that what I have or don't have on under this raincoat is the least of anyone's concerns."

Margrit nodded, and we followed her down the hallway to the elevators. Arnaud took me by the elbow and leaned in close to my ear. "Would you think I was shallow if I told you that what you have on under that raincoat isn't the least of my concerns?" he whispered.

I smothered a laugh, and Benjamin shot an angry glare in my direction.

"Absolutely."

"I don't suppose you'd like to show me later?" Arnaud asked, raising an eyebrow.

I looked at him. Handsome, charming, fun…not kissing me and abandoning me in a church in Malta and then pretending it never happened so that he could jet around the world spying on people and throwing jealous temper tantrums…

"I'll think about it."

20

By the time we got to the bank vault, Gerhardt had arrived, and Ludwig, who Pinkie assured me was more or less unflappable, was looking pretty well flapped.

"What exactly are you expecting to find in this vault?" Gerhardt asked Margrit. "The owner hasn't come near it in seventy years, and Herr Mueller never got a chance to look inside either. It's hard to see what could be in there that would possibly explain a recent murder, don't you think?"

"I don't know what I'm going to find, and if it hasn't been opened in seventy years, neither do you," Margit pointed out. "Maybe there's information about the person who set up the account. Information that we can use to trace back who would have known about the vault."

Ludwig led the way down the stairs, with Arnaud and Hubert right behind him, their expressions grim. Gerhardt brought up the rear, leaning on his cane with one hand and clutching the railing with the other as he painfully lowered himself down each step. By the time we reached the bottom, he was breathing hard with effort.

Margrit observed the handprint entry system with interest. "What kind of security does this vault have?"

"About ten years ago, we updated the old vault to a state-of-the-art system," Gerhardt said. "The hand-recognition and password systems ensure that only named bank employees can access the vaults. The vaults are in zones, so access to the records vault, where Philippe took the ledgers from, doesn't give you access to the long-term deposit vault, which is where the gold is located."

Margrit nodded. "So we'd be able to pull a record of every entry and exit to both the vault area and the long-term deposit vault itself?"

"Of course," Gerhardt said. "But better than that, we can give you film from the last ten years."

"Film of what?"

"Film of the vault itself," Arnaud answered. "When we set up the system, we put video on the entry to the vault area, the entry to the long-term deposit vault, and the inside of the long-term deposit vault, where the boxes are. There's a small area in the vault that's not filmed, where our clients can open their boxes in privacy, but otherwise you should be able to see everything that's happened in the last decade."

"And that's motion activated, right?"

Arnaud shot an unreadable glance at Gerhardt.

Gerhardt cleared his throat. "Continuous feed."

Margrit looked at him in disbelief. "You have continuous feed video going back ten years? Why on earth would you do that?"

Gerhardt flushed. "It just seemed to me that motion activation would leave the potential for tampering. No matter what the security consultant said."

Margrit shook her head. "Please don't tell me that I'm going to have to look through ten years of VHS tapes."

Gerhardt looked offended. "Of course not. We're a modern bank. Everything's on a web page."

"A *web page*?"

"Private cloud," Arnaud murmured.

"And we just need to set you up with a password," Gerhardt continued.

"After we authorize your IP address and provide you with a token that generates random numbers synchronized to our security system," Arnaud added.

Gerhardt waved a hand in irritation. "Arnaud keeps track of this kind of thing. Talk to him."

Margrit made a note in her phone. "All right. Let's see what we've got."

Hubert and Gerhard pulled keys out of their pockets and

inserted them into matching slots in a panel next to the door. Hubert looked at Gerhardt, and they both turned the keys with a smooth movement that spoke of long years of practice. Each of them entered passcodes into the panel beneath the key slot. The massive door slid open on oiled hinges, revealing a large room filled with numbered safety deposit boxes.

"Do two partners always need to open the lock?" Margrit asked.

"Yes," Hubert said. "There are only four keys, one for each partner—Gerhard, myself, Arnaud, and as of two weeks ago, Reiner."

"I thought Reiner only became a partner on Friday," Pinkie said, his voice suddenly sharp.

Hubert shook his head. "Friday was the dinner, but Reiner was legally invested with the partnership two weeks ago. He got his key then."

"Do the partners leave the keys in the bank? In their offices, perhaps?" Margit's tone was one of idle curiosity, but the look in her eyes was far from casual.

"Heavens no," Hubert said. "The keys are always with us or locked away in our homes. In all the years of bank history, we've never had an episode of a lost or missing key."

"And are there any spare keys?"

"There is one spare key that we keep locked in a safe at my home," Hubert said. "I see it whenever I open the safe, and I can assure you that it hasn't moved in decades."

We entered the vault. Although large and well lit, the space was claustrophobic, and I felt my breathing quicken. I tried not to think about the tons of rock pressing down on me from above. "You don't have earthquakes in Switzerland, do you?" I asked Arnaud.

"Not often," he said cheerfully.

My breathing upped another notch.

"It's 7301," Hubert said, scanning the boxes. "We call it a segregated vault, but really, it's just a storage box within the deposit vault. Ah. Here." He gestured to a box on the bottom row, about the size of a mini fridge.

He pulled out a small ring of keys and flipped through them quickly. "Shall I open it?" he asked, looking at Margrit.

"Please."

Hubert inserted the key and pulled on the handle, opening the door.

There was a moment of silence while everyone looked inside. "My god," Pinkie said reverently. Inside the box was a pile of gold bars, each a little bigger than the palm of a man's hand, stacked on top of each other with military precision.

Hubert's voice was hushed. "Two thousand one-kilogram gold bars—seventy-five million francs."

I felt my hand involuntarily reach forward. The urge to pick up a gold bar was almost overwhelming.

"Can you wheel them out or something?" Margrit asked, apparently unmoved by the sight of so much gold. "We need to check the box for papers."

Hubert shook his head. "It's two thousand kilos of gold. It weighs as much as a car. I'm afraid the bars need to be individually removed."

Margrit looked at the small, compact pile of gold. "Dammit. I'll have to get a couple of guys in here to go through it. Individually moving two thousand bars of gold is going to take a while."

While she was talking, Pinkie reached in and grabbed a bar. "Pinkie! Put that back!" I said. I reached out to snatch it from his hand, but as soon as I touched it, a shock of realization went through me.

"It's not…" I started.

"It's not gold," Pinkie said, completing my thought.

"What do you mean, it's not gold?" Hubert asked, aghast. "Of course it's gold. What else would it be?"

Pinkie weighed the bar in his hand lightly before handing it to Hubert. "Plaster would be my guess."

Hubert held the bar in his hand, his mouth open and panic in his eyes. "What does this mean?" He handed the bar to Gerhardt. Gerhardt looked equally shocked.

Hubert reached back in and pulled out a few more bars. "They're all plaster," he said, his voice sounding strangled.

Margrit looked grim. "When was the last time this box was opened?"

"Two weeks ago," Hubert said. "When Reiner's partnership became official. We go through the bank's segregated vaults with all new partners. We open the boxes and do a visual inspection. This one is always the first one we open, since it's one of the oldest."

"Did you pull out any of the bars two weeks ago?"

"No," Hubert said. "We never touch the contents of the boxes."

"So for all you know, this was never gold at all," Margrit said reasonably.

Gerhardt shook his head. "At the time of the original deposit, the gold was certified. It's not like a safety deposit box, where you rent the space and can keep whatever you like in it. In this case, the contract specifies the contents. We took custody of the physical gold. Two partners certified it. My father and Arnaud's father, if I recall correctly. We've been tracking the value of the account ever since."

"So maybe whoever certified the gold back in the '40s lied," Margrit said.

Gerhardt's face darkened. "I realize it's your job to explore all possibilities, but I can assure you that that is not possible. Two bank partners operating in collusion to defraud their own bank? To what end? The idea is preposterous."

Hubert was still standing silently, as if in shock. "I touched it," he said softly.

"What do you mean, you touched it?" Benjamin asked.

"When I made partner. It was many years ago…1992, to be precise, and rules weren't as strict in those days. I picked up a bar, just as Philippe did."

"And…?" Margrit prompted him.

"It was gold," Hubert said simply. His skin had turned gray with shock, and I looked at him in concern.

We all stood in silence for a moment.

Margrit's mouth tightened. "I hate to ask this, Hubert, but it's my job. What exactly would have happened if Horst Mueller had shown up on your doorstep yesterday with the account number and the password?"

Hubert blinked. "We would have come to the vault. We would have opened it," he said, his voice weak.

"And when you found out that there was no gold?"

Hubert pinched the bridge of his nose. "We are responsible," he said simply. "It was in our safekeeping. There's insurance, of course, but the investigation into the theft would almost certainly have gotten out into the press. Nazi gold lost by bank partners."

"So you would have had a public relations problem?"

"This is a private bank. We're not publicly held. That kind of scandal would ruin us. In fact, I think we would have tried to make up the money ourselves. It would have wiped us out personally, but at least we would have had a chance to hold the bank together."

Gerhardt nodded. "I agree. We would have been better off to make up the lost funds. At least then we'd have a chance to stay in business."

"You would have had to make up *seventy-five million francs?*" Margrit asked. "From the bank's money?"

"From our money," Hubert said. "We never changed the structure of this bank. All partners are personally liable for bank losses."

Margrit sucked in. "So if this money had been found missing..."

"We would have made it up," Hubert said softly. "But we would have had to liquidate everything we owned to do it."

I pictured Hubert, turned out of his beautiful lakeside home, forced to start over again in his sixties.

"So the murder of this person saved all of the partners from financial ruin," Margrit summed up.

Hubert looked at her and shook his head sadly. "It doesn't work that way. We are still liable for this gold, whether or not it is claimed. The only thing that the murder means is that we have more time to try to get it back."

21

Benjamin narrowed his eyes as he looked around the vault. "So what we have here is a locked room mystery."

"What we have here," Margrit corrected, "is a matter for the Swiss police. And one that needs to be handled very delicately."

Gerhardt nodded. "The last thing we want to do is cause a panic."

"Why are you tiptoeing around this?" Benjamin asked Margrit, his irritation plain. "You're acting like we've caught your prime minister in bed with the nanny. It's just a bank robbery. Happens all the time."

Margrit looked at him with a hard expression. "First of all, Switzerland doesn't have a prime minister. It has a president, and most Swiss people couldn't care less if he was sleeping with the nanny. We're not quite as hung up on sex as you Americans. But Swiss people *do* care about how their largest industry is doing, and in case you weren't aware of it, it's not doing all that well these days, largely because your government has spent the last two years trying to destroy it."

"Because anonymous banks are used by criminals to hide money," Benjamin said.

"Bullshit. Because your government is a bully. It may have started out because of fears about crime, but at this point you've gone so far over the line that it's ridiculous."

"Are you saying it's not in the world's interests to stop terrorists and criminals from moving money around?"

"I'm fine with stopping terrorists from moving money around. I'm not fine with making other countries responsible for enforcing your ridiculous tax code," Margrit said, her eyes narrowing.

There was a tense moment of silence.

Benjamin held up his hands in surrender. "Look, this really isn't the time to argue over US tax policy."

"This isn't the time for you to be involved at all," Margrit retorted. "We will complete our investigation. Quietly. We will find out who has the gold if at all possible."

"And if it's not possible?"

"If it's not possible, we will make up the difference," Gerhardt said, dropping a hand on Hubert's shoulder. "The next time someone comes to ask for that money, it will be here."

Arnaud nodded, displaying remarkable sangfroid for someone who had been rendered millions of dollars poorer with one stroke. I had to admire his cool. I once accidentally threw away five bucks at Starbucks and kicked myself for a week.

Margrit nodded. "I would expect no less. We'll need to see the records, of course. And the video."

"Of course," Hubert said. "I'll take you to our head of security. Surely a review of the records will tell us what happened. Two thousand kilos of gold can't just disappear." His voice wavered a little at the end, as if wondering at the truth of this statement.

Margrit's phone buzzed, and she held up a finger for silence while she scanned through her messages. She looked up at Benjamin. "You were right. Crimped cases."

"What does that mean?" Pinkie asked.

Margrit shook her head. "It means that whoever was shooting at you in the garage today was shooting blanks. I don't know whether it was intended as a warning or a prank, but the good news is that nobody was trying to kill you. Lucky you."

"Lucky us? Lucky you!" Pinkie said.

"Why me?"

"Because if your brother had graduated from larceny to attempted murder, you'd probably have to switch to the kitten rescue department. Conflict of interest, you know."

Margrit scowled. "I'm still not convinced it was Maurice. But either way, I don't think your lives are in any imminent danger. The best thing you can do at this point is go home."

"Are you sure we can't stay and help?" Pinkie asked. "We've had recent experience fighting crime. Of course that was white slavers, so there may not be a lot of overlap…"

"I'm more than sure," Margrit said firmly. "Go home."

Pinkie's face suddenly lit up. "Hey…you know we had to leave our car at the garage. Can you have someone give us a ride home? Preferably someone really tough? I saw a blonde officer back at the station who looked like he could bench press a Volkswagen, and I for one would feel much better if someone like that was watching my back." He raised an eyebrow suggestively.

Margrit glanced again at her phone. "No need," she said, the barest trace of a smile coming over her face. "Seems that your car is in perfect working order. The techs took prints off of the doors and trunk on the off chance that whoever was shooting did take the ledgers, but the car itself is fine to drive."

"You know," Pinkie said, "I'm thinking you might want to keep it. For evidence. It's really small…it won't take up much space."

"I'm sure we don't need it for evidence."

A look of desperation came over Pinkie's face. "Maybe something got damaged as we went through the barrier. I bet there's all kinds of broken stuff inside that might lead to our fiery deaths. Better safe than sorry, right?"

"You'll be fine."

Pinkie shook a glittery finger at Margrit warningly. "If that car explodes, you're going to feel very guilty. You'll probably have to join a convent or something to atone."

"That's a risk I'm willing to take."

22

Pinkie and I drove most of the way back to the house in silence. There was a lot to think about. First of all, someone had shot at us. Given recent events in my life, this wasn't as exotic as it might sound, but it still wasn't a good feeling. And while the fact that they were shooting blanks made me feel a bit better, I still didn't feel as good as I did when people weren't shooting at me at all.

And then, of course, there was everything else. Right-wing terrorists celebrating a big payday online. The Fat Cat killing someone coming to recover Nazi gold. The possible end of a bank that had managed to survive almost three hundred years. If it were a US bank, I was pretty sure they would be able to find a way out of that mess by some sort of legal wheeling and dealing. A contract written seventy years ago with someone who wasn't even named couldn't possibly hold up in court, right?

But from the brief amount of time I had spent with Hubert, I was pretty sure that he would rather go personally bankrupt than resort to that sort of trick. I shook my head. At least the primary partners had gotten to enjoy many years as wealthy private bankers. Poor Arnaud was just coming into his prime, and suddenly his whole livelihood was gone. Not to mention Reiner, who had probably gone from being pretty comfortable to being about fifteen million dollars in the hole.

"Reiner," Pinkie said.

"I know. I was just thinking about him. I can't imagine how he must be feeling right now, losing a fortune a couple weeks after being made partner. Poor guy."

Pinkie looked at me like I'd gone mad. "Poor guy? Reiner stole that gold."

I looked at Pinkie incredulously. "How on earth do you think he did that?"

"I don't know. But he did. I'm telling you…he's not to be trusted. Think about it. Reiner becomes a partner. The guy who has the password to a fortune in Nazi gold gets killed. The gold vanishes. The sequence of events is as clear as day."

"First of all, you're forgetting about the Fat Cat. Do you honestly think that Reiner is running around spray painting limos in his spare time? You can't be a private banker and a vigilante against the 1 percent."

"He probably intended it to be a diversion so that nobody would suspect him," Pinkie said, setting his jaw.

"The guy at the airport said that the Fat Cat stuff started a month ago. I'm pretty sure Reiner only found out about the gold account when he made partner, right? So what was he doing? Just maintaining a vigilante vandal alibi on the off chance someone was storing seventy-five million francs' worth of gold in the bank?"

"Maybe. I'm telling you…you don't know him like I do."

"Did you ever actually see him do anything? Lying? Cheating? Stealing?"

"Lora, when your senses are as finely honed as mine, you don't need to actually *see* someone committing a crime to know that they're a criminal."

I rolled my eyes. "Maybe you should have told Margrit. I'm sure she would have arrested him on the spot based on your criminal-sensing abilities."

"You'd think so. But she's always been stubborn about the whole 'proof' thing. It's a good thing she's a Swiss police officer. It's terribly inefficient, if you think about it. If she were a New Jersey police officer, they'd boot her off the force in a heartbeat."

We pulled off the main road and began making the climb through the vineyards to get to Hubert's house. As we drove up, I saw a couple on the bench to the side of the house. I frowned. "Isn't that Reiner? Under the grape arbor? With Sarina?"

Pinkie snorted. "Sarina hates Reiner. Passionately." He glanced over, and his jaw dropped as he watched Reiner put his arms around Sarina and kiss her.

"Looks like she feels passionately about him, but maybe hatred isn't what's going on." But even as the words came out of my mouth, I could see that something wasn't right. Reiner was aggressively leaning into the kiss, his hands crushing her body closer. Sarina was stiff, her fists clenched, arms by her sides.

"Oh my god. She's drugged. Or maybe some kind of spider bit her tongue and she needs Reiner to suck the poison out or she'll die." Pinkie looked at me. "What else could possibly explain this?"

Reiner got up, stroked Sarina's face tenderly, and walked off toward the back of the house. Sarina sat on the bench, her eyes fixed on the ground as he walked away. "I have no idea. Maybe she's one of those women who are attracted to people they hate. Some girls love a bad boy."

"I love a bad boy, too, but Reiner's not a bad boy. He's a sleaze. A dorky sleaze, which is the worst kind of sleaze. Trust me. She doesn't like Reiner. Nobody likes Reiner."

I shrugged. "Whatever it is, it's none of our business."

Pinkie's pocket suddenly buzzed, and he pulled out his phone. "It's Hubert." He held the phone to his ear and listened. "Two weeks?" he said, outrage clear in his voice. He listened again. "Well, I don't know how much Swiss police pay their tech guys, but I'm sure that you can hire a computer whiz to do it faster than that." He paused. "Yes, I understand that privacy is a concern…wait a minute."

"Lora? Does your brother do any private security work? Say…analyzing ten years of digital video and security records?"

"He could probably be convinced, but aren't the police supposed to take care of that? I doubt they're going to take the word of a semi-employed hacker from Delaware. This is a major crime."

"The Swiss police are going to do it, but their tech guy just told Margrit that it's going to take two weeks, and Hubert really needs to know as soon as he can."

I gestured for him to give me the phone. "Hubert? I'm happy to talk to my brother. If everything's computerized, he can probably sort it out pretty quickly. He's kind of a genius that way."

Hubert breathed a sigh of relief. "Is he discreet? Gerhardt is concerned about allowing someone from the US to access the files. He's afraid they might get back to the government. If the scandal of the missing gold doesn't kill this bank, the idea that our video surveillance was leaked to the US government certainly would."

"I wouldn't worry about my brother leaking the files to the government. He's more or less been at war with authority figures since he let the air out of his kindergarten teacher's tires. But I should let you know that he's not exactly legitimate. I mean, I'm pretty sure that he has engaged in criminal behavior."

"Criminal behavior? What kind of criminal behavior?"

"Uh…he put deviant porn up as the public home page of the CIA." I hoped he wouldn't ask what flavor of deviance. Given Hubert's conservatism, I didn't relish trying to explain plushophilia to him.

"Oh," Hubert said. He sighed, and I realized how desperate he must be. "I guess the most important question is whether or not you trust him."

"He's my brother. I trust him with my life," I said simply.

"That's good enough for me. If you would be so kind, please give him a call, and see if he's willing to help us. The bank will pay him whatever he usually charges, of course. I'll meet you back at the house in an hour."

23

My phone had been lost in my flight from blank-shooting pseudo-hitmen, so Pinkie showed me to Hubert's office, which was liberally sprinkled with pictures of Helen, Hubert's late wife. I felt a little pang when I saw them. It had been years since Helen had died, but it was obvious that Hubert thought about her every day.

What would have happened had her life not been cut short? Maybe she would have gotten fat and splotchy, and the old pictures would have gradually come down. I opened the candy dish and helped myself to a champagne truffle. With all this sun and truffles, I was on the path to fat and splotchy myself.

Popping another into truffle into my mouth, I picked up Hubert's phone and dialed my brother.

"How's Street Parade?" Chris asked.

"Most people say, 'Hello' when they pick up a call from a strange number."

"Well, most people probably can't reverse engineer the number and then pull up enough personal information to see that you're calling from Pinkie's godfather's house. And since Pinkie only calls when you're being held by white slavers, I figured the odds were it was you. Why aren't you calling from your cell phone?"

I sighed. "Unfortunately, my cell phone has fallen into the hands of criminals. Again."

"Haven't you learned that hanging out with white slavers is bad?"

"I'm not hanging out with white slavers. I'm hanging out with Swiss bankers."

Chris snorted. "Maybe you should try spending time with people with morals. Why would a Swiss banker steal your phone, anyway?"

"It wasn't a Swiss banker. Petty criminals stole my phone along with my bag."

"Because you were wearing a French maid costume and barfing into a gutter somewhere to celebrate Street Parade? How traditional of you. Nice to see you getting into the swing of the local culture, though."

"Because I was fully dressed fleeing for my life from people who were shooting at me," I said. It's hard to surprise my brother, so I have to take the most of the opportunities that come my way.

I heard some tapping. "Shots fired at a parking lot near the police station? That was you?"

"Well, it wasn't me shooting, obviously. Jesus. Is that in the papers already?"

"What are these 'papers' of which you speak? Twitter search. Come into this century, already."

I sighed. "Since you seem to have all the knowledge of the world at your fingertips, perhaps you can tell me who was shooting at Pinkie and me. Apparently they were shooting blanks, so it might have just been some Street Parade fan with a sadistic sense of humor."

"Hmm. You have to admit that that's probably the most likely explanation. Zurich's not exactly Mogadishu. It's not like it's loaded with violent criminals."

"Actually, they seem to be making up for lost time on the violent criminal front," I said. I briefly recapped the murder, the theft of the ledgers, our discovery of the anonymous account, and the missing gold. "Pinkie swears that nothing ever happens in Switzerland, but things haven't stopped happening since we got here."

"Well, that does change the situation," my brother said. "Given what you've told me, it seems the most likely reason someone was shooting at you was because they wanted to take the ledgers."

"Pinkie thinks his cousin Maurice might have staged the shooting so that he could steal the ledgers. They're having a dispute about a family watch."

"Hiring fake shooters so that you can keep a watch?" Chris sounded skeptical. "It seems more likely that it has something to do with the missing gold. I mean, I'm sure it's a very nice watch, but it's not eighty-three million bucks' worth of watch, is it?"

"That's what we thought, too, but the ledgers they stole are from 1972. I could understand if we had the ledgers from 1945 or last week, but Hubert said that the gold was real in 1992, when he was made partner, so I can't imagine what possible relevance a ledger from the '70s might have."

"Maybe whoever shot at you didn't know you had a ledger from the '70s," my brother pointed out. "Maybe he just knew that you had a ledger."

I thought about that. "Anyone who knew we were there would have known which years' ledgers we were taking. It's like a library. They get checked out."

"Well, if it's not the ledgers and it's not Pinkie's cousin, I suggest you ask Pinkie who he's been doing business with recently. Some of the guys that he numbers as friends are into some pretty dodgy shit. Art forgery, insider trading, god knows what else. He's a shameless eavesdropper, and there's a very real chance that he overheard something he shouldn't have. It could be that this was intended as a warning and Pinkie's just too dense to figure out what he's being warned about. In which case the best advice I can give you is to warn Pinkie and then stay far away from him until he either figures it out or gets murdered."

"That hardly seems very supportive."

"Getting yourself murdered because Pinkie's friends are fancy scumbags isn't supportive, either. Who would pour Veuve over his grave every year on his birthday?"

I had to admit that was an excellent point. "Look. The main reason I called was to ask you to do me a favor. The video security files from the vault need to be looked at, and the Swiss police are saying that they'll need at least two weeks to look through the files."

"Two weeks? What are they...Betamax tapes?"

"They're digital. Cloud," I said, remembering Arnaud's comment. I wasn't sure what that actually meant, but I assumed it would mean something to my brother.

"So why two weeks?"

"Apparently it's August. Vacation."

Chris snorted. "If I ever become a criminal, remind me to move someplace with a good work/life balance." He thought for a moment. "Look, if everything's digital, it shouldn't take me too long to write a program to do the scanning. But if you're talking about...what did you say...two thousand bars of gold...shouldn't that be pretty obvious? I mean, like someone opening the door and backing up a forklift?"

"I have no idea. Maybe you'll see a forklift. Maybe you'll just see a big blank spot where the tape has been tampered with."

"And that will at least give you a time frame. Okay, I get it. A bit simplistic for my tastes. Unless you want me to locate the video online and break in there? That could be interesting."

"That won't be necessary. I'll ask Hubert to put you in touch with his security guy."

"Boring."

"Oh, and speaking of boring, you also need to promise me that whatever you find on those tapes goes no further than Hubert and me."

My brother sighed audibly. "God, you really can suck all the joy out of a job, can't you? I can never figure out how you make a living making other people's events fun when you're so not fun in real life."

I sniffed. "Other people's fun is serious business."

"Apparently."

"Other than that, are you doing okay? Have you left the apartment recently?" My brother was a borderline agoraphobic, which he insisted was the only sane way to be when you knew way too much about what other people did in their supposedly private time.

"I did, actually. I had to go to the drugstore to pick up a new prescription. My doctor says it should help even me out."

"Great!" I said with real enthusiasm.

"Yeah, except that I need to watch myself carefully for rashes while I'm taking it."

"It causes rashes?"

"No, but in rare occasions it can apparently cause all your skin to peel off."

I let that hang in the air for a moment.

"Are you kidding?"

"Unfortunately not. But it's really rare, and...if you survive the horror, risk of infections, and debilitating pain, apparently your skin looks just like a baby's when it grows back."

"I think we're done here," I said, shuddering.

"Yeah. Mom says hi, by the way. And she told me to remind you that condoms save lives."

I sighed. "Did you tell her again that I'm not a hooker?"

"I would have, but since I'm looking at a small but real risk of being peeled like a banana, don't you think I should be allowed to have a little fun in my life?"

"No. Tell her I'm fine and that an event hostess is not the same thing as a prostitute."

"I promise to pass on at least half of that message."

"I'll have Hubert send you the info. In the meantime, try to keep your skin on."

"Will do."

I wrote out my brother's phone number and email address on a piece of paper and left the office to find Pinkie, popping a final truffle in my mouth on the way out. These truffles were killing me. I was going to have to flee this country right after the dinner tomorrow if I wanted to have any chance of wearing any of my clothes again.

Pinkie had managed to score another bucket of ice from the kitchen, and was fully dressed and body-glitter free, sipping from a small bottle of Veuve through a crazy straw. In his other hand he held a paperback book. Despite Pinkie's intellectual lightweight act, he actually read a lot of serious literature. I glanced at the back of the book, expecting something by Camus or maybe Nietzsche. Janet Evanovich.

"Really, Pinkie? Janet Evanovich? Was that on the reading list when you were studying classics at Oxford?"

Pinkie sighed. "I know, but I can't help myself. I think I'm in love with Ranger."

"You and every fifty-year-old housewife in America. Look…I talked to my brother, and he's willing to look at the files. Can you please give Hubert his contact info?" I handed the slip of paper to him. "I've got to take a shower and put some clothes on, and then I'm going over to Dieter Schumacher's house to tell him that I don't have a cell phone."

"Get Sarina to look up the number and call him," Pinkie suggested. "There's no need to drive out there."

"I *want* to drive out there. I'm going to get the lay of the land. See if I can get myself into a Swiss frame of mind. Maybe there's still time for me to come up with something spectacular that will blow Jack Green's mind and ensure that Dieter gets the contract."

"Ensure that Dieter gets the contract or ensure that Vanessa St. Germain fails epically and preferably publicly?"

"Both," I admitted. "I've had it with her trying to steal my clients."

"And with her really thick, wavy blonde hair," Pinkie said.

"That, too."

"Well, far be it from me to stand between you and vengeance." Pinkie waved a hand in dismissal. "Have at it. Tell Dieter I said hi."

"Tell him yourself. You're coming with me."

"Why do I have to go?" Pinkie whined. "I hate cows."

"Because I'm not leaving you here alone. Chris thinks that the whole shooting thing today might have been a warning to you, so you need to spend some time thinking over your sins so that you can come up with a couple of likely suspects."

Pinkie looked taken aback. "Me? The target of hired killers? Why does he think that I'm the target?"

"Probably because he knows a lot about you."

Pinkie considered. "I really don't think I've done anything worth getting killed over lately."

"Given what a pain in the neck you've been recently, I'm pretty sure you've done something worth getting killed over in the last twenty-four hours. Cast your mind back. I'm sure you'll come up with something."

"And anyway, they were using blanks, right? So worst-case scenario: I would only be the target of hired actors, which isn't nearly as scary as hired killers. Although I've heard that Russell Crowe is absolutely terrifying, so maybe it is a good idea to stick together."

I shook my head. "Maybe this time was just a warning. Maybe they'll kill you next time."

"Why do you always assume the worst?"

"Call it experience. Downstairs in half an hour. And see if you can't come up with at least one person capable of planning your gory murder, will you? Besides me."

24

The drive over to Dieter's house was much easier in the Smart Car than it had been on the bicycle. Given Pinkie's hatred of cows, I was tempted to leave him in the car, but I figured we'd be better off staying together until we knew more about what was going on.

Dieter's inn was more or less deserted at this hour, except for a chubby blonde in a red checked Oktoberfest costume folding napkins in the corner.

"Hi," I said to the girl. "My name's Lora Godwin. I was looking for Dieter Schumacher?"

"Lora!" I heard a voice behind me. "The dinner's tomorrow! Have you got your schedule confused?" Dieter, a friendly looking man the approximate size of a bear, came in to give me three kisses. He was dressed in a white shirt and a red vest, a golden earring dangling from one ear. I guessed it was traditional Swiss dress for men, but it looked a little like something an organ grinder's monkey might wear.

"Dieter," I said, pulling back to take a look at him. "How long has it been?"

"Two years. Did you manage to get to the regatta last month?"

Dieter was a fanatical follower of sailboat racing. We had met several years ago, when I was accompanying a private banker Pinkie knew to a regatta in Monaco. My job had been to get the banker some face time with an Arab sheikh he had been trying to land for months. After I'd finally managed to finagle Pinkie's friend the interview, mostly by flattering the sheikh regarding his recent creation of a ridiculous ski resort in the desert, I'd gradually melted into the crowd and ended up chatting with Dieter about boats and Switzerland. Once we realized we were both in what could loosely be termed the hospitality industry, we spent a lovely evening chatting about some of our more hellish clients before swapping cards and promising to stay in touch.

"I was on a yacht last month, but I'm afraid we weren't racing."

"Well, that's nice, too. Relaxing, right?"

Since the only part of that trip that hadn't been spent figuring out who was trying to kill me had been spent trying to get away from the people trying to kill me, relaxing really wasn't the right word. But now probably wasn't the time to get into that. I gave him a noncommittal smile.

"And who is this with you? Prince Philippe!" Dieter said, his smile broadening. "I haven't seen you since you were a teenager! What have you been doing with yourself?"

Pinkie vanished into Dieter's massive arms for a friendly hug. "A little of this, a little of that. I'm mostly in New York these days. But since Lora was coming to do an event for you, I had to come with her. I couldn't pass up the chance to see you and Hubert." He looked around the inn. "It's amazing. It seems like nothing has changed."

"That's what people come here for. Traditional Switzerland." He rubbed his hands together. "Tomorrow evening, you'll be able to hear the sound of our alphorn player all up and down the lake. It will be spectacular."

"Sounds great," I said. Privately, I wondered how his neighbors would feel about that.

"So what can I do for you, Lora?" Dieter asked. "You're not here to check up on me, are you?"

"Of course not. Actually, I just wanted to come over to tell you that my cell phone was stolen at Street Parade, so if you need to contact me, you'll need to leave a message at the house or call Philippe."

"That's terrible! Murder. Stolen cell phones. It's like a crime wave in Zurich these days."

"You don't know the half of it," Pinkie said. He whipped a business card out of his pocket and handed it to Dieter. "If you need to talk to Lora, just call the number there. But I should warn you that if I don't pick up, it might be because I'm running for my life or lying dead in a gutter somewhere."

Dieter's face creased with confusion. "Dead in a gutter?"

"Don't worry. It'll probably come to nothing. The last person who shot at us was using blanks."

"Shot at you?" Dieter put his hands on Pinkie's shoulders. "Are you in some sort of trouble, Philippe?"

I cut in before Pinkie could blow things out of proportion. "There was an incident earlier today. We were in a parking garage, and someone fired a gun at us. They were firing blanks, so we weren't in any danger. Probably just some random Street Parade thing."

Dieter looked thoughtful. "Street Parade does cause a lot of chaos, but most of it is just people having fun. That sounds like something altogether more serious. Did you report it to the police?"

I nodded. "They're looking into it. But since we weren't in any danger, they sent us home."

Dieter took this in silently.

"If you're concerned about your safety, I'll understand if you want to cancel," I added.

Dieter shook his head. "Thank you for telling me, but I wouldn't dream of cancelling. And besides, even if someone did come after you again, my guns don't shoot blanks." He gave me a reassuring smile.

"Your guns?"

"Surely you know that all Swiss men do military service," Dieter said.

"I thought Switzerland was neutral."

"Neutral yes, helpless no. Every Swiss man does military service, and then we have to do a few weeks of training to keep up our skills every year. Virtually every house in Switzerland has a gun in it."

"Just like in America."

Dieter laughed. "The difference is that most of the guns here don't have any ammunition. But don't worry. We're one of the few units that keeps ammunition at home, and one of my guys is the sharpshooting champion of the canton. There won't be a safer place to be than here tomorrow night."

"Well... If you're sure…"

"I'm sure. Let me focus on running the event and keeping everyone safe from random blank-shooting vandals. You just focus on charming Jack Green."

"From what I've heard, I think I got the tougher job."

"I've heard that same thing," Dieter admitted.

25

When we got back to Hubert's house, Hubert had arrived and was pacing around, a glass of whiskey untouched on the mantel beside him.

"Where have you two been?" he asked.

"Dieter Schumacher's. I had to tell him I'd lost my cell phone."

"Your dinner tomorrow. Of course. I'm sorry, I'm afraid I haven't been much help providing you with authentically Swiss things."

"Yes, well, all things considered, I think that's understandable. And anyway, Dieter seems to have the Swiss part of the dinner well in hand, so I'll just focus on keeping Jack entertained."

Pinkie gave his godfather's shoulder a squeeze. "How are you holding up?"

"I've been better," Hubert said with a weak smile.

"Did your security guy get in touch with Chris?" I asked. "What did he say?"

Hubert nodded. "He said he should be able to get back to us tonight." He picked up the whiskey and took a sip, grimacing like a man who didn't drink hard liquor very often. "I just can't imagine how this could have happened. Our security is good. Our people are trustworthy." He shook his head.

"Have you told Reiner yet?" Pinkie asked.

I shot a look at him, hoping that he wasn't engaging in a bit of schadenfreude, but for once Pinkie looked genuinely concerned.

"Not yet," Hubert said, taking another sip. "I would prefer to wait until we have something more to tell him."

We all flinched as the phone rang, and Hubert jumped on it like a man possessed. "Hello? Chris? Can I put you on speaker? Your sister and Philippe are here as well."

My brother's voice came over the line. "Hi, guys. How are things there? Mom said to tell you to stay away from the chocolate, by the way. She said you have the self-control of a…"

I interrupted him before he could go on. "Chris, Hubert needs this information as soon as possible. My chocolate consumption is the least of anyone's concern here."

"I don't know," Pinkie said. "If we stay here much longer, you'll have to wear a bathrobe home, so I have to admit I'm a little concerned."

"Get to the point," I told Chris, shooting Pinkie a dark look.

"Jeez, Lora… Chill out already. Okay. Here's the deal, Hubert—I looked at your video files. I mean, I didn't really look at it, obviously, because it was ten years long. I mean, who does that?"

"Faster, please," I said.

My brother continued in the same unhurried tone. "So when you're talking about security, there are lots of different ways to go about checking a tape like this. The first thing I looked at was the time stamp in the corner. That's a very basic protection, of course, but if someone had just taken a snippet of video out of the file, we'd see a gap in the time stamp. Now a good criminal would cover his tracks because the time of the crime can go a long way toward pointing to a suspect. In this case, though, chances were excellent that this crime would never be detected, so whoever did it might not have bothered to cover their tracks."

"Is that it?" I asked. "That doesn't seem like it would take a hacker to figure out."

"Of course that's not it. Even you could have figured that out, assuming you had time to watch ten years of video on fast forward. I was just starting with the basic check."

I gritted my teeth and tried to remember that my brother rarely got a chance to talk about his craft to actual people.

"I also wrote a little program that looks for unexpected activity in the file itself."

"What do you mean 'unexpected activity'?" Hubert asked.

"People who come into the vault and vanish would be the most obvious case, but even in a vault, things don't always stay the same. Dust, failing lightbulbs, spiderwebs... The program I wrote ensures that if something is there in one frame, it doesn't just cease to exist in the next."

"And did you find anything?" Pinkie asked, a hint of exasperation coloring his voice.

"Nope. So I went one level deeper. The security guys who set up the original system put in a digital watermark."

"Faster and also in English," I said.

Chris sniffed. "That was English, but I'll try to use small words so that you can understand. Part of the security system dropped something like a code into the video stream. It's not something that you can see, but it's something that you can extract, but only if the video hasn't been tampered with. I could extract it, so that would tend to indicate that the video hadn't been tampered with."

"So the video hasn't been tampered with," I said, trying to speed this along.

"Ah, but it's also possible to tamper with the watermark. I mean, it would take skills. Skills that few people have. But if you're talking about a lot of money, then it's possible they are skills you could buy. So I had a look at the actual compression scheme. Video files follow a pattern that remains consistent over time, so if you're willing to look at that level and you see an interruption of the pattern, that can indicate tampering."

"So the video was tampered with?" I was completely lost at this point.

"No. The video was clean."

"You're sure?"

"If you want me to take you through the process again, I will," Chris threatened. "In detail this time."

"That won't be necessary," Hubert said. "I just need to think about what this means."

"I've thought about that, too. When was the last time you knew the gold was real?"

"When I was brought in as a full partner. I picked up a bar just out of curiosity. It was definitely real then."

"And that was how many years ago?"

Hubert did a quick mental calculation. "Twenty-three years ago, to be precise."

"And there's no way to access that room other than the doors, which are filmed."

Hubert nodded. "The vault is cut into the stone on three sides. There's only one way in or out."

"Well, then. Since the tape hasn't been tampered with, you know the gold hasn't been touched since the system went in ten years ago. That leaves you with a gap of thirteen years during which someone must have stolen it."

"Well, obviously," Hubert said, "but how do you steal four thousand pounds of gold? How do you even get it out of the building?"

"You're probably looking for a distraction. A fire, an earthquake, a flood...something that would have caused the vault to be opened at a time when people might not have noticed."

Frustration was evident in Hubert's voice when he answered. "It's Zurich. Nothing ever happens here. That's why you put your money in Zurich."

"What about when the security system was being installed? You would have had strangers there. They would have needed tools."

Hubert rubbed his head. "I don't know. We took turns letting the workers in, but they were always supervised by one of the partners. And you've always needed two partner keys to open the vault."

There was a pause on the line.

"If that's true, then I think you should probably be looking at the people who had keys to the vault during those thirteen years. It's either a conspiracy between two partners or maybe just sloppiness...keys left around, procedures not followed. It's human nature. But either way, it's hard to see how this could have happened without a partner being involved.

"That can't be true. I won't believe it."

"Once you eliminate the impossible, whatever remains, no matter how improbable, must be the truth," Chris said softly. "Sherlock Holmes."

"I need to think about this," Hubert said, rubbing a hand over his face. He looked shaken, and it occurred to me that he had been hoping that something on the tape would prove that an outsider had managed to breach their security. Because as bad as that was, it was certainly better than believing that one of your partners had betrayed you.

When he spoke again, his voice was tight. "Thank you for your assistance with this matter, Chris. Please send me a bill for your time."

"Consider this one on the house, as long as you promise to let me know how it comes out."

Hubert shook his head. "I'm not sure we'll ever know, but if we do, I'll make sure you're informed."

Hubert hung up the phone and looked at Pinkie and me. His eyes were flat and shiny, and I wasn't sure whether he was fighting back tears or in a state of shock. "If you'll excuse me for a while, I think I'll go lie down. This has been a very taxing day, I'm afraid."

Pinkie walked across the room and gave Hubert a hard hug, his eyes a little shiny as well. "Take as long as you need."

26

Once Hubert had retired for the evening, Pinkie and I went up to his room and cracked open a couple more splits of Veuve.

"I feel like a terrible human being for drinking champagne," I said, taking a long sip. "It's hardly the time for a celebration."

"Veuve's not just good for celebrations. It's also good for when you're feeling low. Or when you have a headache. Or sometimes when you're really angry. Or when you have to travel. Or even when you're thirsty."

"I get it. It's the Swiss Army Knife of beverages."

"Right, except that unlike most Swiss beverages, this one is drinkable. Did you know they make a soda out of milk here? Seriously." He shuddered.

"Hand me that box of truffles, will you?" I said, pointing to the box on Pinkie's nightstand.

"Honestly, Lora, I don't know why you keep picking at those things," Pinkie sniped, handing over the box. "Why don't you just upend the box over your open mouth? You'll wind up eating the same number."

I paused, a truffle in midair. "What if that's what happened?"

"What if you ate so many truffles that you had to wear a garbage bag home? That's looking like more of a *when* than a *what if.*"

"No, idiot," I said, popping the truffle into my mouth. "What if the gold wasn't taken all in one shot? What if it was taken piece by piece?"

Pinkie looked at me like I had gone mad. "There were two thousand pieces."

"No, think about it. How many pieces of gold could one person carry? Four, maybe? They have to leave their bags at the desk, right?"

"Actually, no," Pinkie said, suddenly interested. "You have to leave your bags at the desk if you're going into the records vault. If you're going into the long-term deposit part of the vault, you can bring your bag with you so that you can carry out whatever's in your box. Since the only thing you have access to is your box, there's no need to search your bag."

"Okay," I said, starting to get excited. "So imagine that you have a box in that part of the bank. You go in, supposedly to visit your box, and you pick the lock on the other box. You take out as much gold as you can carry. How much gold do you think that would be?"

"For a very strong man? Maybe twenty bars."

"So we'd be looking for someone who visited the vault a hundred times during those thirteen years."

"I don't know… That seems like an awful lot. Don't you think someone would have gotten suspicious?"

"Why? He's not bringing in an empty bag and leaving with a full one. He's bringing in a bag full of plaster bricks and leaving with a bag full of gold bricks. And the beauty of it is that most of those boxes aren't even segregated accounts. They're just regular safety deposit boxes—if he got caught with a bunch of gold bricks, who's to say that he didn't get them out of his own box?"

I nodded, increasingly sure that it was possible. "A hundred visits over thirteen years. It's once a month. It's not that crazy."

Pinkie looked at me thoughtfully. "Hand me those truffles. I think you might be on to something." He popped a candy into his mouth. "This all assumes that somebody found out about the box."

"Well, obviously there was something to find, because someone found the account number and the pass phrase quite recently. What if someone only got half of the information? They knew where the box was and they knew what was in it, but they didn't have the pass phrase?"

"We need to get someone to look at the visitor registers for those time periods," Pinkie said, pursing his lips.

"You think they wrote down the names of the visitors to the vault?"

Pinkie rolled his eyes. "It's Switzerland. Of course they wrote down the names of the visitors to the vault."

"Should we get Hubert?"

Pinkie shook his head. "Chris was right. The police are going to start looking at the partners. Hubert's going to be under suspicion. Hubert and Gerhardt both. They were there when the gold was stolen. And if the murder is linked to the theft of the gold, Arnaud and Reiner will come under suspicion as well."

"How can they be under suspicion? They were just kids when the gold was stolen."

"They had family members who had keys at that time. What if Reiner's uncle stole the gold and left it to Reiner? And then Reiner killed that guy to cover his tracks." He narrowed his eyes and stroked his chin. "It's all becoming clear to me now."

"Leave the detective stuff to the professionals. Call Margrit, and ask her about the vault logs. I'm sure they'll let her take a look."

Pinkie picked up the phone. "Fine. But mark my words. Reiner stole the gold and killed that guy."

"Consider your words marked."

Pinkie dialed. "Hello, Margrit? It's Philippe. Lora's here. I'm putting you on speaker."

Margrit's voice came over the line scratchily, almost drowned out by a thumping disco beat in the background. "Are you still at the station?" I asked.

"Yes."

"Are you having a party?"

"Street Parade," Margrit sighed. "And lack of air conditioning. We can either work with the windows open, or we can boil."

"Can you boil for just a little while?" Pinkie asked. "We had an idea about the gold problem."

"Just a minute." We heard a bottle breaking, then the thump of a window shutting. "God, I hate Street Parade. Okay. It's quiet now. Now, before you start talking, perhaps you want to tell me why you are investigating the disappearance of this gold when you are neither police officers nor bankers and you have no more information than I have on this topic."

I cleared my throat nervously. "Actually, we do have a little more information than you do."

"And what information could you possibly have come up with between the time that you were standing here in your underwear and now?" Margrit asked, her irritation clear.

"We know that the gold went missing more than ten years ago," Pinkie said.

"You had someone look at the tape?" Margrit's voice was taut with barely restrained fury, making me happy that we weren't having this conversation in person.

"Technically, the bank contracted with an IT security company to verify that their security system had not been breached," Pinkie said.

"Technically you are about a hair away from being put in jail for interfering with a police investigation."

Pinkie was indignant. "Well, what did you expect? Two weeks without knowing what's going on would have killed Hubert."

"I'm not discussing this. Thank you for the information. I will, of course, need to verify it with our own experts before I can act on it. And while this does help with the time frame, it doesn't particularly help figure out how someone moved a Volkswagen's weight in gold out of a safety deposit box in a vault that required two partners to open it."

"We were thinking about that too," Pinkie said. "What if it didn't get moved all at once?"

"There are two thousand bars of gold there, Philippe. Even best-case scenario, you're looking at what…hundreds of visits, right? Don't you think that would have shown up on someone's radar?"

"A hundred visits over thirteen years," I said. "And maybe longer. Think about it. Hubert said he touched one of the bars and it was gold. Well fine, that bar might have been gold, but if they were moving it out piece by piece, what if they left the bars on top til the end? Anyone able to pick the lock of the box or get ahold of the key could have been pulling gold out of that box for decades without anyone realizing. For all we know, it could have started the day the gold was deposited."

Margrit was silent.

"What do you think?" I asked.

"It's possible," Margit finally admitted. "In that case, we're going to need to look at the records for people visiting the long-term deposit vault. And at least part of those records are going to be paper, I'm sure. Dammit!"

"Are you sure you don't want to deputize us?" Pinkie asked. "Lora and I are getting really good at this crime fighting thing. We can probably have this whole thing wrapped up by the end of the night."

"I'm very sure I'm not going to deputize you, Philippe. But I will put someone right on it. It seems very likely to me that if we figure out who stole the gold, we'll know who killed Horst Mueller."

"Exactly," Pinkie said.

"Don't 'exactly' me, Philippe. You need to stay out of this starting right now. At least one person has died, and while I still don't know what happened with you two in that parking garage, it's possible that was supposed to be a warning. Take Lora out for fondue. Go check out some cows. Drink some more of Hubert's wine. Just mind your own business."

She hung up.

Pinkie looked at the phone. "Honestly, the police are the most ungrateful people. Here we practically hand them the thief—and possibly the murderer—and they tell us to go drink bad wine." He huffed and took another swig of his Veuve. "Should I open another round? These bottles are so tiny."

"Not for me," I said, putting my split down on the table. "Hubert wanted me to talk Sarina out of jetting off to Pakistan to cause an international incident. I guess now's as good a time as any for that conversation. In the extremely unlikely event that I can convince her to change her mind, at least Hubert will have some good news."

27

Sarina's room was at the corner of the house, overlooking the vineyards and gardens rather than the lake. I took a deep breath before knocking. Sarina and I hadn't exactly hit it off so far, and I wasn't sure what I was going to accomplish by talking to her, but given how distressed Hubert was, I was willing to give it a try.

I knocked gently.

"What?" came a muffled voice through the door.

"It's Lora. Your father asked me to talk to you. May I come in?"

There was a long pause, and I thought for a moment that she was going to tell me to get lost, which I would have been more than happy to do. I finally heard the turning of the key inside the lock and found myself face to face with Sarina. A scant two hours ago we had seen her with Reiner on the bench outside, but she didn't look like a woman in love. Her eyes were puffy, and her lips were colorless and pinched. She looked like a woman who had just stared into the face of the zombie apocalypse.

"Yes?" she asked, cracking the door just enough to poke her head outside.

"Have you talked to your father today?" I assumed that was the cause of her pallor.

"No, why?"

I looked at her expectantly, and she sighed and motioned me into her bedroom. Unlike the rest of the house, it was furnished in a modern style that revealed a keen eye for design and color. I looked around for somewhere to sit, finally perching lightly on a chair that looked as though a strong wind would blow it over.

I wondered whether I should start by explaining the missing gold thing. Maybe the knowledge that her father's bank was in the midst of an existential crisis would cause her to rally behind her father. But then again, given her disdain for the bank, it was just possible that she would run straight to the press and sink Richter and Partners for good. No, it was better to let Hubert tackle that particular topic.

"Hubert asked me to speak with you about your plans to go teach in Pakistan."

Sarina snorted, sitting on the edge of her bed across from me. "My father doesn't understand. He's spent his entire life looking after rich people's money. And his father did the same. Three generations of Richters, all who devoted their entire lives to other people's money. Can you imagine a bigger waste of time? And nothing would make him happier than for me to do the same thing."

"I take it you're not contemplating a career in private banking."

"I'd rather live in the street."

It had been my experience that people who told you that they'd rather live in the street generally didn't have a lot of experience living in the street, but I decided that pointing that out would probably not advance my case. Plus, the way things were going, private banker at Richter and Partners probably wouldn't be a great resume-builder anytime soon. "Okay, I'll agree, private banking isn't for everyone. Have you considered any other careers?"

Sarina shrugged. "I studied art for a while, but what's the point? You pour your heart into something, and 90 percent of the people don't get it. It doesn't matter how real it is; it just matters whether you can find the right gallery to represent you. And that has nothing to do with how good it is. It's just connections, like everything else."

She gestured over to a wall that was filled with a haphazard collection of paintings, printed graphics, and freestyle drawing. "My art class had people with way more talent than I had, but I was the one who got an offer to exhibit. Care to guess why?"

I looked at the wall critically. The pictures had a vibrancy and playfulness that seemed at odds with the puritanical face Sarina presented to the world. "I'm not an art expert, but you clearly have talent."

"Maybe, but that's not why I got the offer."

"Your father pulled some strings," I guessed.

"Exactly," she said, smiling bitterly. "And everyone knew it. I turned it down, of course, but I couldn't even show my face in class for the rest of the semester."

I sighed. "I understand that you want to prove yourself, and I really understand the desire to want to make a difference in the world, but going to a dangerous place to lecture men about how backward their treatment of women is—even if it's true—is probably the least useful thing you can do to advance the cause of women."

Sarina shook her head. "No offense, but you make your living attending parties, so I don't think you're exactly an expert in this area."

"I make a living helping people get along," I said sharply, "and if you ever want to make a real change in people's lives, it's a skill you'd do well to cultivate."

Sarina opened her mouth to argue. I held up my hand. "Hear me out. Imagine you show up in some village tomorrow to open a school. First, you're going to have to talk to the head of that village. Your argument is what? That the way of life they've followed for years is wrong? That you, a person barely out of adolescence, who has never actually lived any place that wasn't perfectly safe and organized, know what's best for them? What the hell do you expect them to do? Bow down to your superior knowledge?"

"I'm not saying it will be easy. But I'm not willing to sit by while injustice is done just so that everyone feels good about themselves."

"I'm not asking you to sit by. I'm asking you to put aside the romance of being the great white savior. You've got an education. You've got connections. You want to change the world? Start talking to people who can make a difference."

"So your solution is for me to hold a fundraiser?" she sneered.

"Who do you think saved more kids from malaria?" I snapped back. "The missionary who went down into some remote village and handed out a few bed nets or Bill Gates, who pulled together knowledge, money, and people to change the way entire countries act?"

Sarina scowled. "The people who hand out nets in those villages are heroes. They put their lives at risk."

"I'm sure they are, but here's the thing—charity work doesn't exist so that rich people can make themselves into heroes. It exists to help people who don't have the resources to help themselves. It's not about you growing as a person. It's about actually making a difference. And if you believe that, I'm pretty sure you'll agree that traipsing off to some village to become a martyr is a pretty selfish act when you have the connections and the knowledge and—yes—the money to make an actual difference!"

Sarina stopped, her mouth slightly open in shock.

I was a little shocked myself. For someone who made a living through persuasion and tact, this was an epic fail. *That would teach me to drink a split of champagne on an empty stomach*, I thought remorsefully.

"Uh…" I said, trying to get us back on more normal conversational footing. "Are you okay?"

"No," Sarina said, her voice suddenly broken. "No, I'm not okay. And you're right. This isn't about helping other people. I mean, it was about helping other people. I want to help. But I have to leave. I can't stay here."

"Why not? You've got a father who loves you, a bright future ahead of you, a boyfriend…" I struggled to think of something nice to say about Reiner. "A boyfriend," I repeated.

"A boyfriend?"

"Reiner. We saw you two together on the bench when we drove in from the city this afternoon. I'm sorry—we didn't mean to spy on you, if that was supposed to be a secret."

"Reiner," she said, her voice breaking into something between a hiccup and a bitter laugh. "He's not my boyfriend. He's the reason I need to leave."

"I don't understand," I said, scooting the chair forward so that I could take her hand. My mind flashed back to the stiff way she had sat while Reiner was kissing her. "Is he forcing you to do something against your will?" I couldn't imagine how that was even possible, unless Reiner had managed to order a working hypno-ring from the back of a comic book.

Sarina sat for a moment, looking down at her hand in mine. For a rich girl, her hands were a wreck: dry skin, uneven fingernails, and flecks of a bright orange fingernail polish that she had apparently been unable to scrub away from the cuticles. Something about the color struck me, and I suddenly looked back at the wall of her school work.

One picture in particular caught my eye. A flashy, cartoonish stencil of a snake coiled around a stack of bank notes. Now that I looked at it closely, the similarities were obvious.

"It's you. You're the Fat Cat," I blurted.

She looked like she wanted to deny it, but she finally let out a sigh. "I guess it doesn't matter anymore. I *am* the Fat Cat, and Reiner's blackmailing me. But I didn't kill anyone."

28

It was times like this that I understood why people said the road to hell was paved with good intentions. My attempt to lighten Hubert's load of troubles had resulted in me discovering that his daughter was a vandal and his partner was a blackmailer. God, I needed some truffles. I looked around Sarina's room, hoping that another one of those magically refilling candy boxes was close at hand.

"Are you looking for the Fat Cat stencil?"

"Um, yes. The stencil."

Dammit! Why were there no truffles around when I was having an emergency?

"Reiner has it," Sarina said, her voice stronger now that she had confessed. I couldn't even shave five minutes off my workout without confessing everything to my personal trainer the next day. I couldn't imagine the pressure she had been under all this time.

"Why don't you tell me what's going on? How did this whole Fat Cat thing get started?"

Sarina sighed and put her head in her hands. "It was after I got offered that art show. I mean, people I was in class with knew that I came from a pretty well-connected family, but they also knew that wasn't who I was. I've always been a big fighter for the underdog. My mother was the same way.

"So suddenly, the teacher comes in and announces that there's going to be a show. Major gallery, big launch party, lots of exposure. The kind of chance that can literally make someone's career. And guess what? My work has been selected."

"Maybe they selected your work because it was the best. I don't know too much about art, but even I can see that it's good."

She shrugged. "It's good enough, but there were people in that program who were great. They were doing things that nobody else had even thought about doing. No, it wasn't my work that got me chosen. And the worst part is that everyone knew. It took about thirty seconds for the other people in the class to figure it out. It was so fucking obvious."

She wiped a shaking hand across her eyes. "It was like being a leper. Nobody would talk to me because they thought I was such a hypocrite. My best friend, Khalid, he's from Africa and he came here on scholarship and he's brilliant—really brilliant—and he just stopped talking to me. He said that he thought it would be different here. That Africa had taught him that rich people never had to follow the rules, but that in Switzerland it wasn't supposed to be that way. But it was. The most democratic country on earth, and it was exactly the fucking same."

"So you decided to make a statement."

Sarina shook her head. "I wasn't trying to make a statement. I was just trying to get back at my father. I made the stencil. I waited until it was late at night. I went down to the bank offices and I spray painted their office. I don't even know what I was expecting to happen. Nothing, I guess. It's Zurich. I figured they'd clean off the building and forget about it."

"But that didn't happen."

"No. People in this country were rocked by the banking crisis. I mean, you guys had Occupy Wall Street. Did you know that we had Occupy Paradeplatz?"

"Really?"

"It lasted for only a couple of weeks. Weather here isn't really great for long-term outdoor protests. But it was just a sign of how angry people were. During the crisis, the stock price of Switzerland's biggest bank went from eighty francs to eight. People got laid off in droves. Pension funds evaporated. And this is Switzerland, where we're supposed to be safe. People were angry.

"Someone took a picture of the graffiti and published an article in the free newspaper about how popular culture was revolting against these fat cats. It was a fluff piece, really. There wasn't some vast underground movement. Just a pissed off rich kid throwing rocks at Daddy. But people started talking about it, and suddenly it seemed like people were thinking about the issues. About income inequality and fairness and privilege."

"So you kept doing it."

"I knew it was crazy. But my father had never let me do anything risky, and suddenly I understood what I'd been missing. I was part of a secret. I was breaking the rules. And I told myself that as long as I was sparking conversation, I was helping people." She shook her head. "I must sound like an idiot."

I rubbed my temples. I couldn't argue with that.

"How did Reiner get involved in all of this?"

"Reiner," Sarina said, her voice dripping with contempt. "Reiner has wanted me since I was fifteen years old."

"Because he loves you?"

"I don't think Reiner is capable of love. He wants to own me, I think. This has always been a family bank, and Reiner wasn't really part of the family. A nephew, not a son, you know. I think that was part of it."

"He asked you out?"

She shook her head. "No. He knew me well enough to know that I wasn't interested in him. I wasn't rude about it, but I certainly made it clear enough over the years. But he stayed close. He listened to what I said. He watched what I did. He waited, mainly. When I got to college, he would occasionally drop by to say hi, or to bring some of those chocolates my father keeps all over the house."

She shuddered. "I actually felt a little guilty about the whole thing. I mean, I didn't have any good reason for not liking him."

"But you didn't like him."

"He makes my skin crawl. I can't even tell you why. Until he started blackmailing me, I would have said it was something chemical."

"How did he find out that you were the Fat Cat?"

Sarina chewed on a cuticle thoughtfully. I suppressed the urge to yank her hand out of her mouth.

"I should have been more careful. I knew Reiner. Banking is a relationship business. The best bankers keep tabs on their customers. They know their birthdays, their kids' names, their hobbies. That kind of thing. It allows them to connect on a personal level. But with Reiner it's more than that. He reads every Internet post. He dissects every online picture. He knows who they had dinner with last week. And he's like a terrier. When he sees something suspicious, he just keeps digging and digging. I think it's some kind of sickness with him. He needs to feel like he's in control."

"So you think he saw you vandalize something?"

Sarina grimaced. "I don't know. Maybe he followed me. Maybe he went through my room. Maybe he even figured it out from the style of the work. Reiner's incredibly smart, and he's spent ten years studying everything I do. If anyone could have figured it out, it would have been him. But the night you got here, my stencil and paint went missing, and today Reiner told me that he had it."

I felt a chill run up my spine. "The stencil went missing the night we got here? That means he had it when Horst Mueller was murdered."

"I know." She blinked back tears, and I realized for the first time that she wasn't just afraid of being exposed—she was physically afraid of Reiner.

"Did Reiner kill him?"

"He says he didn't. He said it was just a copycat. But I don't know. I've just been sitting here for the last few hours trying to figure out what to do. If I go to the police, they'll know I'm involved. My fingerprints are all over the stencil, the paint…" she trailed off. "What if they think that I did it? But what if Reiner killed that man?"

She looked at me, all traces of arrogance washed away in fear. "What do I do?"

I sighed. "I think there's only one thing you can do, and it's not fleeing to the tribal lands of Pakistan."

"You think I should call the police."

"Let's wake up your father and get Pinkie to call Margrit. I'm sure she'll be happy to hear from us."

29

Thirty minutes later, Pinkie, Margit, Sarina, Hubert, and I were back at the police station. Benjamin was also there, looking grimmer than usual.

I pulled him aside to talk to him quietly. "Why are you still here? Isn't this a matter for the Swiss police?"

"Unfortunately, until we figure out what happened to Horst Mueller, it's also a matter for Homeland Security. "Whenever you've got eighty-three million dollars and a potential right-wing terrorist threat, we like to keep an eye on it. Call us crazy."

He looked at the rest of the group, who were arranging themselves into uncomfortable-looking straightback chairs. "Your boy toy isn't here?"

I frowned at him. "If you're referring to Arnaud, he's not my boy toy. And given that I'm off your 'to do' list, you don't really get to comment on my love life."

Margrit gave us a sharp look. "Are you two coming over here, or do you have some personal business that you need to attend to?"

Pinkie rolled his eyes. "It's sexual tension. Just ignore it. At some point they'll wind up in bed together, then it'll either be boring or it'll be great, in which case they'll probably end up married, at which point it will definitely be boring."

"Enough, Pinkie," I snapped. "We're here to talk about serious stuff. Vandalism. Murder. A little focus would be nice."

Pinkie huffed but folded his arms and turned his attention to Sarina, who was twisting a Kleenex to shreds between her hands while she waited.

Margrit looked at her, her face neutral. "Before we begin, I'd like to make sure you understand that you have the right not to speak, and you are permitted to bring in an attorney. At this point, I'm treating you as someone who is here voluntarily to provide information about a crime. If what you're telling me implicates you in that or any other crime, we will deal with that separately."

She looked at Sarina searchingly. "Do you understand?"

Sarina nodded, making a visible effort to compose herself. She reached out and took her father's hand. "I am the Fat Cat vandal." She paused, as if waiting for an explosion of shock.

"Lora already told us that part on the phone," Margrit said, apparently unimpressed. "What else do you have?"

Sarina walked Margit and Benjamin through the story she had told me, ending with Reiner's claim that he hadn't murdered anyone and his promise to keep her secret. Although her voice shook from time to time, she didn't cry. Hubert, on the other hand, was wiping his eyes throughout the entire recitation.

When she finished, there was a moment of silence. "Why didn't you come to me?" Hubert asked. "I would have cancelled the show. I just wanted to give you a head start in your career. And your work was good, really good. You would have gotten a show in time."

Sarina brushed her eyes. "Maybe, Dad, but I would have gotten the show when I deserved to get the show. When I was ready. Do you have any idea what it's like to grow up knowing that you'd be nothing without the help of your father?"

"You wouldn't be nothing. You'd find your own way."

"But as long as you keep 'helping' me, I won't ever know for sure."

Hubert shook his head. "God. I wish your mother had been with us all these years. She always saw so much more than I did." He coughed and cleaned his glasses again before looking up at Margrit. "What happens now?"

Margrit sighed. "I'm not going to lie to you, Hubert. This isn't going to go away. But it's not something we need to deal with right now. What we do need to deal with right now is finding Reiner and finding that stencil."

"Reiner told me that the Fat Cat sign on Horst Mueller was a copycat," Sarina said.

Margrit shook her head. "The police lab thinks it's the same. When you cut something like a stencil, little variations are introduced. Of course, unless the stencil is laid down perfectly on whatever you're painting, it's hard to find a 100 percent match, but they're pretty sure."

"Does that mean that Reiner killed that man?" Sarina asked.

Margit shrugged. "It's hard to think of another scenario that works, isn't it? He was carrying the stencil home to add to his stash of blackmail evidence when he just stumbled across a man who was coming to claim seventy-five million francs from the bank where Reiner is a new partner? Maybe that kind of thing works in fiction, but in real life, coincidence doesn't happen that often."

Pinkie nudged me. "I told you Reiner was evil," he whispered.

"You told me Reiner was a jerk. Not that he was a murderer. If everyone you told me was a jerk turned out to be a murderer, there wouldn't be a person left alive on the Upper East Side."

"You have to admit that there are a lot of jerks running around on the Upper East Side," Pinkie mused.

"I don't understand," Hubert said, looking at Margrit. "Reiner didn't even know about the gold until two weeks ago, when we opened the books to him as the new partner. And if the gold was stolen more than ten years ago, there's no way he could have been a party to that either. It just doesn't make any sense."

Pinkie drew himself to his full height, which made him a whopping five foot seven. "I've been pondering this very point. May I?" He looked at Margrit with raised eyebrows, waiting for permission.

"If you must," she said, shaking her head.

"Thank you. What if the story doesn't start with Reiner, but with Reiner's uncle? Bear with me a moment. Imagine that Reiner's uncle managed to steal that gold over the years. And then one night he's old, he's sick, and he realizes that his time has come. On his deathbed, he calls Reiner. 'Reiner,' he says, 'you've always been like a son to me. So I must entrust this secret to you.'" Pinkie clutched my shoulder and looked at me with the closest thing he could muster to the look of a dying man being consumed by his sins.

"'Reiner,' he says, 'seventy years ago a man came to us with two thousand kilograms of gold. Nazi gold. And being your uncle, and being evil just like you, I stole that gold, piece by piece, over many years. And while the real owner of that ill-gotten gold will most likely never darken the door of this bank, if they do, you must be willing to kill. To kill to protect the family name!'"

Pinkie gasped, choked, then went limp, collapsing into a chair.

"Jesus," Benjamin said, looking at me for direction. "Are we supposed to applaud?"

Pinkie snapped his head up and gave a little bow. "Applause is probably a little gauche under the circumstances, but feel free to send a bottle of champagne to my room later." He fluttered his eyelashes at Benjamin.

Margrit let out a sigh and rubbed her eyes. "Obviously I need to get some sleep, because as absurd as that was, I don't think I've got a better scenario at this point. Of course, there are still holes in the story. It takes two partner keys to open the vault, right? But in any case, I'm going to send some officers over to search Reiner's apartment. If we find the stencil, we've got grounds to hold him and question him. And I will get the truth out of him, never fear." She rolled her shoulders and looked at us balefully.

"In the meantime, I'll be sending Officer Denkel home with you." She gestured to a tall, dark, and handsome officer who looked as though he had been poured into his uniform.

"Oh my," Pinkie said, flushing from head to toe. "Is his job to look after Lora and me? Because Lora's brother was pretty sure I was the target, so he should probably stay really close to me. There's a trundle bed in my room, as a matter of fact. Safety first, you know."

Margrit rolled her eyes at Pinkie. "Given the number of strange things we've seen around this family recently, I'm not completely convinced that the earlier incident in the parking lot was a prank, but Officer Denkel's primary concern is to make sure that Sarina doesn't decide to run off in the night. Right now I don't have anything against Sarina except her own words, so I'm not going to hold her, but until we get this damned thing figured out, I want someone keeping an eye on her."

Sarina shook her head. She looked broken. "I didn't commit murder, and I'm ready to face the punishment for the Fat Cat vandalism. I trust the justice system."

Benjamin shot me a look that, for once, I understood without any problem. Who would be crazy enough to trust the justice system? But for all I knew, Switzerland had a completely functional justice system. Although really, that wouldn't make any sense at all. America had way more criminals than Switzerland did, so we had plenty of practice. The Swiss were bound to be rank amateurs at the whole criminal justice thing.

"You have my word that everybody in this family will face whatever repercussions are appropriate as a result of their actions," Hubert said. He squeezed his daughter's hand.

"Great," I said, yawning. "So if that's all we've got, I'd be more than happy to go back to Hubert's house and get some rest." Pinkie gave Officer Denkel a nakedly predatory look. "By all means, let's all head off to bed.

30

I was woken up again by the rooster, at seven o'clock, which was about two hours earlier than I had any wish to be awake. I consoled myself by eating truffles and thinking about Reiner. The conversation with Sarina had convinced me that Reiner was a sleazeball, but I still couldn't make things add up in my head.

Pinkie's theory that Reiner would kill to protect the family name seemed a little farfetched to me. I mean, *Hubert* might kill to protect the family name. He seemed pretty old school that way. But Reiner seemed like the kind of guy who'd just change his name and figure out another way to ingratiate himself with the gullible or blackmailable.

And if Reiner's uncle had stolen eighty-three million dollars in gold, where was it? I didn't see Reiner sticking his neck out to hide the crime unless he had gotten a significant cut, and if he had gotten a significant cut, I couldn't figure out why he was still hanging around sucking up to Hubert and whatever Russian oligarch happened to roll into town to visit his money and buy some watches.

And on a more personally relevant note, I still hadn't managed to make heads or tails of us being shot at in the parking garage. I didn't think Maurice would be able to pull off something so quickly, and I had never really subscribed to the theory that it was just some Street Party denizens with a bad sense of humor. And as much as I hated Vanessa St. Germain, a knife in the back was way more her style than guns in a parking garage.

If someone had been after us, why were they leaving us alone now? Had they gotten what they wanted? Maybe they were just really desperate for a nice Louis Vuitton tote. Or my red Prada dress, come to think of it. I chomped another truffle to console myself for the loss of that dress. That dress was almost worth shooting someone over.

Or maybe they weren't leaving us alone. Maybe they were just biding their time while they waited for Officer Hottie to leave so that they could swoop in and murder us both. I nervously chewed on a fingernail and looked at the window. The heavy velvet curtains were closed, and I felt a sudden sense of alarm. What if a psychotic killer was lurking outside right now?

Heart suddenly pounding, I swung my legs out of the bed and sidled over to the French doors leading out onto the terrace. I put one hand on the curtain and braced myself to fling it open. Suddenly I felt silly. I was in Switzerland, for heaven's sake. It was literally the safest place on earth. I mentally scolded myself for being such a flake, and pulled open the curtain. A dark figure spun around to face me, inches away.

"Ack!" I yelled, staggering backward.

"Shh! It's me," Benjamin said through the glass.

I took in the sight of Benjamin, dressed in dark jeans and a black T-shirt, crouched in front of the French doors. My heart was still threatening to hammer its way out of my chest. "You..." I croaked, unsure as to whether I wanted to collapse in relief or beat him to death with a hammer.

Apparently I looked like I was opting for the hammer because Benjamin held his hands up as if he were pacifying a crazy person. "I know this looks bad, but can you please open the door?"

I opened the door. "You think this looks bad?!" I hissed. "You think that finding you lurking outside my window at the crack of dawn looks bad? Buddy, you have no idea. What the hell are you doing here?"

"I wanted to talk to you."

"Most people try the front door. Or the telephone. You remember the telephone? It's that thing that people use when they want to stay in touch with someone."

Benjamin winced and stepped into the room, closing the door behind him. "This is why I wanted to talk to you alone. I kind of got the impression that you were upset that I hadn't called."

"I can't *imagine* how you got that impression. Why would I care if you called? I mean, strange men kiss me in churches all the time."

He gave me a hurt look. "I know. I wanted to call. But last month I was in a place where it just wasn't possible."

"Really? What kind of place would that be? The end of the world?"

"Peshawar," Benjamin said. "So the ass end of the world, if you want to be specific. I got my orders right after I left you. I wanted to get in touch, but I couldn't." He ran his fingers through his hair distractedly. "I'm not even supposed to be telling you this. I don't know why I'm telling you this. Dammit, I'm not good with this kind of thing." He stepped over the threshold of my room and swept me into a hard embrace, his mouth crushing mine with an urgency that left me breathless.

I want to say that I resisted. I really meant to resist. But I had been thinking about that kiss in the church for a month now, playing it over in my head, wondering if that butterfly feeling in my stomach had been a fluke. But this was no fluke. I opened my mouth and kissed him back, lacing my arms around his neck. He moaned, spinning me around so that my back was against the wall.

He slid the silk nightgown I was wearing up and ran his hands over my body, then worked his way down my neck, kissing, nipping, biting. "God, I've been thinking about this ever since I saw you," he whispered throatily.

I caught my breath as his teeth grazed my earlobe. "The bed," I said urgently.

Gathering me up in his arms, he turned to the bed and dropped me on it, climbing over me, still kissing my neck. He shifted his weight as he fumbled for the hem of my nightgown, causing the headboard to bang against the wall.

A peevish voice interrupted us. "Lora?"

Pinkie, apparently awakened by the rooster, the headboard, or just his sterling sense of bad timing, was standing in the doorway. Resplendent in a silk kimono and lime-green face goop, he was holding a cell phone and goggling at Benjamin.

I sat up and struggled to rearrange my nightgown so that it covered all of the relevant parts of my anatomy.

"Pinkie, I'm kind of busy right now," I said, trying to stop panting.

"I can see that," Pinkie said, showing no inclination to leave. "Good morning, Benjamin...I didn't hear you come in."

"I...uh..." Benjamin started. He looked at Pinkie in frustration. "Why are you here?"

"I'm here to tell Lora that Margrit is on the line for her. But, you know, if you want to let a little thing like a murder investigation get in the way of whatever it is that you were doing..."

I snatched the phone out of his hand. "Hello, Margrit."

"Was I interrupting something?" I wondered how anyone could sound so crisp at seven o'clock in the morning after running around all night catching murderers. Clean living, I guessed.

"Not at all," I said, turning my back on Benjamin, who was giving Pinkie a murderous glare.

"We talked to Reiner last night."

"Did he have the stencil?"

"He did. And a can of paint as well, so that part of Sarina's story checked out."

"Great." I paused. "Maybe I'm not clear on the way Swiss police share information about an ongoing investigation, but is it normal for you guys to call up the houseguests of potential suspects just to keep them in the loop?"

"I'm not calling to keep you in the loop. I'm calling to ask you for a favor. Can you come down to the station first thing this morning?"

"Are you going to tell me why?"

"Not while you're standing in the middle of a house filled with people who are intimately involved in this crime."

"Fine. Do I get to take Officer Hottie, or does he need to stay here?"

"Officer Hottie? Ah. Officer Denkel. No, he needs to watch Sarina. Do you want me to send a car?"

I sighed. "I'll take the Smart Car. It's kind of growing on me." I looked up at Benjamin. "Is there anyone else I should bring? Pinkie? Benjamin?"

Margrit's voice sharpened. "Do you happen to know where Benjamin is?"

"I...uh...yes. He stopped by for a chat this morning."

"A chat? What would he be chatting about with you? Not the

investigation, I hope."

"Nope. Personal stuff." The silence on the other end sounded like an accusation. "He was looking for restaurant tips. You know, in New York. Because I live there, and with my job…" I trailed off.

Margrit let a thoughtful silence stretch out between us on the phone. "Lora, would you be offended if I offered some advice?"

Probably, I thought. "Not at all."

"Don't ever go into crime as a career. You are quite possibly the world's worst liar."

I blushed.

"Bring Benjamin with you. And try to be discreet. The last thing this case needs is more gossip."

31

Twenty minutes later, Benjamin and I piled into the Smart Car. I dreaded making small talk with a horror that was only eclipsed by the possibility that we were going to have to have a serious relationship talk. Did we mean something to each other? Was there a future here? Had he somehow gotten the impression that I was just a complete slut (which was totally false, but at this point, I could see how he might think that)?

After five minutes of driving in awkward silence, I finally turned on the radio. Tina Turner, singing "What's Love Got to Do With It?" I cringed and flipped the station. Tina Turner again, but this time "We Don't Need Another Hero," which seemed slightly less dangerously relevant.

"Big Tina Turner fans here," I said.

"That's because she lives in Switzerland. We'll drive by her house on the way into town."

"Huh."

We drove on in uncomfortable silence.

When we got to the police station, the parking attendant who had turned Pinkie and I away before was again guarding the garage.

"Police vehicles only," he said.

"Do you remember me?"

"I remember the car," he said, smirking. "I told you last time. Police vehicles only."

"The last time you told me that, my friend and I went over to the parking garage down the street, where someone shot at us. So today, I'm parking here."

"I don't see how someone trying to shoot you in the parking garage down the street is really my fault."

"I'm not saying it's your fault. I'm saying that you can call Detective Margrit and get clearance to adjust your definition of police vehicles to include miniature Tupperware cars advertising sex toys or you can arrest me for parking right here, but this car is parking in this garage."

He looked at me hard, then opened the gate. "Americans," he muttered. It didn't sound like a compliment.

Margrit met us at the entry and quickly walked us to an interrogation room. Through the one-way window, I could see Reiner. I expected him to look ravaged after a night of questioning, but he looked as crisp as if he were walking into the bank to start a day of work. Only his eyes were different, and I realized it was because the mask of politeness had slipped. For the first time since I'd met him, I understood what Pinkie had caught a glimpse of—a man who would do whatever it took to get what he wanted.

I shuddered. "He looks like a killer."

Margrit shrugged her shoulders. "Killers can look like anyone. Don't be fooled."

"Is he still saying he's innocent?"

"He is. He's admitting to doing that Fat Cat stencil that we found at the scene, but he says the guy was dead when he found him."

"I don't understand. Why would anyone decide to paint graffiti on a dead body?"

"Before I get into it, I'd like to ask if you'd be willing to call your brother," Margrit said.

"My brother? What does he have to with this?"

"Nothing at all. And I'd like to keep it that way, at least officially, but Benjamin provided me with some information about your brother's unique skill set that makes me think he might be able to verify some of Reiner's story. I can't hire him directly, unfortunately. We have a computer department, and they will check into it. It's just that…"

"It'll take two weeks," I said.

Margrit shook her head. "If you ever decide to commit a crime, August in Europe is definitely the way to go. Everybody's on vacation. That's why I called so early—I wanted to see if we could catch your brother before he went to sleep."

I laughed and reached for the phone. "He doesn't sleep."

"A man after my own heart," Margrit said, raising an eyebrow.

The phone rang only once when Chris picked up. "Have you been arrested?"

"What would I be arrested for?" I asked, putting him on speaker.

"Prostitution, I would guess, although isn't that legal in Switzerland?"

"I'm not a prostitute," I ground out.

"Well, I believe you, but it's an easy mistake to make, I think you'll agree."

Margrit, tapped on the table impatiently.

"I'm here with the Swiss police," I said. "They were wondering if you would be willing to do a little pro bono work for them."

"Hmm. Pro bono. I'm not sure I like the sound of that. You wouldn't believe how much you need to tip a delivery boy these days. Not to mention the price of Red Bull." He sighed dramatically. "Plus, it's hard to see what I could do for the Swiss police. I mean, even I can't reach over the Internet and direct traffic or rescue kittens from trees. I suppose I could technically give directions to tourists, but with smartphones the way they are these days…"

A vein jumped in Margrit's forehead. Sometimes I forgot how deeply annoying other people found my brother. "This is Detective von Hofstedtler, with the Zurich Police Department. We're currently holding someone on suspicion of murder. He's come back to us with what seems like a highly unlikely story, and we want to trace back his digital steps to see if there's any chance he's telling the truth."

"First missing Nazi gold and now murder. I thought Switzerland had a low crime rate."

"Will you do it? It would have to be kept completely confidential, of course. We'd owe you a favor."

"It's hard to think what kind of favor I'd need from a Swiss police department."

"That's true, but if your sister's recent history is any indication, she'll probably need a favor somewhere down the road."

"Touché. But truth be told, you've piqued my interest. Tell me about your little problem, and I'll see what I can do to help. On one condition. Lora has to stay in the room."

"This isn't civilian business," Margrit said. "There's no reason for her to be here."

"If she's not there, I'm not doing it. I don't like talking to strangers. Plus, she's the Watson to my Sherlock Holmes."

"More like the Sherlock Holmes to your Moriarty," I said.

"Which makes me the evil villain sitting unseen at the center of a web stretching across the globe," Chris said thoughtfully. "Hmm. You're right. That's much better. I told you I needed her there."

Margrit gave me a hard look. "What we talk about here stays in this room. You can't tell Hubert or Sarina or Philippe. Especially Philippe. That man has absolutely no sense of discretion."

"Fine."

"Reiner Hoffmann, our suspect in this case, is a partner at a private bank here in Zurich. Our victim, Horst Mueller, was a reasonably successful businessman with a chain of car washes who had somehow managed to discover the account number and password for an account in the bank Reiner works for. That account was an anonymous physical gold account opened at the end of the second World War. The gold in the account is currently worth around $83 million."

There was frantic typing on the other end of the line.

"Are you listening?" Margrit asked.

"Yep. Don't worry about the typing. I think best when I'm fending off Orc attacks."

Margrit glared at the telephone, but continued. "When we started investigating Horst Mueller, his name brought up a flag, and we got a call from American Homeland Security. They had been investigating Horst Mueller for funneling funds to right-wing terrorist organizations."

I turned to Benjamin. "That's what you were doing in Switzerland."

"In Germany first," he said. "I was sent to look into some currency transfers to terrorist groups targeting Israel. Our computer guys told us that Mueller was using his business to help launder money for neo-Nazi causes. Car washes are great for that."

"I know. I saw *Breaking Bad*, too."

Benjamin continued. "Until a couple of weeks ago, Horst Mueller was just a minor player with known right-wing sympathies.

We suspected him of money laundering, but the amounts weren't huge, and we were more worried about the bigger fish. But about two weeks ago, the online chatter started going crazy about some money he had come into."

"Chatter?" I asked.

"The message boards these guys use to communicate," Benjamin said. "Before last week it was more or less just your normal hate speech stuff, but suddenly people started talking about big money, big plans. 'The Legacy,' they called it."

Chris snorted on the phone. "Typical. Why do all white supremacist code names sound like they're coming out of Age of Empires?"

"Point taken, but in this case it might actually be a legacy. Mueller's grandfather was pretty high up in the Nazi Party during the war. He worked in rail transportation. He organized shipments of prisoners to the concentration camps and the distribution of guns and military supplies."

"And let me guess...he also organized the shipment of eighty-three million bucks in gold to a friendly little neutral country next door where anonymity and chocolate were both freely available."

Benjamin nodded. "Hubert told us the account was opened in the last days of the war. Whether Mueller's grandfather intended it to be money for the Reich or a little personal insurance policy, I think it's a pretty safe bet that he was the one who opened the account."

I frowned. "Wait. If he opened the account in the '40s, Mueller's grandfather could have accessed it any time. Why has it just been sitting there? Did he feel guilty and decide to take his secret to the grave?"

Benjamin shook his head. "He died during the Allied invasion. I think the likeliest story is that he just didn't have a chance to tell anyone. But he probably wrote it down somewhere, because somehow Mueller figured out what was waiting for him here in Zurich. I followed him here to watch him, and he was murdered."

"That doesn't give me great confidence in your watching skills," I said.

Benjamin sucked air in, looking guilty. "That was my fault. I was watching him the day of the murder, but once he'd gone back to his hotel, I figured he was in for the night and went back to my room to sleep. I got there at five the next morning, and the body had already been found by a street sweeper. To be honest, we didn't expect this to turn lethal. At this point we still didn't have any solid information about what this legacy was."

"Benjamin, is it?" my brother asked.

"Yes," Benjamin said warily.

"You work for the US government?"

"Yes."

"Which branch?"

"Homeland Security."

"That's a pretty big place. Can you be more specific?"

"It's not relevant to this discussion."

"Oh, if you're looking for the killer of this Horst Mueller, I think it's very relevant."

"Why?" Margrit asked.

Chris made a tutting noise. "Think about it. You've got Horst Mueller suspected of funding terrorist attacks on one of America's allies. The US government sends out a guy who works in Homeland Security to 'watch' him. The guy suddenly realizes he's the heir to eighty-three million bucks in gold. The guy is found dead, and eighty-three million bucks' worth of terrorist cash stays out of circulation. I'm a computer genius, not a math genius, but even I can add those points up."

Benjamin rolled his eyes. "That's ridiculous. I work for the US government. My job is law enforcement, not assassination."

"Because the US government would never, never proactively kill someone funding terrorism, right? I mean, I'm sure that if it came down to a choice between working with German, Swiss, and Israeli police to painstakingly build a case against a German citizen versus just sending over a bag man, they'd be all for the paperwork."

Margrit looked at Benjamin silently for a moment, pondering. "Listen, I'm no fan of the US government either, but we haven't found any evidence that they were involved in the murder."

"Well, you wouldn't, would you?" Chris said cheerfully.

Benjamin looked around the table. "This is ridiculous. I didn't kill Horst Mueller."

"Because you've never killed anyone in the line of duty?"

Benjamin stiffened all over. "I'm done with this topic. We're here to talk about Reiner Hoffmann."

I looked at him in shock. I mean, I knew Benjamin was

involved in spy stuff, but surely he wasn't some kind of government hit man, right? I tried to catch his eye, but he refused to look at me. I kicked him hard under the table.

"Ow," he said, looking up at last. "What was that for?"

I looked into his eyes, not sure what I was hoping to see. His gaze slid away to the side, and I felt a sickening sensation in the pit of my stomach.

"Nothing," I said.

"Can someone please either pull up Skype so I can see or tell me what's going on?" my brother asked pointedly. "Is Laura playing footsie with Mr. Secret Agent Man?"

"Nothing's going on," I said again.

"Fine. Then can we please get back to whatever I'm supposed to be doing to help you? My Ogre King is getting his ass handed to him thanks to you people."

"Reiner Hoffmann," Margrit said.

"Gimme a sec." We heard a few seconds of tapping. "Okay, got it."

"You have a file on Reiner?" Margrit asked.

"No, I had to kill a Daywalker. I hacked into Reiner's computers the first time you mentioned his name. Home and work. So...let's see what we've got here. Newest partner in Richter and Partners? That's nice for him. Pretty young for that role, I'd think, but I guess with the family connection..."

Margrit looked somewhere between impressed and horrified.

"I can tell you that he's also a bit of a computer geek," my brother said. "Nowhere near my league, of course. But then again, nobody is. Let's see...looks like he altered some of his transcripts from college." He clicked his tongue. "He changed his grade from a C to an A in ethics? That's hilarious. I mean, it's also a little trite. I sometimes wish people would be less predictable in their moral lapses."

"Can I fill you in on the rest of the story so we can get on with this?" Margrit snapped.

"By all... Oh my god! Is anyone in imminent danger of sleeping with this person?"

I glanced around the table before checking out Reiner, who was looking into space in the questioning room with every appearance of zen-like calm. "I really don't think so."

"Well, if it does cross your mind, just don't. You wouldn't

believe the stuff this guy has been looking at on the Internet. I'm going to have to clean my brain after this."

"Getting back to the relevant information," Margrit said, clearly wishing she'd never met any of us, "one of the things at the scene that threw us was the Fat Cat symbol that was sprayed near the body. Have you been following this Fat Cat vandalism case in Switzerland?"

"Have I been following a vandalism case in Switzerland? How much time do you think I have, lady?"

I held up a hand to forestall any comment from Margrit, who looked like she was spoiling for a fight.

"They've had a vandal running around spray painting this orange fat cat onto high-end stuff," I said. "Banks, Gucci stores, that kind of thing. It was supposed to be some sort of statement against the 1 percent."

"Ah. Probably some spoiled rich kid with daddy issues."

Benjamin chimed in. "Exactly. Turns out it was Sarina, the daughter of Philippe's godfather. She created the stencil and did the vandalism, but Reiner stole the stencil from her the night of the murder. We found it in his apartment."

"Why did he steal the stencil from Sarina? Why not just report it?"

"He was trying to blackmail her into sex," I said.

"Trust me when I say that if she knew what he was into, it would take more than the threat of jail time to make that deal worth taking."

"So Reiner does admit to spray painting the body," I clarified.

Margrit nodded. "He does, but Reiner says that Mueller was already dead when he found him."

"Why on earth would he spray paint a dead body?" Chris asked.

"Reiner knew who Mueller was, and he figured that if we ever managed to figure out the connection to the bank, he'd fall under suspicion. He used the stencil to give himself an alibi."

More typing from my brother. "Because he was in Singapore for two of the previous Fat Cat vandalisms. Right here on his calendar. Hmm. Wow. Color me impressed. That's thinking on your feet. But how did Reiner know who Horst Mueller was? I thought it was an anonymous account."

"Reiner says that the first time he heard about the account was two weeks ago, when he did the partner inventory. He said he was curious, so he started going back through his uncle's records to see if there was anything that would help him trace the identity of the person who opened the account."

"The account hadn't been touched in seventy years, and the bank would have been much better off if it had never been touched," my brother said. "Why would he start snooping around?"

Margrit shook her head. "We figured he was looking to get a piece of it somehow."

"Maybe not," I said. "Sarina told me that he collects information on people. His clients. Her. He's always looking for something that will give him that extra bit of leverage."

"Well, in any case, he found something in his uncle's records and managed to trace it back to Mueller's grandfather. And then he traced the family tree through to Mueller himself."

"Did he contact Mueller and tell him about the gold?" I asked.

"That's where this story starts to go wrong for me," Margrit said. "He says that he never had any intention of contacting Mueller. He just wanted to make sure he had enough information to—and I quote—'properly evaluate the bank's liability.'" But he decided to keep tabs on Mueller, and he found out about the right-wing connection. A few days after he started watching Mueller, he started hearing chatter about this 'legacy' on those boards. And then Mueller booked a ticket to Zurich, and Reiner decided to meet him in person. He said they had an appointment to meet at midnight the night of the murder."

"He was at the partner dinner with us until ten or so."

Margrit nodded. "That matches his story. He left at ten, planning to go meet Mueller. He says that before he left the grounds, he stopped by Sarina's room, 'to drop off an earring he had found,' he said. She wasn't there, but he says that he saw the template on her desk, realized what it meant, and took it because he was afraid someone else would see it."

"Like hell," I said. "I bet he went to Sarina's room to feel around in her underwear drawer."

"Probably," Margrit conceded, "but that's not really the most pressing concern. He says that the trip to Sarina's room made him miss his train, so instead of getting there at 11:30, he got there at 12:30. He says he literally stumbled across the body."

"Wait," Chris said. "Back up a step. Why did Reiner set up a meeting with Mueller, at midnight, no less, if he wasn't planning on killing him? And why would Mueller agree to meet anyone at midnight? I'm not buying it."

"Reiner told Mueller that he knew about the account, and told him that he was willing to make an offer—they would give him access to the funds, but they would also hold and 'invest' the money so that his withdrawals would be under the table. He was offering to launder the money, in effect. He said the time was Mueller's idea. Mueller wanted to go to the bank the next day, and he didn't plan on waiting."

"But the gold legally belonged to Mueller," I said. "Why would he need money laundering?"

Margrit sighed. "Because the law has changed. The second he touched that gold, he'd need to go through the new system that's designed to prevent thugs of all brands of crazy from moving money around. 'Know Your Customer' laws. If he left it there and let Reiner sell and move the money anonymously in small chunks, the bank would profit, Mueller would keep his anonymity, and nobody would have to open up that whole Nazi gold can of worms again."

Benjamin looked intrigued. "That's not all. If someone could prove that the gold was looted from victims of the Holocaust, you'd be looking at a real possibility of a civil suit. If the gold was originally stolen from Jews, for example, a court might require part of it to go to a fund for Holocaust survivors." He tapped the table thoughtfully. "I've gotta admit…it's a pretty good story. Except for the timing. No way did Mueller stumble across the gold at the same time Reiner did. Reiner told him about it and decided to improve the bank's balance sheet with a little murder."

Chris tapped a few more keys. Elf attack, I guessed. "So if I'm reading you right, you want me to find evidence that Reiner contacted Mueller before all this 'legacy' talk started."

"Right," Margrit said. "Reiner finds out about an account that's been dormant for seventy years, and within three weeks the owner is standing on his doorstep ready to claim it? What are the chances?"

"I've gotta admit, Reiner telling him seems much more likely. But I'll need to take a look at where Reiner's been hanging out. Aside from the sex sites, of course. I think I scarred my prefrontal cortex with what I already saw."

"How much time do you think it'll take?"

"Oh, not much. Bear with me." He typed away for a few minutes while we all sat in the room, looking tensely at each other.

"Son of a bitch," he said softly.

"If you tell me it's Orcs again, I may come to the US to arrest you in person."

"No. Well, yes, actually, but I was referring to your Reiner problem. I told you that Reiner used to be a bit of a computer geek, right? Well, if you look back through his computer history, it's all there. He starts by searching for three different names."

"Probably from his uncle's papers," Margrit said.

"Presumably. Then he narrows by geography and date, which is just common practice. He cross indexes by Nazi rank and by the kinds of jobs that would have allowed someone to move a bunch of gold. He cross indexes again by the hundredth anniversary Steiner jewelry show. Maybe there was a note in his uncle's papers about picking something up for the wife…Die, nightwalker!...and then up through the present generation…and then to Horst himself, and then onto his skinhead extra-curricular activities…and then over to sites reviewing some of the cases against banks holding wartime assets…"

"Ha," my brother said. "Reiner did tell Mueller about the legacy."

"I knew it," Margrit said, standing up.

"Sit down," Chris said.

"How did you know she was standing up?" I asked.

"I just do."

"What's the problem?" Margrit asked, sitting back down again.

"The problem is that he didn't do it on purpose. He managed to figure out that Mueller was into neo-Nazi causes. It's not too hard to do—even a reasonable hacker could find his way onto the site, but apparently he tripped a security measure."

"What kind of security measure?" Benjamin asked, leaning forward.

"Basically, he came in on an unverified computer, and the server went out to verify where he was coming from. And apparently, and this is so idiotic that I almost can't believe it, he was coming from his work computer."

"It's not that idiotic, actually," Margrit said. "It's a private network protected by the banking secrecy laws of Switzerland. It's probably the safest place he could have done it."

"Well, yeah, except that someone apparently passed that information onto Mueller, who must have started wondering why a partner in a Zurich private bank was checking him out."

"But how did he know about the password and the account number?" Margrit asked.

"Well, far be it from me to speculate," my brother said, "but since it would have looked like meaningless jottings to anyone who hadn't heard the story, Mueller's grandfather probably just fucking wrote it on a sticky note and dropped it into his desk drawer. Or a non-sticky note, come to think of it, since sticky notes hadn't been invented yet." Chris snorted. "Not everything's that complicated, you know. Maybe there were family rumors about a lost legacy— we'll probably never know at this point, but the main thing here is that there's no coincidence. Reiner didn't lure him here to kill him, at least not as far as I can tell. In fact, the topics that he was looking at support his story. He was trying to figure out the legal situation. I'd say he was looking to cut a deal."

"That still doesn't explain who killed Mueller or how the gold went missing," I pointed out.

"As much as you all seem to just think that I can solve all the world's problems by sitting here—and I'm not debating the fact that you're largely right, by the way—I think that's going to take some actual police work. The guy was a neo-Nazi about to come into a shitload of money. Mossad. Benjamin. Jews for Jesus. To be completely honest, I doubt you'll ever know. But Reiner's story, at least, holds together. All of which is not to say that Reiner didn't change his mind at the last second and kill the guy. Are we done here?"

"Why?" I asked. "Facing rebellion from your ogre underlings?"

"No. I'm expecting a steak to show up any minute, and I'd like to put on some pants."

"Uh, right. When are you going to stop billing me for Lone Star delivery, by the way?"

"When I feel that the karmic debt you owe me for rescuing you from white slavers has been repaid."

"So...never?"

"Bingo."

32

"So," I said after we had hung up the phone. "What's going to happen to Reiner?"

"I'm going to hold him for the time being," Margrit said. "Your brother has shown that he's not lying about everything, but at the end of the day, we still don't know what happened when they actually met up that night. Maybe they argued. Maybe Reiner knew about the missing gold all along and went there to kill him. Right now, he's still the most likely suspect. We'll finish the investigation, and if we don't find any other options, he'll probably be charged."

"Do you think he did it?" I asked.

"Frankly, I have no idea," Margrit said, sighing. "Up to now, I couldn't figure out how someone managed to kill Mueller and then materialize outside to spray paint the body without going through the only exit. If Reiner's telling the truth, the murderer was someone who was already in the hotel when the last person came through the lobby at eleven o'clock, killed Mueller at twelve, and stayed in the hotel through the morning."

"So it's probably one of the hotel guests, right?"

"Right. Except the rest of the hotel was booked by guys from the Sioux City Rotary Club a year in advance. Apparently they come here every year for Street Parade. The only reason the room was available for Mueller was because one of Rotary guys got a kidney stone two days before he was supposed to leave. I just don't see a connection."

"What about Sarina? Are you going to arrest her?"

"Sarina will have to plead guilty to vandalism, but I doubt she'll see a day in jail. Once you take the murder part away, you're looking mostly at charges of graffiti, and the Swiss have a pretty relaxed attitude toward graffiti artists."

"Yeah, but a rich girl like that… Do you think the Swiss will try to make an example of her by putting her in jail?"

Margit regarded me curiously. "Someday you'll have to explain to me how your American justice system works. We try not to use ours to fight about unrelated social issues."

"Well, that's where you're going wrong. Maybe you should check out a few episodes of *Law & Order* so you see how it's supposed to done. I think you've got, like, thirty flavors to choose from."

"I'll keep it in mind."

"Do you need me here anymore? I've got that hostessing job for tonight, so I'm going to have to prepare myself for an evening of pop yodeling and alphorns."

Margrit snorted. "I'd rather be chasing murderers."

I thought about Vanessa St. Germain. "Me, too." I looked at Benjamin. "I presume you're staying here?"

Benjamin nodded. "I've got some loose ends to tie up, but since it looks like we're not going to end up with eighty-three million dollars in the hands of right-wing terrorists, I doubt Uncle Sam will pay me to hang around eating chocolate and seeing the sights. If it's okay with you, I'll stop by Hubert's once I'm done to say goodbye."

"Okay," I said neutrally, not sure whether it was okay with me or not. "But I've got a lot of things to get done. How should I get in touch with you if something comes up?"

"You lost my card already?"

"Your card, my bag, my phone, and my Prada dress so far. Oh, and thanks to those truffles that Hubert has set in little stashes around the house, I think you can add my figure and my shot at not getting Type 2 diabetes."

Benjamin flashed a smile at me and fished another business card out of his pocket. "This one's slightly more official."

Jonathan Benjamin Joker, Adjunct Professor of Criminal Law, John Jay College of Criminal Justice. Below that was a number.

"Joker. Subtle. And still an adjunct professor? Don't you ever get promoted?"

Benjamin shrugged. "It's a lifestyle choice."

Margrit put her hand on my arm. "It looks like we'll be pretty busy here for the next few days. Lora, if I don't have the chance to talk to you and Philippe again before you leave, please send him my love, and tell him I'm sorry that he wasn't able to find the proof he needed to get his watch back."

"I'll tell him," I said. Silently, I wondered whether it wasn't better this way. Pinkie wouldn't have his watch, but he also wouldn't have to risk his relationship with Hubert. And while I found it hard to believe Hubert would really cut Pinkie out of his life for being gay, I couldn't swear it wouldn't happen.

I said my goodbyes to Margrit and went out and went to retrieve the Erotik Megamart Smart Car from the police parking lot, tossing Benjamin's card onto the seat next to me and giving a jaunty wave to the scowling attendant on my way out. "Jerk," I whispered under my breath.

I glanced in the rearview mirror as I pulled out, just in time to catch the word he mouthed after me like a curse. "American."

33

I pulled up to Hubert's house and sat in the car for a second, trying mentally to go through the list of everything I had to do that day. I wanted to go up to Dieter's house and run through the setup and timing of the acts. I also wanted to pack, because we were leaving tomorrow, and packing while hungover was about the worst way to spend a morning imaginable. Not that I was planning on being hungover—I never plan on being hungover—but I seem to end up that way despite my best efforts, and since kirsch and beer would probably be on the menu for the evening, I figured that the chances of feeling rotten in the morning were approaching 100 percent.

Sighing, I reached over to grab Benjamin's card. It was nowhere to be seen. I remembered distinctly putting it on the seat. Had it self-destructed? I thought for a moment. Given what I knew about Benjamin, that wasn't out of the realm of possibility, but chances were slightly better that it had just fallen under the seat somewhere, particularly given the braking on the Smart Car, which was best described as "choppy."

I put my hand under the passenger seat and felt around blindly, hoping that I didn't run across any used discount sex toys. I felt something square and flat under the seat. Struggling slightly, I managed to work it free. It wasn't until I got it out that I realized what I was holding. It was one of the 1972 bank ledgers that Pinkie and I had checked out of the vault. It must have slid down under the seat while we were fleeing for our lives in the parking lot.

I briefly considered taking it to Margrit on the off chance that it might have something to do with the investigation, but decided to give Pinkie a look inside first to see if he could find any notes about his father's watch. We were leaving tomorrow, so this was probably his last hope, and while I didn't figure our chances were that good with only one out of the four books, it was still worth a shot.

I put the book on the seat and felt around until I found Benjamin's business card, then grabbed the ledger and headed into the house. "Pinkie!" I called. No response. I walked down the hall and knocked on his door. "Pinkie? Are you there?"

I opened the door a crack.

"Don't look at me," Pinkie cried, throwing his arms over his face. "I'm hideous!"

"What is going on, Pinkie?" I slipped into his room and closed the door. I looked him over. He was still in bed, wearing his kimono, looking disheveled. His face was smeared with powdered sugar and a half-empty box of Teuscher truffles lay beside him.

I sat down on the side of the bed. "It's ten thirty in the morning." I looked over at his nightstand, which contained a box of tissues and a glass filled with clear liquid. I felt a jolt of alarm. I picked up the glass and sniffed it. Just as I had feared.

"Are you drinking *water*?"

"Maybe," Pinkie said, mumbling around a mouthful of truffle.

"Okay…I'm putting these truffles away. I think you've had enough." I picked up the box and moved it across the room, fighting the urge to eat one. "Let me pour you a nice glass of Veuve. You'll feel better."

"I'm not in the mood for celebrating."

"Since when have you only had Veuve when celebrating? For the love of god, what happened to you? I left you two hours ago, and you were perfectly fine. I come back now, and you're a wreck."

"I got a call from the girl at Patek Philippe. She found the entry for my father's watch."

"It was your uncle's watch all along?" I asked, shocked. Pinkie never made mistakes like that.

"No. It's even worse than that. The watch is registered to von Hofstedtler. Just the family name. So basically it could belong to anyone. Me, Margrit, Maurice. Why would anyone register a watch with just the family name?"

"Because they didn't expect their family members to steal their stuff after they died?"

Pinkie gave me a withering look. "We're *royalty*, Lora. We always expect our family members to steal our stuff. If they wait until we die, that's the best-case scenario. Fratricide is a long and time-honored tradition in our family. No, it's over. I'll never see that watch again." He dabbed at his eye. "Maybe it's for the best."

"Are you crying?" I asked, feeling a rush of maternal tenderness.

"Of course not," Pinkie said, sniffling. "It's just that perfume that you're wearing. It's terrible. Just terrible." He stifled another sob.

I gave him a little hug. "I know. You're right. It's just terrible. Look, I don't want to get your hopes up, but I just found something. It's a long shot, but maybe somebody up there is looking out for you."

"What?"

"One of the ledgers from 1972. I found it under the seat of the Smart Car. It must have fallen out of the bag when we were racing around in the parking lot."

Pinkie took the book reverently. "Let's see. Maybe there's something in here that will finally make sure justice is done."

He flipped the book open, and we both looked down.

"What the hell?" he said.

We both sat there, looking at the book in silence.

"Does this mean what I think it means?" I asked.

"What else could it mean? And if that's what it means, I think we know who stole the gold."

I thought for a moment, mentally putting the pieces together. "Yes, but it still doesn't tell us who committed the murder."

"But we've narrowed the suspect list."

"Narrowed the suspect list, yes, but not enough. The police aren't going to be able to make a case based on this."

"They don't have to make a case. The killer is going to confess."

"And how are the police going to make him do that?"

"Don't you read mystery novels? The police aren't going to make him confess, Lora. We are." He grabbed a tissue and swiped it over his mouth, clearing away the remnants of his truffle binge.

He gave me a steely glare. "It breaks my heart to do this, but it's my job as a prince to ensure that justice prevails. Hand me an ascot, Lora. We've got a lot of work to do."

34

While Pinkie made it his life's work to look like someone who did absolutely nothing productive, the fact was that when he was really determined to do something, he was almost unstoppable. And while he usually saved that energy for the Harrods Christmas sale, it was in full force today. He had briefly outlined his plan to me on the way over, and had been so taken with his own brilliance that he had even forgotten to slouch down in case someone saw him in the Erotik Smart Car.

While impressed with his energy, I was less convinced. "What makes you think that Dieter is going to let us hijack his dinner so that we can play Nancy Drew? He needs this dinner, Pinkie. This is his livelihood." *And mine,* I thought, although I didn't say it.

"First of all, Lora, we're not playing Nancy Drew. We're playing Hardy Boys. It doesn't take a classics degree from Oxford to understand that the Hardy Boys are far superior to Nancy Drew."

"They were written by the same person."

"Yes, but only one of them has boys in it. You can see why I'd like that one better."

"Can we get back to why Dieter should allow you to use his dinner for your amateur detective night?"

"Yes. Two things, really. First is that Dieter is very old-school Swiss. He can't abide criminality of any kind. Or litter. I believe a hatred of litter is actually in the Swiss national anthem."

"And the second reason?"

Pinkie raised an eyebrow. "The second is that this will literally be the most authentically Swiss dinner the world has ever seen. Jack Green's mind is going to be totally blown."

When we finally pulled over the hill to Dieter's house, it looked as though it had been airbrushed into an idyllic Swiss postcard. The paths had been freshly raked, the window boxes had been refreshed with flowers in patriotic red and white, and the hedges had been trimmed with precision that wasn't merely military—it was Swiss military.

Even the livestock hadn't been spared Dieter's squeaky clean ministrations. Down in one corner of the property, a few young men had set up what looked like a car wash, with hoses, buckets, and industrial quantities of shampoo. Another young man was trying to round up cows and push them toward the wash. The cows were ignoring him, chomping methodically through the grass, and a particularly stoic-looking cow had parked itself right in the middle of the road, blocking our car.

We pulled the nose of the Smart car up to the cow. It gave us a baleful look and mooed in what seemed to me like a menacing sort of way. I honked the horn, but the resulting tinny beep had absolutely no effect. The young man looked at us and shrugged, clearly frustrated.

"For the love of heaven," Pinkie said, throwing up his hands. "Wait for me here. I can't watch this incompetence any longer."

"What are you doing? Are you sure it's safe to go out there?"

"Watch and learn," Pinkie said, opening the door and placing one suede driving moccasin delicately on the grass.

I rolled down the window. "Don't you need a red cape or something?"

Pinkie rolled his eyes. "They're cows, not bulls, Lora. But if you wanted to get me a red cape for Christmas, that might be nice. Count of Monte Cristo-style, obviously. Not Superman."

"Obviously," I echoed weakly.

Pinkie crossed over to the young man and spoke to him in German. After a brief conversation, the young man shook his head, obviously not convinced by whatever Pinkie was telling him. Pinkie gently pushed him to the side and locked eyes with the cow that was standing in front of our car. Letting out a loud whistle, he circled around it and its bovine colleagues, moving in a zigzag fashion across the field. As the cattle became aware of this new, absurd little presence in their paddock, they started moving away from Pinkie, clustering together for security.

When he had the cows more or less in a loose group, Pinkie went over to a big cow on the edge and gave it what I could only describe as a predatory stare. Making his pudgy little hands into claws, he moved toward the cow, hissing menacingly. The cow, clearly bewildered by these antics, decided that best thing to do was to get away from Pinkie, which meant moving in the direction of the cow wash. The other cows followed blindly, and soon the young men were scrubbing their way through a stack of mildly agitated bovines.

Pinkie shook hands with the cowherd and walked back to the car, head held high.

"Where in god's name did you learn how to do that?" I asked, flabbergasted.

"There are three things my kingdom is famous for," Pinkie said. "Our wheat beer, our award-winning tractor assembly plant, and…"

"Cows," I finished.

"As I've told you before, being a prince takes a lot more skill than you seem willing to give me credit for."

"I stand corrected. But I'm not sure that an ability to herd cows or assemble tractors is going to help us in this case. Does getting murderers to confess fall into your princely skill set? Because that would really make me feel a lot better."

"Unfortunately not. But I'm a master of human psychology, Lora. Just have a little faith."

The inside of Dieter's house was a scene of controlled chaos. Fondue pots were scattered around the table. Silverware was being polished. Girls in braids and lace-up dresses were running around with napkins and plates of cold cuts. Cow bells were being strung up along one of the rafters.

We were cringing against the wall to make room for three young men carrying enormous, rounded stones when Dieter emerged from the back of the inn, clutching his cell phone and looking worried.

"Lora! Don't tell me you already heard?"

"Heard what?"

"Our yodeling pop group had to cancel. Apparently some sort of stomach flu."

"Oh. No, no, I hadn't heard. That's not good, right?"

"That's why I booked three events," Dieter said. His voice was still confident, but I could tell that he was mentally sifting through how to handle this.

"I, uh…" I started.

The phone in Dieter's hand buzzed again. "Just a minute." He turned his back on me and spoke into the receiver. "What? What do you mean?" He listened intently. "Well, find someone else. What about Andre? No, I see."

He hung up the phone and looked at me, his face grim. "We have a problem. That was our alphornist. He's also come down with the stomach flu." He shook his head. "It's not even flu season, for god's sake. That leaves us with the steinstossen lesson, which is fine. The steinstossen champion is actually a pretty funny guy. Maybe I can ask him to stretch it out a bit."

Another buzz from Dieter's phone. He looked at the display screen. "It can't be." He picked up the phone with an unnaturally hearty voice. "Schumacher. Yes, I…stomach flu? I hear it's going around. Do you know if your brother would be able to come? I see. Well, I'm sure we'll manage."

"Was that the rock-throwing guy?" I asked, horrified.

"It was," Dieter said, putting the phone in his pocket. "Three acts, all sick. What are the chances? And more to the point, what are we supposed to do? I looked at fifty acts to come up with those three." He looked at the ceiling. "Okay, let me think. I know an interpretative dance group. Maybe we can do something with them…"

Pinkie stepped in front of me. "Dieter, I think I may have the solution to your problem."

"Prince Philippe! Have you come to join our dinner?" He glanced at me. "Not a bad idea. A real prince. Very authentic."

"Well, unfortunately he's not an authentic *Swiss* prince," I reminded him.

Pinkie sniffed. "Given the grasp that most Americans have on geography and history, I really don't see that as a problem. But no, Dieter, I'm not here to add authenticity to the proceedings. I'm here to ask you to help right a very grave injustice."

"A grave injustice?" Dieter's brow furrowed. "This isn't related to that car outside, is it?"

"My god, you really do know Pinkie, don't you?"

Pinkie scowled at me. "I count that more as a grave insult to my dignity. The grave injustice is something altogether more serious. Do you have somewhere private we can talk?"

"If you've got a way to get us out of a four-hour dinner with no entertainment at all, you better believe I do," Dieter said grimly, leading us through the tables and into his office. He closed the door and gestured for us to sit down. "Do you two want to tell me what's going on here?"

"We…" I started.

Pinkie held up a hand to stop me. "We need your help to solve a robbery and a homicide that could destroy the entire Swiss banking system."

Dieter took off his glasses and polished them for a moment. "Well, that does sound rather important. But I can't ask Jack Green to come back another day so that I can help save the Swiss banking system, Philippe. I'm in the middle of a crisis here. My business is on the line."

Pinkie shook his head. "I'm not asking you to postpone the dinner so that we can save the Swiss banking system. I'm asking you to let us *use* the dinner to help capture a killer and save the Swiss banking system."

Dieter sighed. "Isn't this one of those things that we pay policemen to do? Unless you're working for the police these days, Philippe?"

"Given my skills in this area, they should be so lucky. But no… Policemen work with hard evidence, and in this case there's simply not enough evidence to convict someone. Unfortunately, that hasn't stopped them from arresting someone. Do you know Reiner Hoffmann?"

"From Richter and Partners?" Dieter asked, shocked. "I do."

"He is currently being held on suspicion of the Fat Cat murder."

Dieter scoffed. "He can't be the Fat Cat killer. That boy's devoted his entire life to becoming a Fat Cat."

"I don't think he's the killer either, but there is evidence tying him to the scene, and the police seem to think that they've got their man."

That was a bit of an exaggeration, but I figured that under the circumstances, I could let it slide.

Dieter shook his head. "What do you want me to do?"

"I want you to do what any savvy Swiss businessman would do when contemplating a major expansion of your business. I want you to bring in your bankers to help you evaluate the opportunity. Invite them to the dinner tonight."

Dieter looked confused. "But I bank with Richter and Partners. You just said that Reiner was in jail."

"That's right," I said, "but there are three other partners in Richter and Partners, correct?"

Dieter looked hard at Pinkie. "If you're saying that one of those men is a killer, I'm going to have to tell you that you're making a mistake. I've known Hubert and Gerhard most of my life, and Arnaud all of his life. I knew his father, too. They are all as honorable as it's possible for men to be."

Pinkie nodded. "I completely agree. I didn't say that one of them was a killer—I just said that I needed them at the dinner. Can you make it happen?"

Dieter shrugged. "Of course. We've banked with them for years. I'm sure they would come if I asked." Suddenly, his focus sharpened. "Scheisse. It's a client, isn't it?"

Pinkie held up a hand. "I can't say any more. Just have them here."

"I'll do it. But what about the rest of the dinner? Do we still go with the Swiss theme?"

Pinkie glanced at his watch. "It's got to be Swiss, but we need something that's going to provide the right atmosphere. Something serious, dignified, and low key."

An elderly man in a fluffy shirt with a hat, pipe, and an earring wandered over to engage a buxom bar maid in conversation. We watched him in silence.

"Serious and dignified," Dieter said, sighing. "I was really going more for 'fun' Switzerland."

Pinkie shook his head. "We've got six hours to make some changes. How many people do you have helping today?"

"Practically an army. Actually literally half of the army company I command."

I was impressed. "You co-opted the Swiss Army to help with your dinner? I didn't know you were allowed to do that. What a perk!"

"No," Dieter said, looking horrified. "That would be completely forbidden. I told the boys that if they wanted to lend a hand for a few hours today, I'd provide a DJ and an open bar for them to throw a party in the fields behind the inn afterward."

"And that worked?"

"There's nothing to do in Maennedorf," Pinkie reminded me.

Dieter smiled. "Except tonight, apparently. It seems like tonight we're going to be very busy indeed."

35

When it comes right down to it, the difference between being an event planner and being an army commander is one of objective more than technique. And while I prefer being an event hostess to being an event planner (mostly because I prefer drinking champagne to pouring it), I've done my share of both jobs.

So the next time someone tells you that commanding an army is hard work, tell them this: Commanding an army of fit, obedient minions is far easier than commanding a loose collection of semi-employed waitresses, DJs who think they should be spinning disks on the beach in Ibiza, and chefs who manage to subsist on nothing but arrogance and cocaine. In fact, as far as I can tell, the only thing that keeps event planners from taking over the world is the feckless nature of their support staff. If they had half a company of Swiss soldiers to get things done, the world would be groveling at their Jimmy Choos.

Dieter had made the calls as requested, and Hubert, Gerhardt, and Arnaud had all agreed to come. "I don't get it," I told Pinkie. "They're looking at a loss of eighty-three million dollars and the possible arrest for murder of their newest partner. Why are they willing to show up at Dieter's house to help him with a business deal that hasn't even materialized?"

Pinkie shook his head. "That's exactly why they're showing up. They need to show their clients that nothing has changed, and while Dieter's not the richest client they have, he's a well-respected member of the business community here, and his family has banked with Richter and Partners for decades. If any of this comes out, they're going to be able to point back at this and show that they were able to take care of their clients even in the middle of a crisis.

"Pretty good theory."

"And it's probably even true. Except in the case of Arnaud. That's not why he's coming."

"Why is he coming?"

"He's coming because you're here." Pinkie looked at me seriously. "Arnaud may come across as light and fun, but he's pretty old fashioned in the romance department. I can tell by the way that he looks at you that he's interested."

I shook my head. "I wish I knew how tonight was going to end up."

Pinkie gave me a sad smile. "Be careful what you wish for. Given what we know now, I think it might have been better if we'd never found that ledger."

"Are you having second thoughts?"

Pinkie shook his head. "I know you like to joke about me being a prince, but the one thing I do understand is duty. And we have a duty to make sure we know what happened. Not just because it's the right thing to do, but because lives will be ruined if we don't find out what happened to that gold."

I touched him on the shoulder. "Lives will be ruined either way."

Pinkie sighed. "Sometimes duty involves hard choices." He was silent for a moment and then visibly shook off his black mood.

"And speaking of hard choices, what are you going to do about super spy? I couldn't help but notice that you were on the verge of carnal relations the last time I saw you with him."

I thought back to Benjamin's face when my brother had asked about whether he had killed people. I sighed. "I don't know what that is. He makes me crazy most of the time."

"Crazy like you want to have sex with him or crazy like you want to strangle him?"

"Both, unfortunately."

"I had kind of thought you might give Arnaud a shot."

I thought about Arnaud and gave a sad shrug. "I had kind of thought the same thing. Maybe I still can. I guess we'll see where things stand after tonight."

"And Benjamin?"

"I can't have a relationship with someone whose life is a lie, Pinkie."

Pinkie nodded sagely and put his arm around my shoulders. "But you can have casual sex with someone whose life is a lie. I've done it. It works out fine."

I laughed. "I'll let you know."

Pinkie gave me a serious look. "But if you decide Benjamin isn't what you're looking for, just promise me one thing."

"What's that?"

"Promise me you'll tell him that if he's anything other than a zero on the Kinsey scale, he should give me a call. I don't need the hard truth if the rest of him is hard enough."

"Pinkie!" I laughed.

"I'm just saying that I love a bad boy with repression issues, particularly when he's on the rebound."

"And here I thought you were going to make a play for Officer Hottie."

"I don't like to be tied down. Wait. That's completely not true. I love to be tied down, particularly if the ropes are just a little bit tight…"

I put my hand on his mouth to stop that train of thought. "Can we get back to dinner? We've got six hours to put together an event that's going to land Dieter a business deal with Jack Green, obliterate that cow Vanessa St. Germain, and catch a murderer. What did you have in mind?"

36

After a day spent organizing the world's most authentic, murderer-catching dinner, I had to admit that all I wanted to do was raid Pinkie's Veuve stash and collapse into bed. Instead, I took a quick shower and put on high heels that matched my teal Max Mara dress and climbed back in the Smart Car with Pinkie, who was dressed in light wool pants, a custom made button -down shirt, and a rather somber-looking silver ascot.

For once, Pinkie got into the car without comment, and we rode in silence to Dieter's place, each lost in our own thoughts.

Below us, the lake shone pink as it reflected the color of the setting sun. As we pulled into the drive, we caught sight of the Alps. There was the faintest gleam of white on the highest peaks, a reminder that while summer in Zurich was beautiful, winter was never completely gone here.

The sparklingly clean cows gave us a wide berth this time, no doubt wary of Pinkie. A single light shone in the house, on the porch, where we had set up a bar and some chairs on the terrace. Thanks to our labors of the afternoon, there was literally nothing to do except pour a glass of champagne and look at the lake while we waited for our guests. The chirping of crickets and muffled clanking of cow bells were the loudest sounds to be heard and I felt about a million miles away from my apartment in Brooklyn.

"Do you ever think about leaving New York and moving back to a place like this?" I asked Pinkie.

"God, no. You can't find a decent bagel in this entire country. I'd never survive."

"Just so long as you have your priorities straight."

"Always," Pinkie assured me.

We heard the silky purr of a luxury automobile engine and looked down the drive, where a Mercedes was slowly climbing the hill toward the house. "And that should be Jack," I said.

"Have you met him before?" Dieter asked.

"Not in person, no. People say that he's very tough, very detail focused, and about the size of a house."

Pinkie looked at me. "So more or less like you'll be if you don't lay off the truffles, right?"

We stood up as the car pulled to a stop in front of Dieter's house. Given what I'd heard, I mentally pictured Marlon Brando in *The Godfather*, but possibly with more pink. Apparently Pinkie had the same thought, because when Jack Green stepped out of the car, he gasped out loud.

"Thor!" he whispered.

I stifled a laugh. With his long blonde hair and massive physique, Jack Green did look a lot like Thor. He had the tanned skin and easy grace of a guy who got all of his exercise from mountain climbing, white water rafting, and possibly bear wrestling.

"Mmmm," Pinkie purred. "He's in the hospitality industry, right? What do you think the chances are that he's gay?"

"Pretty good, I'd think." He made a quick scan of our party and locked his eyes onto me in a way that was frankly appreciative.

"Make that zero," I amended.

Pinkie sighed dramatically. "Why are all the good ones straight?"

Jack made his way up the path to the house and took my hand. "Jack Green."

"Lora Godwin. Dieter asked me to help out tonight."

"I heard. I'm surprised you could make it. Vanessa St. Germain gave me the rundown the other night on your recent criminal worries."

I raised my eyebrows. "Really. You'll have to fill me in on that rundown. I find that Vanessa gets things so muddled sometimes."

Jack laughed. "It seems only fair."

I gave him a warm smile and turned to introduce the others.

"This is Dieter, our host, and this is my dear friend, Prince Philippe von Hofstedtler, who will be joining us for dinner." Jack shook hands all around, submitting with a sort of lazy amusement to Pinkie's visual molestation.

"When did you arrive in Switzerland?" I asked. "Oh, and most critically, can I get you a drink?"

"A drink would be great. I got here three nights ago. Thought I'd check out Street Parade. See whether it was something I could add to the Swiss itinerary."

I'd like to say that I tried not to picture Jack wearing something in black leather for Street Parade, but truth be told, once my mind had that picture in it, I was pretty content to let it stay there for a while so that I could appreciate it more fully.

"What did you think?"

"I think it would be a blast. Although we'd probably have to let them go shopping first. Most of our clients don't have a large wardrobe in latex—at least not one that they're willing to admit to."

"You know, by pure coincidence, I happen to know of an Erotik Megamart right outside of town. I'm sure they'd be happy to arrange a private showing for your more bashful clients."

Jack smiled at me. "Well. You seem to be a woman of many talents. We'll have to discuss it further." He looked over at Dieter. "You don't happen to have scotch over there, Dieter, do you?"

"Single malt or Blue Label?"

"Blue, if you've got it," Jack said. He looked around. "Are we it for dinner?"

"Actually, we'll have three additional guests," I said. "Hubert, Gerhardt, and Arnaud. They're the partners of Richter and Partners, which is one of the oldest private banks in Switzerland."

Jack looked confused. "Swiss bankers?"

"What could be more authentic?" I asked, smiling.

Jack looked doubtful but shrugged and took a sip of his drink, a not unnatural reaction on the part of someone facing a lengthy dinner with bankers.

"There they are now," Dieter said. Sure enough, Hubert's Bentley was pulling up the drive. When it pulled to a stop, the three partners made their way up to the porch. I thought back to the dinner we had all attended just a couple of nights ago. All three of them seemed to have aged five years since then. Hubert walked close to Gerhardt, who leaned heavily on his cane as he climbed the stairs to the porch. Even Arnaud looked tired and drawn.

Having never had a fortune or sometimes even enough money to be certain of making rent, I couldn't imagine what it felt like to face the loss of everything I had worked for. If these guys were any indication, it didn't feel good.

"Thank you for inviting us, Dieter," Hubert said, taking Dieter's hand. I made quick introductions all around.

Jack was looking at the bankers speculatively. "So are you here as bankers or as part of the authentic Swiss experience?"

"Can't we be both?" Gerhardt asked, giving him a weary smile. "Our bank has worked with Dieter's family for over fifty years. We are his bankers, yes, but Hubert is also his neighbor, and we are all friends. I guess it doesn't work the same way in America?"

Jack took a sip of drink. "Heck no. I do all my banking on the Internet. I'm all about the convenience."

Gerhardt shook his head. "Convenient, yes, but do you trust the Internet to provide you with understanding about what's happening in regards to your investments, to keep you on course when you hit a rough patch, and even to remember your birthday?"

"Absolutely."

Gerhardt laughed. "It's answers like that that make me look forward to retirement."

I let Gerhardt and Jack trade opinions on the future of banking while I went over to speak to Dieter. "Are we all set with the steinstossen?"

We had decided to go through with the sporting event despite the lack of a coach. We needed something to break the ice, and even without a nuanced explanation of steinstossen's finer points, I figured that a bunch of guys standing around chucking heavy rocks would definitely serve the purpose.

"We're ready." Dieter eyed Jack professionally. "I'll tell the boys from the company not to hold back. Jack looks like the kind of man who likes a little challenge."

I nodded. "Gentlemen, I don't want to interrupt, but before we start our dinner, we have a little outdoor entertainment planned. Dieter, would you care to explain?"

Dieter led the group around to a flat stretch of soil near the barn. A yellow line was laid across one end of the strip, marking the starting point. Lined up in order of size was a series of stones, the smallest of which was about the size of a grapefruit and the largest of which looked like the cornerstone of a castle. Two fit young men were standing around, swinging their arms to warm up.

"Steinstossen is a very old Swiss sport," Dieter said. "It literally translates to stone tossing. The goal is simple. You pick up the rock; you throw it. Your feet cannot cross the yellow line. Whoever throws the rock the farthest is the winner."

Jack smiled and unbuttoned his cuffs. I could tell that this kind of physical sport was right up his alley. He gestured at the row of stones. "Which one do you throw?"

"It varies," Dieter said. "The most famous stone used for steinstossen is 83.5 kilograms—about 180 pounds."

Jack whistled. "That sounds tricky."

"It is, but most competitions these days use top weights closer to 50 kilos. Otherwise too many injuries. I've put out some smaller stones as well so that you can get the feel for it. It's best to start small and work your way up. Johann…do want to demonstrate?"

The young blonde man on the right picked up a grapefruit-sized stone and, lifting it to his shoulder with both hands, steadied it. With a sudden arching motion, he dropped his front hand and pressed the stone forward. The stone arced through the air and landed about ten yards away, which seemed pretty impressive to me.

The other young man quickly ran out to the stone with a tape measure. "Nine point four nine."

Hubert chuckled and raised an eyebrow at Dieter. "What are you doing to these poor boys? Nine and a half meters? When I was young I think the average was ten. Gerhardt himself used to be able to do twelve with a stone that size. Of course, that was a long time ago." He patted Gerhardt on the shoulder.

"Not so long ago," Gerhardt said. He handed Philippe his cane and jacket and walked up to the yellow line, rolling up his sleeves as he went.

I looked at Dieter in alarm. "Uh…I don't think…" I started.

Dieter waved my concerns away, a twinkle in his eye. "Don't worry, Lora. It's good for these young boys to see that not all of us old folks are useless."

Gerhardt picked up the stone, weighing it in his hand. With a slight smile, he hefted the rock to his shoulder and in a smooth, graceful movement, let it fly. Even without measuring, it was obvious that Gerhardt's rock landed a few feet farther than Johann's had been.

Hubert smiled and clapped him on the shoulder as Gerhardt reclaimed his cane and jacket from Pinkie. I couldn't help but notice that Gerhardt was slightly winded.

Jack took his turn next, landing his stone slightly farther than Gerhardt's.

Hubert was impressed. "This is the first time you've done this?"

Jack nodded. "I did some shot put in high school, though. Pretty similar, I guess."

"Ah," Hubert said. "Then you'll need to try the bigger stones. They're completely different."

Arnaud lined up next, landing a respectable throw near Johann's and shooting me a rueful glance. "Not my sport. But you should see me at darts. That's what I get for having studied in England instead of here."

"Yeah, I noticed that Pinkie's not doing much for Oxford's athletic reputation," I said. Pinkie was languidly draped across a bench, champagne in hand, eyes half-closed. To the casual observer, he looked relaxed and perhaps a bit bored, but I could feel the intensity rolling off of him. He was listening, gauging, and preparing for the next part of the evening.

Jack and Johann took turns with a variety of stones, Johann out-throwing Jack on the lighter stones and Jack beating him on the heavier ones, where his massive shoulders and size gave him a clear advantage. Finally, everyone who wanted to had taken their turn, and the contestants collapsed onto benches and sipped their drinks.

"Are all Switzerland's traditional sports so tough?" Jack asked, rubbing his shoulder as he took a sip of his whiskey.

Hubert laughed. "This is the easiest Swiss sport. You should see Waffenlaufen competitions."

"What's that?"

"It's basically running a marathon in army fatigues with a rucksack and a rifle," Dieter said.

"Nice," Jack replied, lifting an eyebrow. "Something to think about for my next vacation." He looked over at Dieter. "What's on the schedule for the rest of the evening? Cow tipping? Yodeling? Cheese-making?"

I took his arm, deflecting his attention. "Dinner."

Jack smiled at me. "Sounds good," he said patting his perfectly flat stomach absently. He turned to start back to the house, and I placed a hand on his chest to stop him.

"Not the inn. Someplace a little more 'authentic.'"

Jack gave a good-natured shrug and allowed me to lead him away from the sand pit and across the fields. The path had been lit with candles in brown paper bags, an effective way both of providing some rustic ambiance and, most importantly, keeping the cows away from our guests. We wound our way through the pastures, which were now almost completely dark. The lights of the towns around the lake were spread out below us.

We came to a stop in front of the tiny building Arnaud and I had seen on our bike ride. Jack raised an eyebrow. "All six of us are going to eat in a port-a-potty?"

"Trust me. It's bigger inside than it looks." I opened the door, revealing a ramp leading down into the ground.

"You gonna fill me in on where we're going?" Jack asked, looking at me.

"All in good time."

"Abandon all hope, ye who enter here," Jack murmured.

I laughed. "I've only been here a couple of days, but I'm pretty sure Hell isn't in Switzerland. Maybe Baltimore."

37

We made our way down the ramp into the bomb shelter. As Arnaud had told me, the room was shaped like a giant igloo, with neatly stacked crates of supplies ringing the outer edges of the space. Although Pinkie and I had spent most of our afternoon directing the work in this room, I still felt my breath catch as I looked around.

Dieter's men had cleared a large space in the middle of the shelter, where we had set up a dining table for six. Eschewing the plain fluorescent bulbs for something more atmospheric, we had strung an old-fashioned candle chandelier over the table, and the twenty beeswax tapers were now flickering, barely illuminating the heavy artillery pieces that were tucked into the corners.

The table itself was a masterpiece in silver and white. In the center, we had placed an antique silver centerpiece that had been in Dieter's family for generations. Modeled in the shape of jagged mountains with tiny rams, it was a thing of beauty. The table linens were a snowy white embroidered by Dieter's mother with a chasing of silver vines. Silver candelabra stood on either end of the long table.

The noise of crickets and cows faded away as we descended the ramp. We had lit only the center of the room, and the faint vision of guns and supplies looming in the shadowed edges of the bunker caused a chill to run over my spine. Like the revelers in Poe's "The Masque of the Red Death," we had created a room filled with luxury and had shut ourselves away from the rest of the world. And just like the ill-fated characters in that story, there was a killer among us.

I looked over the assembly, hoping the careful staging was having an effect. Jack was clearly impressed, but the others were harder to read.

I arranged everyone around the table, putting myself at Jack's right hand and Dieter at his left. "If you all will have a seat, we'll be starting with the first course in a moment. But first I wanted to tell Jack a little bit about where we are and why Dieter and I thought that this place, more than any other, best represented authentic Switzerland."

I gave a quick signal, and one of Dieter's Swiss soldiers materialized with a bottle of wine from a dark corner of the room. Like all of the soldiers here tonight, he was in uniform and wore a rifle strapped to his back.

I waited as the young man filled the glasses. Whether it was the chilly air or the stacked relics of a time when the very survival of the world seemed an open question, the feeling of the company had turned serious—even reverent.

I turned to Jack. "Switzerland has more than three hundred thousand buildings like this. They started building them in the Cold War, but most city codes still require that they be part of any new construction.

"When I first heard about this, I thought it was bizarre, but I've since come to believe that the building of these bunkers, at the cost of literally billions of dollars, says something very fundamental about Swiss culture."

"That they don't like to be bombed?" Jack quipped.

"That they are willing to go to whatever lengths are necessary to protect their people," I said, switching my attention to each of the bank partners in turn. Arnaud nodded slightly. "The Swiss protect their own. At virtually any cost. In America, we think of being neutral as being passive. But in Switzerland, being neutral is a constant struggle. There are bunkers beneath the homes and military bases hidden in the mountains. Every friendly old Swiss man has been trained to handle a weapon—not to conquer but to protect.

"The Swiss tradition of private banks is a good example of that principle in action. Imagine that you have millions upon millions of dollars. You want to put it someplace that it will be safe. Who can you trust? Your family? Your friends? History tells us that doesn't work out very well. When millions of dollars are on the line, your family may turn on you, but your Swiss bankers won't. They will protect your money. They will protect your privacy. They will protect your future."

I spared another glance at the partners, who were listening to me carefully.

"Are you sure about that?" Jack asked. "No offense, but I'm not sure I share your trust in Swiss bankers...current company excepted, of course."

I smiled at him. "I'd hate for you to think I was being naïve, so let me give you an example. A true story, actually. A man comes to a Swiss bank in a time of trouble. He has with him a sizable quantity of gold. Let's call it two thousand kilograms of gold, just for the sake of argument."

I could feel the attention at the table shift, as the partners realized that what had started out as a slightly rambling lesson on history and culture had just gotten dangerously specific.

"A kilogram of gold, by the way, isn't very big."

"About this big," Pinkie said, pulling a phone-sized plate of gold out from under his chair, where we had placed it earlier. He passed it to me, and I handed it to Jack.

"Is this for real?" Jack asked.

"It certainly is."

"Do you always keep one of these in your pocket?" Jack asked, stroking the gold. I understood the temptation. I had held it earlier in the day, and the strange heaviness of the plate and the way it quickly warmed in your hand made it feel almost like a living thing.

"Not in my pocket," Pinkie said. "Ruins the drape of the jacket, you know."

Jack smiled and placed it on the table in front of him, then looked again at me. I could tell that I had his full attention.

"So what happens to our troubled man?"

"The man leaves the gold in the bank, but he sets up very special conditions because he doesn't know whether he'll be able to come back for it right away. In fact, he's heading back into a war, and he knows it's a war that he probably won't win. So he tells the bank that the gold will stay in a private vault. They set up an account number and a pass phrase. And whoever is able to provide those two pieces of information can claim the gold. Tomorrow. Next week. Or in seventy years."

I paused for breath.

"That man goes back to his life, knowing that his gold is safe. He doesn't trust his government or his family, but he trusts his banker. But is his gold really safe?"

Jack raised his eyebrows. "You told me it was safe."

"It should be. The box the gold is stored in a locked box in a vault. The vault is cut into the stone beneath Zurich and the only door can only be opened by the keys of two partners, turned together. To even get to the vault's door requires the bank's manager to open yet another door. The gold itself is heavy...two thousand plates the size of that one there...not something that you can move without a forklift. How safe is his gold?" I look at Jack questioningly.

"Pretty safe, I'd guess," he admitted.

"But the next person who opens that vault, many years later, finds that the gold has been taken. Replaced, in fact, with plaster replicas so that anyone who doesn't actually touch the gold will never spot the difference."

I heard a sharp intake of breath from Hubert, and from the corner of my eye I saw Arnaud start from his chair, as if to jump up and shush me.

"So who took the gold?" Jack asked me, his eyes shining.

"Who do you think?"

Jack thought for a moment. "The vault door needs to be unlocked by two partners?"

"Two partners," I confirmed. "And the partners are responsible for the keys. They are always in the partners' possession, either locked away at home or on the partners themselves."

Jack shrugged his shoulders. "Easy. It's a conspiracy. Two of the partners conspired together to take the gold. Am I right?" He looked at Hubert, assuming, I guess, that he was just confirming the facts of a case that had already been solved. Hubert's face had drained of color.

"That would never happen," he said flatly. He looked at me, a man who had seen more loss in the last three days than most people see in a lifetime. I wanted to drop my gaze, but I looked back at him steadily, searchingly.

"You're right. That's not what happened." There was a

collective intake of breath from the partners, and Arnaud suddenly gave me a questioning look.

I avoided his gaze. "Pinkie, could you please give Hubert the ledger from 1972?"

Pinkie drew the ledger from beneath his chair and walked slowly over to Hubert. Six pairs of eyes tracked its motion as he laid it on ceremonially on the table.

"What is this?" Jack asked.

"This is the key to the mystery."

We all looked silently at the book.

"I thought the ledgers were stolen from your car." Arnaud said. "Where did this book come from?"

Jack gave me a piercing look, realizing for the first time that we weren't talking about ancient history.

"They were, but one of them slipped out of the bag and managed to get wedged under the seat. Whoever took the books didn't have time to count them, I guess."

Hubert touched the cover of the book. "You're saying that the answer to who took the gold is in this book? How can that be?"

"Open it," I said.

Hubert flipped the book open to the middle, and everyone craned their necks forward to see. "What is this?" he asked, shock in his voice. "The whole book has been destroyed. Why would someone do that?"

Whoever had vandalized the book had cut a hole through the pages, leaving the edges of the paper intact. Closed, it looked like a book. Open, it looked like a box.

Jack picked up the bar of gold and slotted it into the hole. It took up precisely one quarter of the space inside the book. "So they could do this. Four bars of gold in each book." He looked at me with a raised eyebrow. "Two thousand bars? That's a lot of trips."

"You're right," I admitted. "It is a lot of trips. More than a hundred visits over thirteen years."

Jack shook his head. "Wouldn't people notice?"

"Not if that someone had a very good reason for being in the vault."

Hubert suddenly looked stricken as he realized what I was saying. "No. You're wrong."

"It's the only person it could have been," I said softly.

Hubert shook his head. "You're saying that my wife stole the gold? Helen never would have done that. She couldn't have. She needed two partner keys," he finished triumphantly. "Maybe she could have gotten mine. The spare key. She knew where I kept it. But none of the other partners would have given her their key." He looked at Arnaud, seeking support. "Right?"

Arnaud bit his lip and shook his head, silent.

I plowed on. "Helen took that gold. But she couldn't have done it without someone's help. And not just someone. The help of one of the partners."

Hubert shook his head. "That's absurd, Lora. What on earth are you talking about?"

"Let me tell you. Two weeks ago, a man came from Germany with a passcode and an account number. He was coming to claim eighty-three million dollars in gold. Gold that his grandfather had stolen. That man, Horst Mueller, was murdered—killed by someone who knew what he was coming for and knew that the gold he was coming to claim was no longer there. Killed by someone who didn't want to see the bank ruined."

"That's ridiculous," Arnaud said. "Gerhardt and Hubert are the only bank partners who were around back then. Reiner's father and my father are both dead."

I nodded. "But responsibility in this bank is passed down from father to son. Any of you could have left that dinner, gone to Mueller's hotel, gone up to his room to wait for him, and killed him and pushed him over the balcony."

Pinkie suddenly sat up straight. "Wait a minute. Not anyone, Lora. Remember what Margrit said? The hotel didn't have an elevator. Gerhardt could never have managed the stairs." Everyone's eyes swiveled to Gerhardt's cane.

Pinkie was right. Gerhardt would have struggled to climb the stairs. He would have been seen. The hotel staff would have remembered. Who did that leave?

Hubert looked at me, confusion evident on his face. "You think I did it? You think I helped my own wife steal from my own bank?"

I shook my head, trying to put the pieces together. "There are four keys to this. First, the person had to know the gold was missing and how it was taken. They could have known that because they helped Helen take the gold, or they could have known that because someone told them about it.

"Second, they had to be able to find who had opened the account. Apparently those accounts weren't as anonymous as advertised. Reiner managed to find the owner in just a few days, using what my brother described as 'pretty basic' computer skills. So I'd say we're looking for someone with computer skills."

"So we're back to Reiner being the killer," Arnaud said.

"I don't think so. Reiner found Mueller and inadvertently alerted Mueller to the gold, but Reiner's next step was to look into ways he could launder the money. There was no money to launder. It wasn't Reiner."

Jack had been watching this unfold with interest. "If it wasn't Gerhardt because he couldn't climb the stairs and it wasn't Reiner because he didn't know the money was missing, that leaves only one answer." He looked at Arnaud. "You."

Arnaud stood up, his eyes wide in disbelief. "You are insane. Lora, for god's sake, I know we haven't known each other for long, but surely you don't think I killed someone for money."

I shook my head, stricken. It all fit. The computer skills. The fact that he stayed with the bank after presumably having inherited a stack of gold. "You didn't do it for money, Arnaud. You did it to protect the bank from ruin. And if your father knew that the gold was missing, I think the real reason you did it was to protect Hubert from knowing that his wife, the woman he loved more than anyone, betrayed him with your father."

A moment of silence descended on the table as all eyes turned to Arnaud. Out of the corner of my eye, I saw a few of Dieter's soldiers materialize from the shadows, guns held at the ready.

Arnaud looked at me, his mouth open to explain.

"Enough," Gerhardt said, his voice a wheeze. "Arnaud didn't kill Mueller. I did."

38

The air in the bunker seemed to waver for a moment as the patterns of history shuffled in everyone's minds. Gerhardt, the ladies' man. Gerhardt, whose wife was an invalid.

"I'm so sorry, Hubert," Gerhardt said, "I never meant for you to find out."

Hubert sat down as though he'd been punched. "How could you?"

"I tried not to. We both tried. We both loved you, you know. But I loved her, too. I would never have said anything to her. But I came over one night, late, to talk to you. Sarina was still very young then, and Helen was on her own. You were away with a client somewhere. She was lonely. And she kissed me. And god help me, I should have run out of that house, but I didn't."

"Did she love you?" Hubert asked in a broken voice.

Gerhardt passed his hand over his eyes. "I thought so at the time. But now I just don't know. She loved danger and excitement. She was like a wild animal trapped in this life. Responsibility, order, duty." He let out a noise that was part cough, part sob. "She loved you, but she told me she felt like she was dying a little more each day."

I weighed the silence, unsure if I should push further. "Tell us about the gold," I said softly.

"Helen loved history," Gerhardt said. "That, at least, was true. And she was a very gifted researcher. She was working in a time before the Internet, you understand, and she had a knack for making connections that nobody else could see. That and, of course, she was very charming. People talked to her, told her things. Sometimes things that would have been better left unsaid.

"She knew about the gold in that vault. We all did. It was part of our firm's history—a point of shame and a point of pride. Someday a man would show up with a number and a phrase. And we would, in effect, hand him seventy-five million francs."

"And if you didn't give him the money, nobody would ever know," Jack said.

"That's it," Gerhardt said, his eyes alight. "There were no paper trails...just a handshake agreement based on trust. We could have taken that money and walked away with it and just denied that the account had ever existed. Nobody would ever have known. It would have been the perfect crime."

"We would have known," Hubert said sharply.

"Exactly. It's who we are. Or at least, who I thought I was. Helen knew these ledgers inside and out. She managed to put together the clues—a comment in Reiner's uncle's ledger, a note in the bank manager's files—and she figured out who had deposited that gold. She knew where that gold came from."

"Where did the gold come from?" Jack asked.

"The account was opened in 1945," Arnaud said bitterly. "I'm sure you can work out where it came from."

Gerhardt shook his head. "There's no need to tiptoe around it. It came from the camps. The Nazis kept excellent records, you know. That gold was taken from teeth and money that they seized from prisoners before they gassed them. It was blood money. We should never have touched it."

"What happened?" Hubert asked.

"Helen told me that she knew where the gold came from. She became obsessed with it. She worried that someone would come to claim it. And what if the person who claimed it was just as evil as the person who had deposited it?"

Gerhardt shook his head. "I told her not to be silly...that the gold would probably never be claimed. But she said we had to be sure. I don't know whether she really believed that or she just wanted something exciting to do. An intellectual puzzle with an eighty-three million-dollar payoff. It wasn't hard to do, of course. She would come in to do research when Arnaud's father and I were on duty. She always had access to Hubert's safe at home, of course. He trusted her implicitly. All she had to do was take the spare key."

Hubert's mouth twisted at this.

"Ludwig, the bank manager, would let her into the vault so that she could start working with the records, and then we would have the daily partners' meeting. With all of us upstairs, the vault was not open to customers. She dropped her bag off with Frau Backer, keeping only whatever ledgers she had checked out the previous evening. She keyed into the deposit vault using Hubert's and my keys, replaced the real gold with replicas she had smuggled in the books, keyed out, placed the real gold bricks into the ledger, and started her research."

"Why bother with the replicas?" Dieter asked. "Why not just take the gold?"

"New partners do a visual confirmation of the gold," Arnaud said. "I did when I was made partner as well. But you're not allowed to touch anything." He shook his head. "Only someone who really knew the bank—knew everything about it, really—could have done this."

We all sat for a moment in silence. In the face of so much pain, I wanted to drop it. But an innocent man's freedom was hanging in the balance. "You knew who the gold belonged to," I told Gerhardt.

"Oh yes," he said. "Mueller. I never would have looked into it myself, but when Helen showed me her research, I hired someone to confirm it. The gold had been deposited by the grandfather, but he returned to Germany to fight to the bitter end. He was killed, and his son never knew about the gold. The family lived in poverty for many years."

"Until the grandson grew up," I said.

Gerhardt shrugged. "When I hired the investigator, Horst was still in school. He was smart and savvy, and despite his family's poverty it was clear that he would make something of himself. But even when he was young, he was involved in these right-wing organizations. Never openly. He was too smart for that. He supported laws that would have closed Germany's borders. He supported expulsion of people who weren't German by race."

"You're saying that the guy who owned that gold was a neo-Nazi?" Jack asked.

Gerhardt nodded. "But not the kind you're thinking of. He

wasn't the skinhead young man covered in tattoos, drunk on the street corner and shouting ethnic slurs at women in head scarves. He was a middle-class businessman who slowly but surely was building a way to get money to right-wing parties. In recent years, he had been moving beyond politics, exploring fringe groups. Violent people. But then, suddenly, the men I had hired to watch the Muellers caught wind of something new. The legacy. And he gave me a call."

"You pretended to go to bed after the partner dinner, but you really went to meet Horst Mueller," I prompted.

"Not to meet him," Gerhardt corrected.

"To kill him," Pinkie said, his voice breaking.

Gerhardt smiled sadly. "Nobody ever sees an old man as a threat, but old men have the most to protect. Our bank. Hubert." He shook his head. "I wasn't sure how I was going to manage it, truth be told. I was hoping I'd catch him, drunk perhaps, on the way back into his hotel, but when I got there, he was already upstairs."

"But Margrit said there was no elevator. How did you get up the stairs?"

Jack banged a hand on the table. "He didn't go up the stairs. He threw a rock!"

Gerhardt gave him a sad smile that held the faintest hint of pride. "I did indeed. He went out on the balcony to smoke a cigarette. I picked up a stone—there were several in the garden. I threw it." He shrugged. "The reflexes are still there. The stone struck him. He fell. I found the stone a few yards away, and I put it back in the garden and walked away."

"Just like that?" Jack asked.

"Just like that. The man was a petty thug who was about to become a monster. I felt no guilt. Not about that, anyway," he said, looking at Hubert.

"The next morning everyone said it was the Fat Cat killer, and I almost could believe I'd had nothing to do with it...but of course I had. And that's all there is to tell, I think."

"Not quite," I said. "You sent people to shoot at us!"

"That's right," Pinkie said, shaking his finger at Gerhardt. "Who were those guys? I mean, you're a Swiss banker, not a Mafia don."

Gerhardt sighed. "In the forty years I've been working for this bank, I've met all kinds of people. When I heard that you were going to retrieve the ledgers, I called an old friend and told him I had a rather delicate situation and I needed some support."

"You called hired killers to take back the ledgers?"

"They weren't killers," Gerhardt said, sighing. "They were actors. You were never in any danger."

"They were very convincing," I said, remembering the terror I had felt as we had been forced to flee the parking garage with nothing but a miniature plastic erotic car between us and killers.

Gerhardt sighed, searching out Hubert with his eyes. "And now, I think that really is all," he said. "Hubert...I know you will never be able to forgive me, but I hope you know that I've lived with this guilt now for twenty years. Not a day has gone by when I didn't wish I could take it back."

Hubert remained silent, his face stoic and his eyes shiny. There would be no scenes of forgiveness tonight, I suspected.

"Aren't you all forgetting something?" Jack asked. "Where's the gold?"

"I haven't the slightest idea," Gerhardt said. "Helen never told me what she was doing with it. She just said that she was keeping it somewhere safe. And then when she died, I just blocked out the whole thing. I'm not a spiritual man. I guess that's clear by now. But I think about that gold sometimes. I think about how that fortune came to be. Money seized from people who didn't get out in time. Teeth pulled out of the jaws of the dead. And I tell you, I think that gold will bring ruin to everyone who touches it."

"There's another possibility," I said, realization dawning on me. "It might still be with Helen."

"Helen's dead," Hubert said flatly.

"Is she? Isn't it possible that she decided to take the gold, not to keep it out of the hands of evil men—not even to right an ancient wrong—but just to fund a life that suited her? How hard is it to fake a death?"

"I'll never believe that," Hubert said, his voice cracking. "She would never abandon us that way. Not just me. Sarina, too. She loved us."

Arnaud looked at me, anger clear on his face. "I think you have what you need. You don't need to keep torturing him, do you? What does it matter anymore? She's gone. The gold is gone. It's over." The look he gave me made it clear that whatever might have been between him and me was over as well.

I dropped my eyes. He was right. A youthful indiscretion with a handsome man, the theft of ill-gotten gains—maybe these things could be reconciled in Hubert's mind. But not the abandonment of her family. If he believed that of her, his entire married life had been a lie.

Dieter cleared his throat. "Boys?"

Four members of Dieter's army company materialized from the shadows, guns at the ready. "Hans," Dieter said, pointing to one of the young men, "I think you'll need to call the police."

"No, you won't," came a voice from the shadows. Margrit emerged from behind a stack of boxes. "Honestly, Philippe, I should arrest you for interfering in police business...again."

"You called Margrit?" Hubert asked, looking at Pinkie.

"Well, someone had to. Otherwise she would have convicted the wrong man. Although I think we can agree that convicting Reiner of something heinous is only a matter of time. He's almost as horrible as that brother of hers."

"We're the Swiss police," Margrit said. "We never convict the wrong man." She looked at Gerhardt sadly. "Herr Kantor," she said formally, "it is my duty to place you under arrest for the murder of Horst Mueller."

Arnaud gripped Gerhardt's arm, clearly torn.

Gerhardt smiled weakly and patted his hand. "Don't worry, Arnaud. I've been waiting for this for twenty years. I think I was really just holding on for my wife. When she got sick, I realized how far I had strayed from being the man I thought I was. I broke it off with Helen the day we got the diagnosis. People always looked at me like I was a saint for taking care of her, but the truth is that she saved me. I'm only happy that she's not alive to see this."

Margrit motioned to a couple of the soldiers. "If you gentlemen can give me a hand, I'd appreciate it."

"And you," she said, looking at Pinkie. "You'd better plan on meeting me tomorrow before your flight. I'll need a statement from you. And you'd better be prepared to come back here for the trial."

Pinkie nodded silently. As Gerhardt was slowly led away, I could see Pinkie brush a hand across his eyes. Pinkie had loved Gerhardt as a boy, and to see his hero disgraced clearly affected him. I spared a glance at Hubert, who was clinging to Arnaud's arm as though it was the only stable thing in the room.

I felt another wave of doubt at what we had done here tonight. Gerhardt would spend the rest of his life in prison. Hubert would forever wonder whether his unfaithful wife had really died or left him to mourn while she made a new life for herself with the money she had stolen from the bank. The partners would still be personally ruined as they tried to make up the loss of seventy-five million francs. And all for what? To punish someone for killing a despicable racist? To keep a blackmailer from a wrongful conviction of murder? I felt sick.

"If you'll excuse us," Hubert said, his voice hollow, "I will ask Arnaud to take me home. I'm afraid I don't feel well enough to continue this evening."

"Of course," Arnaud said, shooting me another hostile look.

"If you want us to stay someplace else tonight..." I started.

Hubert shook his head. "I don't blame you for this. How could I? For three generations, we've been trained in only two things, and one of those things is to put our honor and the honor of the bank above all personal concerns."

"What's the second thing?" Jack asked.

"To keep going even when things are at their darkest point," Hubert said wistfully. "Because sometimes it's hard for even the most honorable men to do the right thing."

39

Once they'd left, Jack, Dieter, Pinkie, and I sat around the table. "That was…" Jack started.

"Excruciating?" I asked.

Jack nodded slowly. "Yes, but probably the most amazing thing I've ever seen. I've gotta tell you, Dieter, Vanessa and Ueli put together a solid program, but this takes the cake."

Dieter looked concerned. "I'm afraid that I can't get someone to confess to murder every time a tour group comes through. We don't have that many murders in Switzerland."

Jack laughed. "No…just this. This place. And the talk about Switzerland, how it protects people. Protects its way of life. It's a whole other way of looking at things. God, I tell you I was expecting raclette and beer and accordions and god knows what else."

"Never," Dieter said. "We had planned a yodeling pop duo, though. Crossed Flags, they're called. Lovely girls. Very popular."

"Crossed Flags," Jack mused. "Why does that name ring a bell…"

"And I hired Antoine Mauer. He's one of the best alphornists in Switzerland. Honestly, I wish he could have made it tonight. He's as Swiss as they come, straight from the mountains. And a memory as long as time. Part of the reason he wanted to come here tonight was because he got into a fight twenty years ago with Ueli, and he knew that we were both auditioning with you for the contract."

Jack held a hand up. "Wait a minute. Antoine Mauer and Crossed Flags. Their names were on two boxes I saw at Vanessa's place when I first got here. She invited me to stop by when I first got into town so that she could give me the rundown on Street Parade."

"What kind of boxes?" I asked, suddenly paying close attention.

Jack scratched his chin. "About so big," he said, spreading his giant paws to indicate a small six-inch square. "They were wrapped in green paper with a yellow ribbon. There were three of them, just sitting on the hall in the entry. I didn't see the name on the third."

"Chocolates," I said, remembering Vanessa coming out of the Teuscher store.

Pinkie perked up. "Didn't she get you a box of chocolates, too, Lora?"

"Yes, she did. She's quite something, our friend Vanessa. Very thoughtful."

"She struck me that way, too," Jack said. "Lovely woman."

"Lovely," I echoed, clenching my hands into fists.

Jack turned his attention back to Dieter. "But back to the program. I don't need a murderer every night, but we've got to have a bar of gold like this to pass around. It's the most unbelievable feeling."

"Don't get attached," Dieter said. "I have to take it back to the bank tomorrow. Philippe asked if I could take one out to show the fit for the book."

Jack patted the gold. "I'm going to get one of these to keep on my nightstand so that I can rub it when I have trouble sleeping." He looked around the bunker. "You know, we never actually got to eat dinner."

I looked over the silver table. "We can have them bring it to us here if you're hungry, but I think we lost a couple of our servers."

"Well, as atmospheric as this place is, I think we can go back up to the inn." Jack picked the ledger up from the table. "I guess you'll need to take this to the police. They'll probably want it as evidence."

I opened the book and traced the cut pages with my finger. "I can't imagine going into the vault day after day and sneaking gold out like Helen did. I'm really not that good under pressure."

"You just managed to simultaneously land a big client and get someone to confess to murder," Jack said. "I was a Navy SEAL for ten years, lady, and I can tell you that you might want to update your definition of pressure."

I smiled. "Dieter, do you have any guys who can run this book over to the police? I think Margrit's probably had enough of me at this point."

"Sure," Dieter said, taking the book. "I always wondered what they kept in these books. He flipped through a couple of the uncut pages at the end. "Nothing interesting. Birthdays, anniversaries. God, being a banker must be the most boring job in the world." Dieter stopped for a second. "Someone from your family is in this one, Philippe."

Pinkie perked up. "You're kidding. What does it say? Does it say that he bought a watch?"

Dieter scanned it. "Let's see. 'Talked to Prince von Hofstedtler about the Patek Philippe he was considering and pointed out that given his recent setbacks, this might not be the best time to spend money. He said he's buying it for himself—he's buying it for the next generation.'"

"Prince vH again! Dammit," Pinkie said in frustration. "That still doesn't tell me which prince."

"There's more," Dieter said. "'Next generation' vH due in November—tell Janet to send a gift. Also pass on story to H. Stern. Possible ad campaign?'"

Pinkie jumped to his feet. "November! *My* birthday's in November."

"And your cousin's birthday?" I prompted him.

"May," Pinkie said. "My god. That's the proof I needed. I'm having this book bronzed. Or better yet, gold plated."

He looked at me. "I'm going with the soldier to take this down to Margrit right this second. Do you want to come?"

I looked at him skeptically. "Isn't that a little tacky? I mean, chasing after your watch when so much has happened?"

"Not at all. Now, making sure that I'm down there when Reiner finds out that I saved him from lifetime in a Swiss prison—that's pretty tacky. But I'm okay with that. I think reality television has desensitized me to tackiness."

"You go ahead. But Pinkie…" I stopped, unsure of what to say. "You remember what Maurice said. About what he would tell Hubert. Are you sure you want to take that risk?"

Pinkie looked at me seriously. "Whatever happened with Jurg all those years ago, I have to trust that Hubert did the honorable thing."

I nodded, and he grabbed the book and followed the soldier up the ramp.

Dieter rubbed a hand over his face wearily. "Jack, if you want to discuss business now, I'm happy to join you. Or I can leave you alone to finish dinner with Lora."

Jack raised an eyebrow at me. "To be honest, I think we can work out the particulars tomorrow. Lora seems like she's more than capable of keeping me entertained. Shall we go on up?" he asked me, gesturing at the ramp. "Ladies first."

40

Dinner went on longer than I expected, mostly because Jack was such good company. He told me horror stories of clients who wanted air conditioning in their Mongolian yurts and gluten-free bread while camping in mountains of Peru, and I countered with a recap of my last job, where I had ended up on a boat full of white slavers.

We laughed a lot, and while I was sure that part of it was just a way of feeling normal again after the revelations of the day, part of it was just pleasure in each other's company.

"You know that I was expecting you to be gay," I told him.

"Gay? Why?"

"It's industry standard. High-end tours? Impeccable taste? I tell you, I've never seen Pinkie so disappointed. How on earth did you manage to get into this profession?"

Jack grinned. "It wasn't so much that I wanted to get into this profession as that I wanted to get out of my last one. Navy SEAL."

"You mentioned that. You got tired of putting your life at risk?"

Jack waved that away. "That was the best part of the job. No, it wasn't that. I got dumped by a really wonderful woman—a veterinarian. Susan. It was my fault. I had stood her up three times. Not out of rudeness. Just a normal part of the job. And when she called me on it, I told her that my job was important, that I was saving people, and that asking me to put that on hold for her was pure selfishness."

"Oof. How did that go over?"

"Not well," he admitted. "She's married to an accountant now. Three kids and three dogs. He's not out saving the world, but she tells me he's home for dinner every night."

"And you?"

"I was pissed, obviously. But eventually I realized that you can be a hero or you can be a person, but you can't be both. I decided not to be a hero." He smiled. "I know. What a complete ass, right? What kind of guy tells a woman he cares about that she should just suck it up and wait because he's out saving the world?"

I gave him a half smile, thinking of Benjamin. "Oh…I've been meaning to ask you. What was Vanessa St. Germain's big surprise? She seemed pretty sure that it would win you over."

Jack choked on his beer slightly. "It was pretty surprising," he admitted.

"Are you blushing?"

"Absolutely not."

"Are you going to tell me?"

"A gentleman never tells. Let's just say that she offered me the opportunity to explore some of Switzerland's less famous peaks and valleys."

My jaw dropped. "Really?" Maybe I *was* the only event hostess who wasn't a prostitute. I probably owed my mother an apology. "Did you take her up on it?"

Jack smiled. "I'm afraid I had to decline. Not my type."

I pictured Vanessa's golden hair and aristocratic cheekbones. "Really?"

"Really."

"Can you clarify 'not your type'?"

Jack gave me a mischievous smile. "Let's just say I like a challenge."

"A challenge," I repeated.

"And that's why I've been putting a lot of thought as to what we should do on our second date," he continued.

"Is that what this was? A date?"

"Nazi gold, a murder confession, the vindication of an innocent man—of course it's a date. What else would it be? Now, I was thinking that we could try our hand at tandem skydiving. Have you ever been?"

"Uh, skydiving? Is there another option on the table?"

"Well, I wasn't going to put it out there," he said, leaning forward, "but if you're up for wild, passionate sex, I wouldn't say no."

I smiled, even though I felt a little bubble of remorse at what could have been with Arnaud. But there was no point in wallowing in regret. "Can we start with dinner and a movie or something? We can make it a challenging movie. Something in French where everyone smokes a lot."

Jack sighed dramatically. "Boring. But in your case I'll make an exception. I'll call you Wednesday when you're back, and we can set something up."

"You're based in DC, right? Isn't New York an awfully long way to go for a date?"

"I once took a three-day camel trip across the desert for a cold beer. What can I say? I don't mind going out of my way when something's really worth it."

I smiled. "Me neither."

41
〜〜

By the time I drove the Smart Car back to Hubert's, I was beyond exhaustion. I should have been happy. I had beaten Vanessa. I had a date with Thor. I had even caught a murderer. But on the whole, I had to admit that I wasn't proud of what we'd done this evening.

We had managed to prove the innocence of a slimy blackmailer at the cost of putting a good, albeit deeply flawed man in jail. We had destroyed the foundation of another good man's life. And my unfounded accusations had managed to completely alienate Arnaud, who seemed like the kind of stable, fun, and loving man that any woman would want.

And the most nigglingly annoying part was that we hadn't found out what happened to the gold, which meant that Hubert and Arnaud, who had done nothing wrong, would be forced to make up that money. It might not happen today or tomorrow, but we knew the evidence was out there, and it was probably just a matter of time until someone turned up to claim that gold. And no matter what happened—whether neo-Nazis got the gold or it went to Jewish charities or, more likely, it got eaten up in legal fees while people squabbled over who had the right to keep it—the fact remained that the one organization that clearly had no claim at all to the gold was the bank.

I parked the car and headed around the house to the French doors that led to my room. Hubert usually kept the doors unlocked, and I didn't really feel like running across anyone else tonight. All I wanted to do was sleep.

I opened the door to my bedroom and threw myself on the bed, wondering if my skin could take one night of not being cleansed, massaged, and moisturized. Probably not.

"I've been waiting for you to get back," a voice said in the darkness.

At one point in time, the voice of a strange man in my bedroom would have caused me to shriek and jump to my feet, fight-or-flight mechanism fully engaged. But given that I was very tired and it was Switzerland and it wasn't the first time this had happened, I just sighed and flicked the light on.

"Benjamin. What a surprise. You continue your streak of turning up at the worst possible time and invading my personal space without invitation."

Benjamin stood up from the velvet sofa and walked across the room. "I think we left some unfinished business earlier today."

I thought back over the course of the day. Oh yes. The almost-having-sex thing. Given all that had happened between then and now, that seemed like something that belonged to a decade where corsets were still the rage. I sighed. "Let me ask you something. What do you want from me?"

"What kind of question is that? You know that I care about you, right? Why else would I be here?"

Given my willingness to throw myself at him earlier today, I was pretty sure I could think of at least one other reason. "I didn't ask how you felt about me. I asked what you wanted from me."

Benjamin looked at me blankly.

"God. You probably speak five languages, and you still can't talk to women, can you?"

"Seven, actually, and I wasn't aware that woman was a language. I just want to be with you. Is that so complicated?" He reached out to stroke my hand, and I snatched it back before I could get distracted.

"So you're expecting what...that I'm going to wait around, having no idea where you are, just hoping that you'll show up, break into my apartment, and 'be with me' for a night before taking off again?"

"Is that not on the table?"

I narrowed my eyes at him.

"Look, what are you asking here? You know the kind of job I

have."

"Adjunct professor of Russian studies? Oh, sorry…Maltese history. Or is it criminal law? It's so hard to keep track."

Benjamin gave me a chiding look. "I don't know where I'm going to be next week. Heck, sometimes I don't even know where I am when I'm there. But I'm doing important work, Lora. I can't just quit so that we can sit around watching *Game of Thrones*."

"So what you're offering is sex—but only when you don't have something more important to do."

"You know it's more than that."

"It could be, but I'm telling you right now that I won't let it be. Listen…I like you, Benjamin. I'm attracted to you. Obviously. But I don't want to spend the rest of my life setting my table for two on the off chance you might walk in the door."

"What are you saying?"

"I'm saying that I'm going to keep looking, and when I'm with a man I care about and you roll into town looking to 'be with me,' I'm going to turn you down cold. Because the guy who's there to rub my shoulders when I've had a bad day is way higher on my priority list than the guy who drops by while he's on shore leave."

"So you're saying you don't want to see me?" Benjamin asked, his face stricken.

"I'm fine with seeing you. When I'm in the mood for it and when I'm not in a relationship with someone who's not too busy saving the world to watch *Game of Thrones* with me."

"That's not fair," he objected.

He reached out to pull me in, but I stepped out of his grasp. The air felt thick between us. If we were going to do this, it had to be on my terms. Holding his eyes in a cool stare, I shook my hair out and untied the wrap on my dress, letting it drop to the floor in a puddle of silk. I stood before him in my underwear and bra, both black and lacy.

"Fair or not, it's about two hours past my bedtime, and I've had what I think even you would consider a pretty full day. So you can take what's on offer or you can go, but decide quickly because either way, I'm looking to be asleep in fifteen minutes." That probably wasn't my best come-on line ever, but I was too tired to play the seductress.

I watched the play of emotions across Benjamin's face. Annoyance. Lust. Tenderness. Lust. Anger. Lust. With a growl of frustration, he pulled me onto the bed, rolling on top of me. Capturing both of my wrists in one hand, he buried his head in the hollow of my neck, kissing, licking, biting. Tearing at the hooks on the back of the bra, he yanked it off and threw it to the floor and moved down to by breasts, pinching the nipples before moving his head down to take them into his mouth. I moaned, running my fingernails lightly over his back.

Maddened, he flipped me over onto my stomach and yanked my underwear off. Wrapping a hand around my hips, he pulled me onto my knees in front of him. I heard the sound of a zipper and then felt him plunge into me with a force that was just short of violence. Even though I was ready, I let out a shriek, partly from pleasure, partly from the shock.

His hands roamed my body, pinching and teasing until I finally couldn't hold back any more, "I..." I started.

Without altering his rhythm, he turned me again, pinning my wrists and looking into my eyes. "Look at me."

I looked up at him. He was staring straight into my eyes, his face filled with triumph as he saw me completely surrender. A moment later he spent as well, letting out a yell before collapsing off to the side.

We lay there in silence for a few moments, breathing.

"Is it always like that?" I finally managed.

"Like what?"

"Like you're trying to keep yourself from killing me. Not that I'm complaining."

He scowled. "You really pissed me off."

"Well, make a list of other stuff that pisses you off so that I know what to do the next time I see you."

He gave an exasperated chuckle. "Based on past experience, I think you'll probably manage fine without the list."

"Probably," I agreed, suddenly feeling a wave of exhaustion hit. "Look, not to piss you off again, but I'm about thirty seconds from passing out here, so if you've got anything else to say, say it now."

"I think you should reconsider your terms," he whispered, running a hand lightly over my arm.

I burrowed deeper into the pillow. "Nope."

"I feel like you might just be using me for sex."

"Yep."

He kissed me lightly on the neck. "I'll be gone when you wake up."

"I figured."

He laughed ruefully and tucked the blanket around me. Thirty seconds later, I was completely dead to the world.

42

I woke up in the morning feeling like I had run a marathon. Well, maybe a 5K. People in my family seemed to be very poorly designed for running.

Benjamin was gone, as promised. He had left a small origami frog on the pillow next to me. I looked at it curiously. My grandmother, who fancied herself a bit of a psychic, had once told me that the frog was a symbol of change. Or maybe he was trying to tell me that my kiss had turned him into a prince. Or most likely a frog was the only thing he knew how to fold.

Shrugging, I took a shower and packed up the rest of my things. I still felt terrible for Hubert and, truth be told, was looking forward to getting back to New York, where the bankers were sleazy and didn't seem to care too much if their wives betrayed them, as long as they were discreet.

The mood downstairs was subdued. Sarina was curled into herself, staring at the table. I wondered how much Hubert had told her about last night. Did she know that her mother was an adulteress and a thief? I hoped he had at least spared her my unthinkingly cruel speculation about her mother's death. Given the fact that she was going to have to defend herself on the Fat Cat vandalism charges, I figured she had enough to worry about.

Hubert was stirring his coffee and staring into space.

"Good morning," I said tentatively, pouring myself a cup of coffee.

"Oh," Hubert said, blinking as he came back to reality. "Lora. Good morning." He looked slightly at a loss as to how to continue the conversation. "Did you sleep well?"

"Yes, Lora," Pinkie said, an innocent expression pasted onto his face. "Did you sleep well?"

I shot Pinkie an evil look. "I slept fine, thank you, Hubert. Were you able to get any sleep?"

Hubert smiled weakly. "Not much."

"Margrit is going to be coming by this morning," Pinkie said. "She said that she has some news for us."

I took a sip of coffee. "Does that woman ever sleep? I think she's been going nonstop since we got here."

"Well, now that everything is wrapped up, she'll probably have a few years to rest before there's another serious crime in Zurich."

We heard the bell ring, and then the maid showed Margrit into the breakfast room. She looked a like a woman who had been running on caffeine and adrenaline for the last four days. She poured herself a cup of coffee and sat down without being invited.

"Do you want to start with the good news or the bad news?" she asked.

Pinkie raised an eyebrow. "Most people start with good morning."

Margrit ran a hand over her eyes. "Sorry. Let me start with the bad, because it gets better after that. The bad news is that Gerhardt died last night."

"What?" Hubert gasped, suddenly snapped out of his lethargy.

"He had a heart attack. We drove him to the hospital, but it was too late." She paused. "It was very fast. I don't think he was fighting it."

"He almost made it," Hubert said.

Margrit looked at him in confusion. "What?"

"If he'd died a week ago, none of this would have happened. We would never have known what he had done."

Margit was silent for a moment. "I think you're missing the point. You might never have known, but he always knew what he had done."

Hubert looked sad. "I suppose you're right."

Margrit shook her head. "Now onto the slightly better news. Murder charges have been dropped against Reiner."

Pinkie clutched his chest. "That's your good news, Margrit? I think you might want to look up the definition of 'good.'"

Hubert's face hardened. "That man blackmailed my daughter. I don't want him anywhere near this bank again."

"Well, lucky for you, he also tampered with a crime scene, so he will have to answer for that."

Pinkie looked alarmed. "Is he going to come back as a bank partner when he's out?"

"No," Hubert said flatly. "He's committed a crime. He can't be a bank partner. He's finished here. He'll never work in this city again."

Seeing Hubert's resolve, I realized that underneath that kindly Swiss banker exterior was a core of steel. No matter what happened, Hubert would make it through this. And while he might not be stronger coming out the other side, he wouldn't break, either.

"Now, as to Sarina's situation with the Fat Cat vandalism..." Margrit began.

Sarina flushed and looked at the table. "I'm ready to pay the price for my crimes."

Margrit shook her head. "Good, because you'll need to show the judge that you're truly sorry for what you've done. I've talked to the prosecutor, and he thinks that he can work out a deal where you pay back the victims for damages and do community service. A *lot* of community service."

Hubert looked both relieved and stricken. "Does that mean that you'll be going off to Pakistan to teach?"

Sarina glanced at me. "No, Dad, Lora and I had a little chat about that, and I've got some ideas about things that I can do here that might make a more lasting impression."

Hubert shot me a look of naked gratitude.

Margrit took a sip of coffee. "In any case, you'll need to come in and make a formal statement. Bring a lawyer."

Sarina nodded.

"And now for you..." Margit said, looking at Pinkie. "Wait here a moment, please."

She left the breakfast room and returned with Maurice in tow. Pinkie and I exchanged glances. Maurice was immaculately dressed, but the air of playful sleaze that he had shown at the airport had been replaced with a hard smile that did not bode well. Cradled lovingly in his hands was a small leather box.

"When I showed Maurice the evidence that the watch had been intended for you all along, he insisted that he come along to give it to you in person."

"Really, that was terribly kind of you," Pinkie said. His tone was haughty, but he was unable to stop his eyes from darting to Hubert nervously.

"Yes," Maurice continued, "your father must have loved you very much to buy such a lovely gift for you."

"Philippe's father loved him dearly," Hubert said. "We all do."

Maurice simpered. "That's wonderful. And it's lovely to see that his godfather can overlook Philippe's lifestyle choices. Many people would not be so accepting."

Hubert looked at Maurice blankly. "Lifestyle choices? What on earth are you talking about, Maurice?"

Pinkie opened his mouth to jump in, but Maurice cut him off. "I'm afraid Pinkie has the same personal habits as your former partner Jurg Hoffmann. You remember—the one you fired?"

Hubert's eyebrows went up in shock. "Philippe, is this true?"

"I…" Pinkie stalled out and looked at me for support. I nodded. "It is," he said simply.

Hubert shook as head, as if to deny an unpleasant truth. "I know a place that can help you. They fix this kind of problem all the time. You don't need to live like this, Philippe."

Pinkie took a step backward, shock and hurt in his eyes. I felt my hands curl into fists at my sides and glared at Maurice, whose face was fixed in an expression of smug glee.

"I don't need to be 'fixed,' Hubert. There's nothing wrong with me. This is who I am. This 'problem' is just a part of me. You're my godfather. You're supposed to love me no matter what!" Pinkie's voice, the voice of a wounded child, broke on the last syllable.

"Don't talk that way," Hubert begged him. "That's what Jurg said as well, but he was wrong. There are options. Don't give up on your future. You can have a real life—a life with a family and children—but not if you stay on this path."

A tear escaped from Pinkie's eye, and I stepped between him and Hubert. "You think Pinkie needs to be fixed? I think you need to be fixed!" I shoved him back away from Pinkie. "How can you turn your back on your godson for being who he is? He doesn't need to change to have children or a family or a life."

Hubert shook his head sadly. "Really? As much as you might love Philippe, you can't seriously be saying that you'd raise children with him. Not with the way he is."

"Pinkie would be a wonderful father," I said, suddenly realizing that it might even be true.

Hubert shook his head. "Lora…heroin addicts can't be trusted with children. Surely even you must admit that."

A moment of dead silence fell over the room.

"Heroin addicts?" Pinkie asked.

"Yes, addicts. You heard me!" Hubert grabbed him by the arms. "It's not the way you are, Philippe. It's an addiction! Let me get help for you."

"You think I'm a heroin addict?" Pinkie asked again, the faintest hint of a smile curling around his mouth.

"I know, Jurg hated to be called an addict, too, but that's what you are. You must face reality!"

"I'm not a heroin addict," Pinkie said, taking Hubert's arms. He took a deep breath. "I'm gay."

Hubert stared at him uncomprehendingly.

"I like to sleep with men," Pinkie added, apparently unsure that Hubert was up with the lingo.

"I know that," Hubert said.

"You know what 'gay' means?" I asked.

"No. I mean, yes. But I meant that I know Philippe is gay. I've probably known it longer than he's known it. His father knew it."

"My father knew?" Pinkie asked wonderingly.

"Of course. We discussed it occasionally, over the years."

Pinkie looked shocked. "Was he…okay with it?"

Hubert waved a hand dismissively. "He was fine with it."

"Really…" Pinkie said. He wiped a tear away. "I never told him. I never thought he knew."

Hubert snorted. "It's not like you were hiding it, Philippe. Simply a *parade* of stable boys through your rooms on school breaks. Honestly. We both did occasionally wish you'd find a nice fellow and settle down."

Pinkie shook his head. "I should have known you wouldn't be so small minded."

"Yes," Hubert said mildly, "you should have. But I forgive you." He gave Pinkie a hearty hug.

Pinkie looked at Maurice, who was standing there, fuming. I

held my breath. Was Pinkie going to slap him? Verbally slice and dice him?

Pinkie smiled. "Maurice, I suppose I have to thank you. Not only did you bring my father's watch back—you also gave me a little piece of my father back. I'm sure there's an official punishment for attempted blackmail…"

"There sure as hell is," Margrit chimed in, grabbing the watch box out of Maurice's hands and giving him a look that promised more pain down the road.

"But I think the best punishment in this case will be watching me put on this watch and knowing that you've made me very happy." Pinkie smiled at him cherubically and held out his hands to Margrit. "Gimme, gimme, gimme," he said, abandoning all pretense of dignity.

Margrit handed him the box, and Pinkie opened it reverently. I snuck a peek, not sure what to expect. The watch was unremarkable. A gold face with lines to mark the hours; a chocolate leather strap. For Pinkie, a man who thought of a pink ascot as casual wear, it was so nondescript as to be invisible.

But when I looked at him, I could see that whatever the watch looked like, it was beautiful in his eyes. His face glowed with happiness as he took the watch out and put it on his wrist. It fit perfectly.

Margrit tweaked the corner of her mouth. "You never really own a Patek Philippe. You just look after it for the next generation. Might want to think that obligation through, Philippe."

Pinkie stuck out his tongue. "Plenty of time. My biological clock runs in slow motion."

43

After breakfast, I finished packing and went to the drawing room to wait for the car. Hubert was alone in the room, drinking a glass of wine and looking at a picture of his wife. I doubted it was his practice to drink wine in the mornings, but I couldn't blame him for seeking comfort wherever he could find it today.

He looked up when I came in. "I wanted to thank you for talking to Sarina," he said, touching my shoulder. "I don't know what you said to her, but she seems to have grown up a lot in the last few days."

"She's had to." I looked at the picture of Hubert's wife. Now that I knew more about her, the vivaciousness looked more like recklessness to me. She was the kind of woman who would steal gold and seduce her husband's best friend. Maybe the kind of woman who would fake her own death.

Hubert seemed to catch my thoughts. "I'll never believe that she left us. She was wild, yes, and maybe I shouldn't have tried to force her into the life of a banker's wife. But she loved Sarina, and I think she loved me. She even loved this place. The time that she spent on the history of the bank, the house, the wine…"

He took a sip of wine. "God, she was talented in so many ways. Even this," he said, raising his glass. "She didn't know a thing about wine when she got here, but she was a quick study. She read up on the topic, and then she told me she was taking over the wine production. She bought these special vats and it was like magic…

Within the course of one harvest, the wine suddenly went from this to something really special."

"Maybe you should keep using those vats," I said diplomatically.

"I tried," he said, wincing as he took another sip. "I'm afraid I didn't have the same results. No, the magic wasn't in the vats. The magic was in her."

An absurd idea came to me. "Hubert, can I see your wine cellar?"

Hubert shrugged. "Of course."

He led the way down into the basement, past rooms filled with massive, carved antiques and mysterious jars of what was once probably fruit. "The basement in an old family house like this is like a little history museum," Hubert said.

"I can see that. That jar of peaches back there looks like it might actually be fossilized."

He chuckled. "I should probably clean it out, but I spent many happy hours of my childhood playing down here. There was always something new to discover."

We finally came to a large room lined with bottles. The walls were of thick stone, covered with plaster. Two large stainless steel tanks sat on a low platform.

I walked over to the tanks and tapped on them. Hollow. "We don't use them for making wine anymore," Hubert explained. "I never really got the hang of the new equipment."

I checked the rest of the room quickly. Stone and bottles.

"What's under this platform?" I asked, tapping the platform under the tanks.

"The platform? I don't know. Helen had them put it in. Maybe it made it easier on her back?"

I examined the platform carefully. While there were no obvious doors, one of the panels looked like it might open. I pulled at it with my fingernails, then pressed around the edge. The panel opened, showing a selection of mysterious-looking stainless steel objects.

Hubert looked faintly surprised. "I didn't know it did that," he said. He peered at the objects. "My god, no wonder I could never get those tanks to work. I was probably missing half the equipment. I wish she'd told me what she was doing down here."

I got down on my knees and started methodically emptying the cabinet.

"What are you doing?"

"Bear with me." With the cabinet empty, I checked the dimensions again. "This cabinet is too small."

"Too small for what?"

I stepped aside so that he could see. "The outside is bigger than the inside. Do you see?"

"Yes," Hubert said, pushing his glasses up his nose. "I wonder why they built it that way."

I reached into the cabinet, grunting as I felt around the edges. Sure enough, there was a catch. I released the catch and held my breath. A panel in the back of the cabinet slid open.

"Oh my god," Hubert said.

I stood for a moment staring at what I'd found. Block after block of gold. I reached in and picked one up. It was smooth and heavy and warmed almost immediately to my touch.

I handed it to Hubert. "You know what this means?"

Hubert looked at the gold in his hands and then looked up at me. "The bank is saved! I have to tell Arnaud."

"Yes, but more than that. It means that whatever else she might have done, she didn't abandon you. I think you were right. She loved you and Sarina. She loved this place. I don't know why she took the gold—adventure, danger, some twisted sense of justice from a war fought seventy years ago—but she didn't take the money and run away. It's here. It's always been here."

Hubert looked at me searchingly. "How did you know? How did you know where she'd kept the gold?"

"Well, the fact that she kept shooing you out of here was probably a hint, but really, it was because you said the wine got better right away."

Hubert looked confused.

"The only thing that she could have done to improve the wine in the short run was replace it. And replacing your wine with someone else's doesn't require a lot of equipment. Just a great big jug of someone else's wine and a day when you were out of town."

"Lora!" Pinkie's voice came to us faintly. "The limo is here! Lora!" We heard footsteps descend halfway down the stairs. "Are you down here?"

"We're here. We'll be up in a minute." We stood up and walked out to meet him.

"Be careful," Pinkie fussed from the stairs. "The last time I was down in that basement, a spider the size of a Frisbee dropped on my head and started trying to suck my virginal blood."

"If your blood was virginal, that must have been a really, really long time ago," I said, stepping into the light.

"I'm just saying that there is nothing on this earth that could convince me to step one foot farther into this basement!"

Hubert held up the block of gold so that Pinkie could see it.

"How about two thousand of those?" I asked.

Pinkie shut his jaw with an audible snap. "I stand corrected."

44

"Vanessa," I said, taking a seat in the lounge at the Waldorf Astoria.

"Lora," Vanessa said, putting aside her phone. "I'm so glad you called. I've always said we should be friends."

We sat in silence for a few moments, smiling at each other with the kind of smiles you save for your best friends and your worst enemies.

Our waiter, a darkly handsome young man in a black apron, came over to the table, white teeth flashing in a friendly smile. "Hello, ladies, I hope you're having a lovely afternoon. Can I get you something to drink?"

"Oh gosh," Vanessa said, "I'm not much of a drinker, I'm afraid. Maybe just an herbal tea?"

"Of course."

"Would you like a tea as well?" he asked me.

"Absolutely not. I'd like a glass of Veuve, please."

"Excellent choice," the waiter said. "Something to eat?"

I glanced at him. "No. We're not going to be here long."

"So," Vanessa said after he had left. "Champagne. To celebrate winning Jack Green's business?"

"Oh, life's too short to save champagne for a celebration."

The waiter returned, placing a small teapot in front of Vanessa and a champagne flute in front of me.

"I'm sure you're right," Vanessa said. "I was just talking to Ricardo about a celebration he was planning. You remember Ricardo? He's with the Spanish consulate…lovely man. He's one of your clients, too, isn't he? Or at least he used to be…"

I sipped my champagne and smiled at her. "Oh, I'm pretty sure he will be again."

"Really? Because he seemed quite open to the possibility of me helping out with his next party. I mean, he really is a lovely man. And he throws so many events. Surely we could share, right?"

"I don't think so. I think you're going to call him up and tell him that you're not available to help him. And then you're going to call up any of my other clients you've tried to poach and you're going to give them the same message."

Vanessa blew delicately on her tea before taking a sip. "And why would I do that?" she asked, her voice silky.

"Because right before we left Switzerland, I asked Pinkie's policewoman cousin, Margrit, to do me a little favor. I asked her to analyze some chocolates that you left for me. You know, the ones that Hubert and his housekeeper both saw you drop off."

Vanessa's face became very still. "Really."

"Really. And it was a good thing that I did because they had apparently been laced with syrup of ipecac."

"I'm afraid I have no idea what that is."

"Well, apparently it used to be used to induce vomiting in children." I took another sip, watching her closely.

"Vomiting! My, I'm so sorry. Honestly, you pay a fortune for these chocolates, only to find out they're contaminated. I tell you, can nothing be trusted anymore?"

"Well, funny you should ask. I actually saw you buying those chocolates, so I could give the police a very exact window of time. And as it turned out, several boxes from that very batch had gone to longstanding customers, none of whom had any problems with their chocolates."

Vanessa smiled weakly. "Well, that's a relief."

"Yes, but unfortunately some people did get sick. Specifically, the alphornist and yodeling pop singers who were going to play at Dieter's dinner. And the steinstossen Swiss world champion who was scheduled to give a lesson at the event. Apparently you had sent them boxes of chocolates as well."

Vanessa's face showed the first signs of strain.

"Are you sure I can't get you a drink?"

"I'm fine. Yes, I did send them chocolates on Ueli's behalf. He wanted to show that there were no hard feelings. You know, because they were performing at Dieter's event."

"Except that Ueli says he did no such thing."

"Well, of course he would say that, wouldn't he?" Vanessa gave a short laugh. "I mean, are you honestly implying that I tried to poison you?"

I smiled at her.

"Look," Vanessa said, pushing her tea aside and leaning over the table. "I'm not admitting anything. What are you getting at, Lora? Are you threatening me?"

"I would never, ever threaten you. I'm just informing you that my clients are off limits."

Her lip curled. "Or?"

"Or I will make sure that everyone knows that you tried to poison the competition."

"You have no proof of that."

"This business is built on reputation, Vanessa, and I'm pretty sure that if Jack Green and Prince Philippe and Hubert tell a few of their friends about this—particularly with the Swiss police test to back it up—your reputation is going to be...what's the word I'm looking for here? Ah yes. Shit. Your reputation is going to be shit."

Vanessa narrowed her eyes at me. "And if I stay away from your clients?"

I shrugged. "I'm not afraid of a little competition. And it'll be nice to have a number to give people when they think that part of a hostess's job is to put out."

"I would never," she said hotly.

"Oh, I'm sorry." I picked up my phone. "Give me a minute. I need to get back to Jack on that pop yodeling trio. We're still wrangling over the contract, but as I know Jack would be the first to say, nothing worth having is easy."

She flushed a mottled red.

"I'll stay away from your clients," she said, her voice strangled.

I raised my glass. "Perfect. Then I don't think we really have anything else to discuss." I drained my glass and set it on the table, standing up and picking up my bag. "This round's on you, let's say." I sauntered out of the bar, feeling her eyes boring holes in my back as I went. I had to say that I had burned through the "one" that the Swiss police owed my brother in near record time, but I felt that it was a favor well spent.

EPILOGUE

"Horseback riding," Pinkie said.

"Ooh…" I said, lifting my glass of Veuve in a silent toast, "good countermove. Less chance of dying."

"Or of peeing your pants out of terror."

"Right. And a couple more weeks of the South Beach Diet, and I should look pretty good in jodhpurs and boots, don't you think?"

Pinkie took a sip of champagne. "Possibly, but not as good as I would look."

"I bet you Jack would disagree with that."

"I bet he would, but the fact that he proposed hang gliding for your second official date just shows that the man has poor judgment."

I laughed. "Well, he did say he was open to counteroffers. Let's hope horseback riding works for him."

"Didn't you say that he also proposed hot, wild sex?"

"He did," I admitted.

"Because I'd be all over that."

"I think I'm going to take it slow."

"Slow hot, wild sex is also good," Pinkie pointed out.

"Enough with the hot, wild sex."

"Well, if he wonders what advice I gave on this topic, just tell Jack that I had his back."

"You wish."

"I do."

A loud ringing interrupted us. "You got the doorbell fixed!"

"I had to," I said, getting up to get the door.

"Why?"

"Hold that thought." I opened the door, expecting the postman. Instead, it was a man in a suit holding a medium-sized box.

"Courier service, ma'am. I need you to sign here. And here. And here."

I scribbled my signature three more times. "Jeez. I know this stuff is expensive, but this is ridiculous."

"Too rich for my blood," the man said with a wink.

I put the box on the coffee table and picked up my champagne. "Back to the doorbell—remember Heather? That crazy vegan mommy blogger from across the street?"

"How could I forget? She's called the police on me what— twice now?"

"Three times. Well, apparently she came over to complain about the bad example you were setting for her kids, and since she knew I was home and I wasn't hearing the bell, she thought I was blowing her off."

"What bad example was I setting for the kids?! I'm a sterling example for the youth of tomorrow. Wait…because I'm gay? Who hates gay people anymore? Not even Hubert, and he can't even use a telephone without a cord! You'd think she would have moved on to hating Coca-Cola executives and investment bankers like the rest of the world."

"It's not because you're gay. For the last time, nobody cares about that any more. She said that your frequent use of limousines is destroying the environment and fostering an 'unhealthy attachment to material possessions' in her kids."

"Little Jimmy wants a remote control car, and suddenly that's my fault?"

"Little Emma wants a Louis Vuitton purse, apparently."

"That actually could be my fault," Pinkie mused. "Hmm. I'll get Heather a subscription to the meat of the month club to apologize. I bet little Emma would love prosciutto. She's obviously going to turn out to be a girl of taste despite her mother's best efforts."

"Enough. Do not engage. I forbid it. But if you're dying to send someone a meat of the month club membership, send it to me. I'm already a girl of taste."

"Speaking of delicious objects coming by mail," Pinkie said, gesturing to the box the courier had dropped off, "What's that?"

"I ordered some matcha tea the other day," I said, taking a sip of my champagne. "I'm detoxing."

"Ah. Sometimes it's hard to tell with you. Is it any good? Maybe I should get some."

"It's absolutely disgusting. That's how I know it's good for me. Why else would people drink something that tastes so utterly vile?"

Pinkie slid the box over to look at it more closely. "This isn't tea, Lora," he said, his voice suddenly excited.

"Really?" I snatched the box out of his hands. "From Richter and Partners. Oooh...Hubert sent something. I hope it's chocolate. No, I don't. Yes, I do. Dammit!"

I quickly undid the wrapper, exposing a box emblazoned with the word *Breguet*. Flipping open the box, I stifled a gasp. Nestled around a tiny ivory pillow was the most beautiful watch I had ever seen. A white gold bezel with diamonds surrounded a mother of pearl face on which a clock and a moon dial twined into an intricate figure eight.

"Let me see," Pinkie said. He peered into the box. "Ohh...it's perfect," he breathed. He looked at me seriously. "Reine de Naples. Somebody must like you very much."

"There's a card," I said, flipping opening the envelope. I read the letter out loud. "We hope you'll accept this small token of our appreciation. Like the bank you saved, it comes from a small firm that's been in the same family for years. I hope you'll come back to visit under happier circumstances. Love, Arnaud and Hubert."

Pinkie looked at the watch again. "It's nice when people know how to say thank you, isn't it?"

"Wait," I said. "There's a PS. 'Dear Lora, I hope you'll forgive me for my anger the night of the dinner. Like all Swiss people, my instinct is to protect those I care about, but protecting people from the truth rarely turns out well. Right now Hubert and I are focused on helping the bank recover from the loss of two partners, but I hope that we can remain...at least...friends. Arnaud."

Pinkie peered over my shoulder. "Nice use of ellipses."

"'At least' friends. Does that mean what I think it means?"

"It means that once you get sick and tired of broken bones and bruises from Jack's half-witted adventures, you can break it off with him and go do some skiing in Switzerland. And by skiing, I mean sex with Arnaud. Possibly on skis… I try not to speculate."

"He doesn't seem like the kind of guy who's just looking for a good time."

Pinkie waved a hand in the air. "All guys are just looking for a good time. It's just that Arnaud would probably consider a house full of kids and Friday nights at the ice cream parlor to be a good time." He shuddered. "Really, you'd be crying with boredom in a week. But I doubt that that'll come up right away."

"Because I'll be having such a great time with Jack?"

"Because I got a note this morning from Mr. Chang. How do you feel about Singapore?"

"I feel like we'll cross that ocean when we come to it," I said. "For now, pour me another glass of champagne and order us some pizza. I think I'm up for a little domestic bliss."

THE END

MORE PINKIE AND LORA

Missed the first book? Check out *Champagne Float.*

Lora Godwin, professional hostess to the rich and feckless, makes her living being flattering, witty, and decorative. When she agrees to manage a yacht trip for a reclusive Russian oligarch and some potential business partners, she figures the worst problem she'll face is keeping her professional distance from the sleazy yet seductive Greek playboy who seems keen to end her six-month, one-week, and three-day sexual dry spell. But when she accidentally stumbles across a woman being held prisoner on the yacht, she finds her "to do" list suddenly includes dodging white slavers, escaping kidnappers, covering up homicides, and trying not to get pulped by the Russian Mafia.

VISIT NISSAALEXANDROV.COM
for updates, excerpts, and much, much more

-and-

Join the conversation at
www.facebook.com/nissaalexandrovbooks.

ACKNOWLEDGMENTS

The beauty of a second novel is that you've already got the dream team together.

There's my brother, Chris Van Trump, who does beta reading for all the parts that aren't dirty.

There's my editor, Jason Whited, who has given me a healthy respect for my ignorance when it comes to *The Chicago Manual of Style*. He was also the first (okay, the only) person to mention Oscar Wilde in the context of my writing, which makes him especially dear to me.

There's Simon Avery, who does covers that are unique and fun and different and who has a rare ability to put up with the fact that I can explain what I don't like, but can't explain why I don't like it.

There's my husband, who has an unwavering belief that I write very funny books despite the fact that he doesn't "get" fiction.

There's my son, who loves books in general enough to give me the time I need to write mine.

Of course, the key members of the dream team are the readers. My fondest wish for all of you is that you'll laugh loudly and often as you read, and that you'll tell others about the books so that they have the chance to do the same.

I raise my glass to all of you. Thank you.

ABOUT THE AUTHOR

After a childhood spent in the Wonder Bread suburbs of Delaware, Nissa Alexandrov fled the country in search of a more global perspective. She has lived in Beijing, Bulgaria, Moscow, and Zurich and visited everywhere from Albania to Zimbabwe. *Champagne Gold* is her second novel.

www.ingramcontent.com/pod-product-compliance
Lightning Source LLC
Chambersburg PA
CBHW020400210626
46816CB00006BB/2059